TH ART OF VICTORY

PARADIGM
PRESS

MARTHA KEYES

Chapter One

OAKWORTH VILLAGE, KENT, 1816

I put a hand over Lucy Ellis's fidgeting ones, sending her a reassuring smile as she looked to the ballroom door for the tenth time.

"Forgive me," she said, clasping her hands tightly in front of her gown. She looked beautiful tonight, her blonde hair glinting in the candlelit assembly room. When we had first met at the seminary a few years ago, Lucy had been a young and naive thirteen. She had since grown into her eighteen years. "I am just so very nervous. Oh, Diana, what if he becomes terribly angry at you? Or at me?"

I laughed lightly. "What precisely do you imagine he will do in a place like this?" I gestured to the couples dancing down the set in the middle of the room, chock-full of people.

Lucy's eyes grew wider as though she saw nothing to joke about in my words. "There is no telling what he will do. My uncle is a most disagreeable man."

I frowned at the woman who jostled me as she tried to make her way through the crowded room. Despite taking place in the

1

village just a mile from my home, I hadn't attended a country assembly in years, and tonight was serving as a strong reminder of why. There was no room to breathe here, let alone dance. Even if that had not been the case, though, I had little interest in events where matchmaking was the objective. I didn't intend to marry; I hadn't the proper personality for it.

A gentleman I didn't recognize looked at me with patent admiration in his eyes, and I turned my gaze away. I couldn't help but touch a hand to the honey-colored ringlets framing my face. Surely, they were to blame for attracting his attention. Men might look at me with approval in their eyes, but once they knew me, they were quickly cured of any desire to marry me. "Of course he is disagreeable," I said. "Why else would he refuse an entirely reasonable match to someone as good and kind as you are?"

"Edwin says it is because he cannot bear to surrender control."

I didn't respond to that, for it was inconceivable to me that her uncle *wouldn't* wish to cede responsibility of a charge like Lucy. She was sweet and innocent and young—and in serious need of constant guidance. It was only because Mrs. Agnes Westwood was providing that guidance that her guardian uncle could sit back and relax.

Lucy deserved happiness, though, and I couldn't imagine why her uncle had refused to give his approval for the match she sought. I had only met Mr. Edwin Pike twice, but he was entirely unexceptionable, particularly for someone like Lucy. She had been living in the care of her cousin Mrs. Westwood since the death of her parents many years ago. Her orphan status did not exactly make her the most desirable of brides.

Mrs. Westwood was approaching us now, looking more stern than usual as she passed a young man and young woman exchanging whispered secrets. As the head of the nearby Mrs. Westwood's Seminary for Fine Young Ladies—which both Lucy and I had attended—she was tasked with turning giddy and foolish girls into respectable and marriageable young women. Bringing her to a public assembly, where behavior was not always the most circumspect, was some form of torture. I wondered how many times she had already stopped to provide unsolicited censure to those in attendance. It was her specialty, after all.

Just the sight of Mrs. Westwood was enough to determine me more than ever to help Lucy gain the approval of her uncle, who was also her guardian. Lucy deserved more freedom than she had enjoyed under Mrs. Westwood's care, and I had promised myself to be an advocate for her the moment I had met her at the seminary. If that meant speaking with her stuffy old uncle, I was more than happy to do it. My own father was just such a stuffy old man—a naval admiral, in fact—and having associated with his fellows all my life, I'd had plenty of occasion to learn how to appeal to even the most rigid of old men. I loved a good challenge.

"An overabundance of company leads to an underabundance of super-vision," Mrs. Westwood tittered as she came up beside us, shooting another disapproving glance at the whispering couple she had passed. I had heard this particular maxim a handful of times from her. It was the reason she took on fewer young women at her seminary than most. She needed to be able to devote the proper amount of attention to each one.

She surveyed the room with displeasure. "One would *think* that—"

"He is here!" Lucy called out, rudely—but mercifully—inter-rupting her cousin.

Surprised to hear her sound so animated at her guardian's arrival, I whipped around to the doorway, curious to see my opponent.

But it was only Edwin Pike, the man Lucy had fallen in love with. When he caught sight of Lucy, his mouth drew up into a smile. He was a handsome young man, with sandy hair, a broad smile, and an amiable personality. He pushed his way through the crowd toward her, receiving her hand with his. I thought he might kiss her glove, but he settled for a bow.

His eye caught mine as he came up from it, and I smiled at him, acknowledging the wisdom of his decision. Mrs. Westwood seemed to look upon Mr. Pike's courting of Lucy favorably enough, but her tone had undergone a marked shift since Lucy's uncle had expressed his disapproval of the match. Mrs. Westwood might be a chaperone and companion to Lucy, but it was her uncle who made the decisions for Lucy's future.

I wished he might have witnessed this moment, though. Surely no one could be heartless enough to deny marriage to two people who looked at one another the way Lucy and Mr. Pike were regarding each other. I knew a pang of jealousy at the sight of it, like the slice of a papercut. I had long given up hoping to be regarded in such a way, but every now and then, I had a moment of weakness— a moment of wishing I was not so very difficult a woman.

But tonight was not about me. It was about softening the heart of Lucy's uncle.

"What is your uncle's name, Lucy?" I asked.

She was still looking at Edwin, as though the physical contact she was denied could only be made up for by communicating the depth of her feelings by eye contact. "Duke."

"What?" I said, dismayed. Surely Lucy would have told me if her uncle was a duke. And surely she would not be spending her time at Mrs. Westwood's if that were the case. Unless, that is, he was a cantankerous, penny-pinching sort of duke.

She turned to me, and Mr. Pike took his place beside her. Whether or not her guardian gave them his approval to marry, Lucy was unlikely to have many other suitors—at least not any who happened to be attending *this* assembly. Their proximity and attitude toward one another spoke quite clearly of their intentions and feelings. A censure from Mrs. Westwood was imminent.

"Well, properly, his name is Marmaduke Russell," Lucy said, "but he has always insisted I call him Uncle Duke, and I daren't disobey him."

My lip curled up in a smile half-amused, half-contemptuous. I saw through this man already. Undoubtedly, he thought if he could only manage to be *called* Duke, he might be regarded with the same awe and deference as someone holding that title. It was somewhat pathetic, and I felt a sliver of pity for the sort of man who would stoop to such methods.

Lucy stiffened, her eyes growing wider as she stared in the direction of the door. "He has come."

Based on the dread in her tone, the devil himself had just stepped into the room.

I turned my head, my curiosity far too piqued to do anything else. I looked for a head of graying hair, the halting gait of a gouty gentleman, and a waistcoat bursting at the buttons. My forehead wrinkled. "Where?"

"*There.* In the maroon waistcoat."

My eyes searched amongst those at the door, finally finding the article of clothing mentioned. The buttons were certainly not in any danger of bursting. My gaze traveled upward, running over a blue coat spread across a pair of strong shoulders, past a broad neck encased in a well-tied cravat, and finally to a sharp-jawed face with light eyes, dark lashes, and even darker, somber brows.

The man couldn't have been much past thirty, and certainly only a handful of years my senior. Why had I imagined him to be so much older? I tried to think back on what Lucy had said about him, but aside from her complaints about his disagree-ableness, I could not remember if she had ever told me his age. Whatever the case, he was not at all what I had expected.

Indeed, had his aspect not been so severe, I might have been tempted to describe him as handsome.

"Oh, Diana," Lucy said, taking me by the arm. "Are you reconsidering your offer to speak with him? I certainly wouldn't blame you."

I blinked, pulling my eyes away from the unexpected sight of the man who, if I was being honest, *looked* like he might well be an actual duke—though far more handsome than the dukes I had seen. He carried himself with enough assurance for the position, certainly. "Nonsense. I am as determined as ever."

"It is very kind of you, Miss Donovan," said Mr. Pike, "but, if I may venture to ask, do you truly think he shall lend an ear to you—a stranger?"

I smiled at the doubt in his voice. "I certainly intend that he shall." From the time I could string a few words together, I had been trained up on the battle strategy of the ancient Chinese war general Sun Tzu. I could list the thirteen principles contained in his military treatise *The Art of War* as easily as I could tell you the names of my three siblings. Managing conversation with a gentleman only a few years older than I was mere child's play.

"Diana is the bravest person I know." Lucy took in a fortifying breath. "Come, I shall introduce you."

You cannot first signal your intentions. The line from *The Art of War* came immediately to mind.

Lucy took up my hand, but I pulled her back. "No, no. If you take me to him, it will immediately set up his back. Let me go about it my own way."

"Surely you do not intend to introduce *yourself* to him, Miss Donovan." Mrs. Westwood couldn't have sounded more surprised if I had stated my intention to ask the Prince Regent to dance.

I sent her a reassuring smile, though the prospect of seeing her expression if I *did* approach Mr. Russell was admittedly enticing. "You needn't worry, Mrs. Westwood. You taught me better than to commit such an egregious error as *that*."

She blinked in relief. "You set my mind at ease, my dear, for you are here under my chaperonage, you know, and I simply cannot allow you to tarnish your reputation."

Since Mrs. Westwood had already acted as a guide and chaperone to me during my years at the seminary, she was the one I sometimes asked to accompany Lucy and me on outings. My mother had died two years ago, but even before that, she had been too ill to attend parties and balls. My father, the only other potential chaperone, was not one to seek out entertainments like this one.

After reassuring her yet again, I made my way toward the Master of Ceremonies, Mr. Booth, who was a friend of my father. He looked at me with a knowing expression as I communicated to him that I wished to be introduced to Mr. Russell, as though I was not the first to make such a request of him. I considered informing him that my intention in dancing with the man was far from what he clearly assumed it to be, but in the end, I decided this was unnecessary information, and he obligingly led the way.

Chapter Two

A t the prospect of the challenge before me, my heart quickened. Mr. Russell was in conversation with a man unfamiliar to me, but the stranger was kind enough to make an end to the conversation when he saw the Master of Ceremonies waiting to speak with Mr. Russell.

Now that I had a closer view of him, I decided it was the combination of his thick brows and light eyes which gave him a severe, piercing look. Little wonder Lucy feared him so.

"Miss Donovan," said Mr. Booth, "allow me the pleasure to present you to Mr. Marmaduke Russell. I saw the two of you without partners and thought you might enjoy dancing together. Miss Donovan is the daughter of the esteemed Admiral Donovan, Mr. Russell. Perhaps you have heard of him."

The man was looking at me in a calculating way as we performed the expected bow and curtsy. I met his gaze unflinchingly, for I had long since outgrown the inclination to blush under scrutiny.

"I have indeed heard of him," Mr. Russell said. "Met him, even."

"Ah, then you will have plenty to discuss, I am certain," said

Mr. Booth. "Now, if you will excuse me . . ." He bowed himself away, leaving me to my challenge.

Mr. Russell did not speak right away, though his gaze was on me, and it would have been easy to let it unnerve me if I had been the type to become nervous.

"Shall we hope for a cotillion?" I asked. "Or is the reel more to your taste?"

"Neither," he said flatly. "I have no intention of dancing this evening."

I found myself grasping for words, a turn of events as rare as it was unwelcome. The only ones occurring to me were hardly the type that would be conducive to my goal. Lucy's description of her guardian as being disagreeable suddenly seemed an understatement.

"I would, however, be more than happy to procure a drink for you, Miss Donovan."

I wanted nothing more than to refuse, but a quick glance at Lucy and her worried gaze and fidgeting hands was all the reminder I needed. Devil fly away with my pride; I was here to win a battle.

"I would be grateful for that, sir," I managed to say with my most charming smile.

His eyes narrowed slightly as he regarded me. "Would you? I think you would rather throw the drink in my face the moment I hand it to you."

Thrown off balance, I could find nothing to do but laugh. "The thought had occurred to me, I admit. Perhaps if you select a claret, it will blend in with your waistcoat."

He looked down for a moment, a little smile playing at the corner of his lips. "A generous suggestion."

"I wouldn't wish to deprive you of a night full of refusing to dance with more young women. Tell me, Mr. Russell, what *is* the purpose of coming to an assembly when one refuses to dance?"

"It is nothing personal." He offered me his arm, and I

accepted it after a brief hesitation. He guided us through the throngs of people, parting the way as effortlessly as Moses and the Red Sea. This was a man used to having his way.

Well, not for long.

"In answer to your question, I am here as a promise to my niece," he said.

I saw my opportunity—a way to bring up the subject of Lucy without being too heavy-handed. "Your niece?"

He shot a quick glance at me as we reached the refreshment table, laden with various drinks and sweetmeats. "Yes."

That was hardly an encouraging response. In fact, it was plain disobliging. "I presume you speak of Miss Lucy Ellis," I prodded, determined to have this conversation.

"You presume correctly," he said flatly. "Do you prefer lemonade or negus, Miss Donovan?"

"Claret," I said.

His mouth quirked up at the edge. "I am afraid they do not have claret."

"No, I suppose they do not. Let it be negus, then. It will do well enough for our purposes."

He reached for a glass of the amber liquid, offering it to me and raising a brow, as though in expectation of my promised revenge for his refusal to dance. The vision of splashing the glass's contents in his face, his stark white cravat becoming soiled with drips of negus, presented itself to me. But it was quickly followed by Sun Tzu's words: *Be subtle! Be subtle!*

"Ah, there she is," I said, nodding at Lucy. She and Mr. Pike were walking to join the set. "How very blissful she looks."

There was no response from Mr. Russell, and I looked over at him to see if he had even heeded me. He was staring at me, cool and calm.

"*This* is why you asked Mr. Booth to introduce us," he said.

I blinked in surprise, and heat shot up to my cheeks.

He smiled in amusement at my embarrassment. "You must be one of Lucy's school friends."

I scoffed at the description that made me sound as though I was seventeen rather than three-and-twenty. "And *you* must be Lucy's decrepit, crotchety uncle."

His smile only grew, making him look more handsome than anyone so disagreeable should be permitted to appear. "Did she describe me that way?"

"No. I did." Though after meeting him, I could hardly pretend he was decrepit. Indeed, he looked capable of anything he set his mind—or athletic form—to.

I took in a breath. I was losing sight of my strategy—to coax and inspire him to agree to the match—but I could hardly help myself. He was maddening and intriguing and disagreeable all at once.

"And you are here to plead the case for her and Mr. Pike, I take it? Save your breath, Miss Donovan. I shan't approve of the match. Would you care to dance?" He put out a hand in invitation.

"I thought you didn't intend to dance."

"You have changed my mind."

I stood speechless. Mr. Russell was proving much more diffi-cult an opponent than I had anticipated, and I wanted nothing more than to give him a set down by refusing his invitation. But if I had changed his mind about dancing, surely I could change his mind about other things.

He was watching me with those vivid, perceptive eyes and a little twitch at the corner of his mouth, as though he knew precisely what my inner struggle was.

"I would be thrilled," I said with a tight smile, "to dance with you, Mr. Russell."

"You would not. But I hope you shall be by the end of the set. Come."

I caught eyes with Lucy as we made our way to the ballroom

floor, and she looked a question at me, the hope in her gaze visible even from opposite ends of the set. I gave her an encouraging smile, then glanced at Mr. Russell.

He raised a brow at me. He had seen the exchange.

I was particularly clumsy tonight, it seemed. Hardly an ideal state for dancing, to say nothing of bringing down an opponent. But perhaps clumsiness was just what was needed to force Mr. Russell to lose some of his composure. *If your opponent is of choleric temper, seek to irritate him,* Sun Tzu said.

I found it difficult to step on his feet, though. In fact, I couldn't have if I wanted to. If any further evidence was needed of his controlling nature, the dances supplied it amply. He was a capable if somewhat reserved dancer, and he led the steps in a way that allowed for no deviation on my part.

"What have you against Mr. Pike?" I asked as the couple beside us made their way to the center of the set.

He shook his head as we came together and skipped down the set. "Let us find another subject, Miss Donovan. I make it a point not to mix business with pleasure."

"And what makes you think this is pleasure?" We separated and took our places across from one another again.

He held my gaze, his face inscrutable. "It is."

There was absolutely nothing flirtatious in his tone—in fact, it was aggravatingly bland—and yet, I found my cheeks warming all the same.

It was not until the final step of the second dance that I managed to press my heel into the toe of his shoe. I smiled at him as I moved back into place and curtsied, and he bowed, returning his own enigmatic smile and giving no indication that anything had happened.

He rose and met my gaze. "Thank you for the dances, Miss Donovan. If you are looking for your next partner, might I suggest Mr. Pike? I would be grateful if you would take him off both mine and Lucy's hands. As an added bonus, as you are already acquainted with him, you need not even ask the Master of Ceremonies to arrange an introduction."

My blood boiled, but I would rather die than give him any sign that he was ruffling me, so I met his gaze squarely. "A kind suggestion, Mr. Russell. Tell me, how long do we have the pleasure"—I drew out the word unnecessarily long—"of your company in Oakworth?"

"I regret to inform you that I leave tomorrow morning," he replied. "I only came at Lucy's behest—guardian duties, you know—and now that that business is taken care of, I must away."

A sliver of disappointment lodged itself under my skin at being denied the possibility of securing a victory against Mr. Russell. "Is it not a guardian's duty to see to his ward's future? You have the opportunity to do just that for Lucy by securing a match for her, yet you dismiss it out of hand. I find it incomprehensible."

"Respectfully, Miss Donovan, it makes no difference to me whether or not you comprehend it. It is none of your business."

Heat rushed into my cheeks. "Saying *respectfully* does not automatically absolve you of the need to utter respectful words, *sir*. Let me be clear. I have been Lucy's friend for years. I would venture a guess that I know her better than you do. If you care about your ward, you would be wise to listen to me."

The fact that there was no anger in his face, only that same impassible expression he so often wore only increased my own frustration. He raised his brows. "Are you finished?"

I said nothing, knowing that if I opened my mouth, a few choice obscenities I had learned aboard my father's ship, the *Dominance*, would undoubtedly come out. That would hardly make him more likely to view me as Lucy's wise and trustworthy friend.

"Now allow *me* to be clear," he said so calmly I wanted to strangle him. "You seem to be an intelligent woman, Miss

Donovan, and a friend to Lucy. My advice to you is to accept both *that* role in Lucy's life and *my* role in her life—and not to confuse them." He held my gaze. "Even more clearly now—in case I have mistaken your level of intelligence or stubbornness— if you try to combat me on this point, *you will fail.* I would hate to see someone with as much promise as you fail." He smiled serenely. "It has been a pleasure making your acquaintance, Miss Donovan. Allow me to convey you back to your chaperone. I believe the next set is forming around us."

Biting my tongue until I was certain it would bleed, I allowed Mr. Russell to escort me. All I could think about was how to defeat him.

And I had every intention of doing so.

Chapter Three

The sun shone down prettily on the road that led to the parish church of Oakham, and Lucy hummed softly next to me as we walked in companionable silence with Mrs. Westwood behind. I had not even bothered telling her that I had failed in my goal. I *hadn't* failed. My goal had merely shifted. I understood now that this was not a short battle. This was war, and I would emerge victorious, despite having to wage it against my enemy from afar. In fact, the distance might even be turned to my benefit, for I would think more clearly with Mr. Russell gone.

"Ow!" Lucy yanked her arm away, staring at me in surprise. She looked down at her sleeve, which was bunched where my hand had been.

"Oh, heavens," I said, smoothing down the fabric and pressing her arm where my nails had been digging in. "I am terribly sorry, Lucy! How thoughtless of me."

She shook her head, though her brow was still furrowed. "Whatever possessed you to . . . to *claw* me in such a way?"

I tried to think of a plausible explanation, but I had none. The thought of Mr. Russell simply had such an effect upon me.

Thankfully, we reached the gate to the churchyard at that moment, and our attention was taken up with greeting those we passed.

Lucy had insisted we come in advance of the service—church was the only time she and Mr. Pike were guaranteed to see one another, and they made the most of it. He was just inside the door to the church, waiting, and Lucy quickly abandoned me for him, leaving me to Mrs. Westwood.

I didn't blame her for it. I could still remember how it felt when I had fallen in love at fifteen with Lieutenant Stokes aboard the *Dominance*, how I had been anxious for every opportunity to see him. I had even managed to convince my father to extend invitations for him to join us at dinner once or twice. That story had ended badly for me—moments I tried not to think on when I could avoid it—but I hoped to ensure that Lucy's story did *not*. Mr. Pike was nothing like Lieutenant Stokes.

Mrs. Westwood was eager to take her seat. She took nothing so seriously as church attendance, hence her willingness to arrive in advance. But rather than join her in the pew, I informed her that there was someone I needed to speak with before the service began. With pinched lips that told me she thought I should be applying myself to pondering for the minutes remaining, she left my side and made her way to her seat, keeping a sharp eye on Lucy.

I hadn't anyone particular to speak to, but I preferred standing by myself to being subject to Mrs. Westwood's conversation at the moment. I took the opportunity to inspect the plaques on the wall—prominent figures who had been buried in the church and a few who had made kind contributions, as well. It was terribly dull, but I preferred a bit of walking to sitting.

"Following me, are you, Miss Donovan?"

I whipped around and found myself facing Mr. Russell. My heart jumped. I hadn't ever thought to see him again, much less just two days after the assembly. How he could speak with such levity after the way we had parted the other night was inexplicable to me. My hands balled into fists at the mere sight of him.

"The shoe is rather on the other foot, it seems," I replied. "You will recall you told me you were leaving the area, which informs me, I suppose, that I may add perjurer to your growing list of *admirable* qualities."

The vicar took his place at the front of the congregation, and Mr. Russell ushered me into the nearest pew. "Crotchety and decrepit foremost among them? My business here is not, as I had thought it was, taken care of, hence my continued presence."

Mrs. Westwood was seated beside Lucy a few pews in front of us, and she turned, sending us a disapproving look, accompanied by a shushing gesture.

I waited until she turned back around before leaning toward Mr. Russell and whispering. "Business here meaning dashing Lucy's hopes and dreams to bits?"

"This is not the moment for such a discussion," he replied, not bothering to keep his voice down.

"And what is your excuse this time?" I hissed. "And no more of your nonsense about mixing business with pleasure, if you please."

Mrs. Westwood turned again, her expression even more foreboding than last time. Mr. Russell settled his own gaze upon me. It was both disappointed and disapproving, and he put a finger to his lips. "Please, Miss Donovan." He spoke a bit louder now. "This is hardly the place for discussing unholy matters— much less in such a strident voice. Surely you can leave such things at the door for just this short time. We are in God's house."

I stared at him, infusing my eyes with as much promised vengeance as I could muster. But he was not looking at me. His hands were clasped in his lap, and he was looking toward the vicar with anticipatory calm, the mere hint of a twitch at the corner of his mouth.

I pressed my lips together and bit my tongue, unwilling to draw any more censuring glances when he was so set upon refusing to speak on the subject.

Never had I sat through a sermon and heard so little. I wasn't sure what to be most annoyed about—the fact that Mr. Russell had managed to force me to sit beside him for the duration of the service or that he refused to speak with me about the only matter I cared to discuss with him. My own family—my father and my brothers Valentine and Phineas—were seated in our family's pew, where I should have been. There would be talk amongst the parish about my sitting beside Mr. Russell, and I had no patience for it.

When there was a short break in the service, he turned to me. "Are you enjoying the service today, Miss Donovan?"

I kept my eyes forward, saying nothing.

His gaze remained on me, waiting for the response I vowed not to give him.

"You refuse to speak with me, then?" he asked.

"My only business with you, Mr. Russell, relates to your niece, and as you refuse to discuss that matter, I can see no purpose to any conversation between us." I paused. "Besides, we are, as you so astutely pointed out, in God's house, and nothing else I have to say to you is appropriate for such a venue."

"Good gracious," he said, his voice infused with amusement. "You scandalize me, Miss Donovan."

I whipped my head around, my face growing hot at what he had inferred from my words. "That is hardly what I meant, as you are well aware. Expressing my true thoughts would be scandalous only because it requires me to use the breadth of sailor cant at my disposal—insults that would leave your ears ringing."

"After church, then," he said. "I am duly intrigued."

He was impossible, but I was as mad at myself as I was at him. Since the assembly, I had been formulating a strategy to help Lucy and Mr. Pike—one that would make use of Mr. Russell's absence and my proximity to the couple—but his sudden and unexpected appearance at church had overset me, taking me off guard and causing me to act in a way that would hardly help my cause. Lucy's cause, that was.

By the time the service was over, I was regretting my rashness. I had inherited my temper from my father—heaven knew my mother had none—and it was not something I was proud of. With a stiff *excuse me*, I left the pew.

I needed to decide how to act toward Mr. Russell in a way that would most benefit Lucy. I couldn't let this battle be about me and my pride. Lucy's happiness and future were at stake.

Perhaps Mr. Russell was right. Perhaps I should mind my own business and leave the two to settle her future between them. But what sort of friend would do such a thing? There was no guarantee, after all, that an offer better than Mr. Pike's would present itself—in fact, it was quite *un*likely, for she was an orphan with no dowry to speak of. This made it all the more flabbergasting to me that Mr. Russell was so set against the match.

As I stepped outside and into the shade the building cast over the churchyard, I found my brothers and father awaiting me.

"Couldn't bring yourself to sit with us riffraff today?" Valentine quipped. He was older than me by two years and by far the darkest in our family—in both appearance and personality. Given how light both my father's and mother's coloring were, he had been teased from a young age about being illegitimate. The fact that he and my father couldn't stand one another had hardly helped calm such speculation. Neither had his insistence on taking pains to thwart and upset my father at every turn. Where *the Admiral*, as Valentine called him, insisted on moral rectitude and frugality, Valentine had garnered a reputation as a rake and a gambler.

"I wasn't aware you were acquainted with Mr. Russell, Diana," my father said, removing any doubt that he had noted where I had sat during the service.

"Barely," I said. "He is Lucy Ellis's guardian, you know."

"One would have expected him to sit by *her*, then," Valentine said, raising a dark, quizzical brow.

"Believe me," I replied, "I would have far preferred that."

"Mr. Russell," my father said, looking behind me.

Valentine's lip twitched, and I shut my eyes as Mr. Russell spoke.

"Admiral Donovan, what a pleasure to see you. I had assumed you would still be away, engaged in naval matters. Your daughter was just telling me all she learned from spending time aboard."

I turned toward him, my eyes widening at his reference to my ability to swear like a sailor. It was not something my father appreciated—in fact, it was that and my failed attempt at a romance with Lieutenant Stokes that had decided him upon sending me home and subsequently to Mrs. Westwood's. He was convinced I had been corrupted by my time aboard the *Dominance* and needed to be taken sternly in hand, something my mother was incapable of doing given her failing health. I had taken pains since his return from the war to refrain from letting any unsavory words pass through my lips.

My father's brows contracted, but it was Phineas who spoke, adjusting his glasses to sit on the bridge of his nose. "Yes, Diana can work the ropes as well as any of us, I think."

It was a sacrifice for Phineas to say such a thing, and I wanted to embrace him for the unusual interjection. He had never been the sailor my father had hoped for him to be. None of my brothers had, in fact. Theo had come very near to it, only to ruin everything when he had resigned from the Navy earlier this year and married my friend Elena.

Phineas had disappointed my father early on, though, begging to attend the Royal Naval Academy rather than go to work on an actual ship—blasphemy to Admiral George Donovan, who valued experience over everything. But Phineas's interest in the Navy had always been limited to what he could read between the covers of a book.

"I *am* quite occupied, as it happens," my father said, "but most of my time is dedicated to correspondence at this point. Which, I fear, is why I must beg your pardon. I have a few pressing matters awaiting my attention at home." He gave a curt bow of the head and turned to me. "Are you coming, Diana?"

"No," I replied. "I promised Lucy I would walk home with her."

"And Mrs. Westwood," my father supplied, though he said it as a question.

"Yes, Father." It was a mystery to me what he assumed I might do in Mrs. Westwood's absence and why he thought she would be a deterrent for anything I was truly determined to do, but I was content for him to think her presence a guard to my reputation if it allowed me more freedom.

"I rather think I shall walk home too," Valentine said.

"Very well," my father said colorlessly. "Good day to you, Mr. Russell."

"And to you, Admiral," Mr. Russell replied.

Valentine looked between me and Mr. Russell, quirked a black brow at me, then turned away while Phineas followed my father.

"I am ready, Miss Donovan," Mr. Russell said.

I turned toward him and raised my brows. "Ready?"

"To have my character torn to shreds in the vernacular of a sailor." He clasped his hands at his waist and waited.

I stared at him for a moment, considering how it would feel

to tell him what I thought of him, how strong my feelings were after such a short time. But, while I had not heard most of the vicar's sermon, I had had a bit of time to reflect, and I had no intention of letting Mr. Russell know the power he exercised over my temper. I envied his calm, cool disposition.

"No," I said.

His brows contracted. "No?"

"No."

He paused, looking a bit disappointed. "Perhaps another time, then."

"Unlikely," I said. "Now, if you will excuse me, I must find Lucy." I gave a quick curtsy and turned to go.

"By that, do you mean you intend to aid and abet her in spending time with Mr. Pike?"

I stopped, waiting a moment before I turned back toward him. "And if that *is* what I intend?"

"Then I hope you will not encourage her to do anything she might have cause to regret."

I let out a breathy laugh through my nose. "Mr. Russell, it was you who so *respectfully* reminded me that I am Lucy's friend, not her guardian. What influence have I compared to yours? If you wish to control Lucy, I recommend you do it yourself. It is none of my business, after all, is it?" I smiled with false sweetness.

"As much as I would love to *control Lucy*, as you so delicately put it, I mustn't delay returning home any longer. I had not intended to spend more than a day here."

I raised my brows. "And your business is truly concluded now? You trust me enough to leave Lucy's well-being in my devious hands?"

"In Mrs. Westwood's, rather."

I laughed and looked away. Those in attendance at the morning's service were slowly trickling out of the churchyard, leaving only a few clusters of conversation amongst the leafy trees and stone grave markers.

"You scoff at my choice?" Mr. Russell asked.

I folded my arms and met his gaze. "Yes. At your choice to neglect your duties *and* at your choice of companion for Lucy."

He frowned. "Mrs. Westwood is an upstanding woman."

"And have you spent any time in her company?"

"Of course I have."

"Then you are familiar with her overabundance of maxims and the way she peppers every conversation with them?"

"I could hardly be unfamiliar with that."

I gave a nod. "And would you care to surrender *yourself* to her care for years at a time? I spent three years under her tutelage, Mr. Russell, and I could tell you plenty of stories to illustrate why your choice is an unwise one."

He held my gaze, saying nothing for a moment. "She is the most proper and sensible person to care for Lucy, Miss Donovan."

"Sensible," I repeated with a laugh. It was not the first word I would use to describe Mrs. Westwood. Her heart was good, but she was rigid and inflexible in her expectations.

"Again, you venture into matters outside the scope of your responsibility or knowledge," Mr. Russell said.

I shrugged. "You asked for my opinion on your choice. I am merely providing it."

"And submitting yourself as a more suitable alternative?"

"I am submitting Mr. Pike for that role, Mr. Russell. I thought I had made that clear. And as our dear Mrs. Westwood says, *No one can know better that which is best for a woman than her husband.*"

I thought I saw the corner of Mr. Russell's mouth quiver. "I am sure Mrs. Westwood would agree that an alternative must be selected until Lucy has such a husband."

"Which, if *you* are the arbiter of her future, will be never."

"You are wrong, Miss Donovan. Intelligent and engaging, but wrong."

I ignored the strange sensation his backhanded compliment produced inside me. "Or perhaps it is *you* who are wrong, Mr. Russell. And I intend to make you see that. What is it you have against Mr. Pike? What is so unsuitable about him in your eyes?"

He smiled slightly. "I ask you again, Miss Donovan, to leave the matter in my hands."

"When you give me no reason to?"

"I am not obliged to give you anything. I mean what I said. If you insist on pursuing this road, you give me no choice but to consider it as provocation. It is a battle you shall lose."

It was my turn to smile. Talk of battle couldn't but draw such a response. "Are you acquainted with the teachings of Sun Tzu, Mr. Russell? *To secure ourselves against defeat lies in our own hands, but the opportunity of defeating the enemy is provided by the enemy himself.*" I stared at him intently. "I assure you, I shall not provide you with such an opportunity."

He put out his hands. "By all means, then, do your best. But when you finally realize your cause is a lost one, I hope you shall remember this moment."

"I rather think I shall remember this moment for other reasons."

"Being . . . ?"

I tilted my head to the side. "The moment you challenged me to war."

His eyes squinted imperceptibly in amusement. "Almost you make me regret having to leave."

"Regret is a feeling with which you will become very well acquainted, Mr. Russell."

In an unexpected gesture, he took up my hand, bowing and placing a chaste kiss upon my glove. Still bent over, he looked up at me through his dark lashes. "Oh, I very much doubt that."

Chapter Four

I watched Mr. Russell walk off to speak with Mrs. Westwood, my heart knocking about in my chest at the way he had just looked at me. Once again, I found myself wondering how to interpret his words and whether there had been a double meaning in them. I couldn't tell if he despised our conversation or enjoyed the challenge I presented, and that made it very difficult for me to strategize.

From the way Mrs. Westwood glanced over at Lucy and Mr. Pike as Mr. Russell spoke with her, I anticipated she would be averse to letting him escort Lucy on the walk home.

I waited until Mr. Russell had departed and Mrs. Westwood was making her way to join Lucy and Mr. Pike, allowing her to hear my remark to Mr. Pike.

"I had a matter to discuss with you, Mr. Pike," I said. "Would it be a great burden for you and your mother to walk with us?"

He met my eyes, a clear understanding there of what I was trying to accomplish. "Not a burden at all, Miss Donovan. Are you agreeable, Mother?" He looked to Mrs. Pike, who had been standing with him and Lucy for the past few minutes. She was a thin, quiet widow, her eyes a bit gaunt and her face pale. Lucy had told me that she was invalidish, and I suddenly worried that I might be asking too much of her. But she assented to the plan with a small smile and a nod. "The fresh air will do me good."

She could keep Mrs. Westwood occupied, I hoped, until we parted ways. I needed this time to consult with Lucy and Mr. Pike, for there was no telling when I would next see them both. There was the added benefit for them, too, of more time together.

And though Mrs. Westwood's lips compressed when the three of us dropped behind her and Mrs. Pike, allowing ample distance between our two groups, she said nothing. Mrs. Pike was obliged to keep a slow pace, which would give us at least ten minutes to discuss plans before we parted ways with her and her son.

"Have you made any progress, Diana?" Lucy asked me anxiously.

"A bit," I said, feeling that even that was a stretch. "But it is always slow at first, you know. I cannot do much until I come to know Mr. Russell better." That was certainly difficult given the fact that I had seen all of him that I *would* see. "So far, he has been very opaque about his reasons for disapproving of the match. Mr. Pike, have you any idea why he might be set against you?"

Mr. Pike's eyebrows went up, and he shook his head incredulously. "I have racked my brain to think what it might be owing to. Perhaps he thinks me too forward in my affections for Lucy?"

"Well, that would just be silly," I said. "One would think he would applaud a man who knew his own mind. He gave no reason, then, for assuring you he would not give his approval?"

Lucy lifted her shoulders. "He said I was too young and that he does not trust Edwin to take care of me."

I raised my brows.

"On account of a few unwise financial decisions I made in

the past," Mr. Pike explained, his brows pulled tight and the corners of his mouth drooping in a self-condemnatory frown.

"What man has not made unwise financial decisions?" I said. "Indeed, I should like to ask Mr. Russell if he is immune to such foibles." I turned to Mr. Pike again. "Lucy mentioned you believe it is also a matter of him not wishing to relinquish control over her."

Mr. Pike went a bit red about the ears. "I should not have said that, perhaps, but I have known a guardian or two with strong personalities like Mr. Russell's, and often they are eager to assert their control."

"I know just the sort of person." My father was such a one. He was accustomed to being obeyed, and when he was not . . . well, one need look no further than Valentine to see the sort of rancor that might result. If Valentine had not been in financial distress at this particular moment, he would certainly not have been spending his time at Blackwick.

"We must persuade Mr. Russell that he is wrong in his assessments," I continued. "We need a strategy to gain his approval for the match."

"What if we never succeed?" Lucy looked at Mr. Pike with a touch of anguish. "He is so very stubborn—so very demanding. I believe that is why he himself has not yet married. No woman could ever meet his expectations."

I scoffed. "I should think not. Not that any woman would ever *wish* to." I calmed myself, remembering the point of our conversation, which was not to enumerate Mr. Russell's worst qualities but to make a plan and assuage Lucy's very obvious doubts. "We shall succeed, Lucy. Of that I am confident. But there is always Scotland if the situation becomes desperate." I winked at Mr. Pike.

"Scotland," Mr. Pike repeated, looking at me with wide eyes.

"You mean Gretna Green?" Lucy's voice was filled with dismay.

"I am only teasing," I said. "Scotland is a last resort, and we have not yet tried any other strategies. There are plenty available to us. You may be sure of that."

"Of course," Mr. Pike said. "You are too right, Miss Donovan. That is not at all how I wish to have my Lucy." His gaze went to her, and tenderness filled his eyes. "I want to do things the right way—the way she deserves."

I looked away from the intimate moment they were having in the middle of the road. What must it feel like to be regarded such a way? Would I enjoy it? Or find it nauseating? Either way, I wasn't the sort of angel that deserved such a gaze, and any man who could believe I was would be too dull to keep my feelings engaged. I would certainly not be his choice of wife. I was too masculine by personality, too practical and abrupt. Men wanted sweet and docile Lucys to protect, women who made them feel needed and important, and I needed no one to protect me.

"I need a better understanding of Mr. Russell," I said, refocusing my attention again. "What else can you tell me about him, Lucy?"

"Precious little. Aside from short communications about my allowance and other such business matters, my interactions with him have been few and far between."

I pursed my lips pensively. "How, then, have you come to your opinion of him? You said he was disagreeable—a word with which I agree, mind you, now that I have met him—but how did you come to that conclusion?"

Her brow furrowed. "He has always . . . avoided me, I suppose. Hardly speaks a word to me. It has been that way ever since I can remember. Properly, he is my uncle, but there has been nothing avuncular about him. I had hoped that might change when he became my guardian, but if anything, he has been even more aloof and distant since then. After the death of my parents, he seemed upset with me—as if he disliked being saddled with my care." She frowned. "And he looks so severe all the time."

"Well," I said, "Mr. Russell's temperament we cannot change. We must work with what we have, and what we have, my dear, is *you*. You have been far too compliant and easy a ward, I think."

Mr. Pike looked at me curiously, while Lucy directed her wide, blue eyes at me. "I do try not to be a burden."

I smiled at her sympathetically. "And that does you justice. But is it any wonder your uncle is loath to surrender responsibility for you when you are so easy a charge? You must *become* a burden. That way, he will be eager to hand you over to Mr. Pike here."

Lucy looked doubtful but Mr. Pike admiring.

I continued. "We will only be asking him to do the things any guardian must be prepared to do. And, if all goes well, he will be less averse to the idea of abdicating his responsibility and allowing someone who is eager to see to your needs"—I looked at Mr. Pike—"to take it up."

Lucy looked to him. "I do not like to bother my uncle, but if it means I shall be able to be with Edwin . . ."

We arrived at the crossroads which required the Pikes to leave us, and we bid the two of them farewell.

Mrs. Westwood turned to us once they were out of earshot. "I cannot feel that it is wise of you to continue seeing Mr. Pike now that your uncle has expressed his disapproval of the connection, Lucy."

"Oh, but surely he does not disapprove of Edwin entirely," Lucy said in alarm.

Mrs. Westwood's mouth grew prim. *"Those who take liberties with the names of the opposite sex are bound to take liberties in other areas of propriety.* You should not be making free with Mr. Pike's given name, Lucy. It is not at all proper. And you may be right about Mr. Russell's opinion on the topic of Mr. Pike, but I would hate to assume such a thing and discover myself to be wrong."

I had been listening to the exchange in silence, but an idea occurred to me—one that made me smile inwardly. "There is no need for anyone to assume *anything*. It is best to apply to Mr. Russell himself to clear up any matter upon which there is a question."

Mrs. Westwood looked at me thoughtfully, considering the suggestion, and I pressed my advantage.

"You should not have the burden of such decisions on your shoulders, Mrs. Westwood. You already have a great deal occupying your mind and time, of course, and you cannot be expected to guess at the wishes of Lucy's guardian. He has assured me he takes his position quite seriously; I cannot think he would be anything but eager to do what lies within his power, even if it is only easing your mind." I paused. "No matter is too small upon which to ask his opinion, in fact, for he seems a particular sort of man who expects his wishes to be understood and obeyed with precision."

Between Lucy's and Mrs. Westwood's communications, Mr. Russell would be obliged to respond to a hitherto unreached level of correspondence. It would also be a burden upon his pocketbook, paying for the receipt of each piece of post.

Supreme excellence consists in breaking the enemy's resistance without fighting. This would be a perfect application of Sun Tzu's philosophy.

Chapter Five

My father was enough occupied with naval matters these days that he hardly took notice of my doings. The war might have ended for England as a whole, but its repercussions had certainly not ended for the Royal Navy. Despite the fact that he would not have noticed my leaving unaccompanied, I brought my maid, Tait, along with me on my walk the next day. I needed to ensure the letter Lucy wrote her uncle had the proper tone to it, but I didn't wish to be lectured on proper decorum by Mrs. Westwood when I arrived at the seminary.

It was near the center of Oakworth, just beside the circulating library, a fact which Mrs. Westwood had had ample cause to regret. More than once, I had been chastised for slipping inside and returning with one of the novels that so scandalized her. The thought brought a nostalgic smile to my face. All in all, though, I did not miss being a student at the seminary.

It was midsummer holiday, and all of the girls were home for the next four weeks, leaving it oddly quiet inside. I found Lucy in her room, sitting at her escritoire with a quill in hand, staring through the window. A few crumpled papers were scattered on the floorboards near her feet.

She jumped as the door squeaked, then hurried to her feet. "There you are, Diana! You must help me write this letter. Cousin Agnes will be positively furious with me if I waste another piece of paper, but I cannot at all decide what to say."

I came over to her and peered at the greeting she had written and the sentences that followed it. It was just as I had thought, full of phrases like *forgive me, at your convenience,* and *not at all an urgent matter.*

She looked up at me with a hint of guilt written on her face.

"Lucy," I said, looking at her in mixed amusement and consternation, "do you wish to marry Mr. Pike at your uncle's convenience? Is your future not at all an urgent matter?"

She smiled slightly. "When you put it into such words . . ."

"Let us try again."

Together, we crafted a letter to Mr. Russell, explaining that Lucy was in need of more money to purchase trimmings for a new bonnet.

"*Two yards of ribbon will be more than enough, I think,*" I dictated slowly enough for her to keep pace with me. Normally, I hated correspondence—my hand could never keep up with my thoughts—but dictating was different. And this was for an important cause. "*I found the most enchanting color yesterday, the hue of red apples, or perhaps cherries would be a more apt comparison—*"

Lucy had stopped writing. She looked up at me.

"What?"

"Need we trouble my uncle with the color of the trimmings?"

"Most certainly, we must. It is bound to bore him to death, which is all the more reason to draw out such details, my dear. If he intends to assert his guardianship now, of all times, he must accept all which that entails, down to the most trifling particulars of your life. Shall we carry on?"

She nodded, turning back to the page and dipping the quill again.

"At thruppence per yard, I would need half a shilling to afford them. Do you think it is too dear a price for red silk ribbon? I should not say red, perhaps, for that gives one to think it was rather plain, when it was anything but that, as I mentioned. There was another spool that caught my eye at tuppence per yard, though I am told that lime green is not so wholesome a color as something more subdued—pear, for example. Cousin Agnes says that the colors a woman wears should be as restrained as her character. But apart from that, I would be pleased over anything if the ribbon matched my pelisse, which is, if you remember from church, a sort of scarlet color, which I think shall go quite nicely with the red but not nearly so well with the lime. Oh, please do tell me your thoughts! I shouldn't wish to do anything of which you might disapprove."

I smiled at the thought of Mr. Russell reading it.

Once we had finished the long and drawn out ending, Lucy sprinkled the ink with sand and turned to me. "Do you think Cousin Agnes is serious about my not seeing Edwin anymore?"

"I think she is afraid of your uncle accusing her of encouraging you, Lucy. But you cannot avoid seeing Mr. Pike entirely. Your uncle must be reasonable enough to admit that. You are in the same parish, after all, and I imagine you must see him in the village too."

"Not often, no," she replied with a frown. "I have only ever seen him at the apothecary. He is there often, you know, on account of his mother's ill health."

I raised my brows at this helpful piece of information. "Next to The Feather and Fawn, you mean, where letters are posted?" I raised an enigmatic brow. "Come, let us take this letter, then. Who knows what we shall find when we do?"

She waved her hand and turned away to fold the paper. "Oh, Sarah can do that. There is no need for—" Her head whipped around, eyes fixed on me as understanding dawned upon her. "Oh." Her mouth drew up into a smile. "Yes. Yes, let us go."

"I have a mind to stop at the apothecary myself," I said, donning my bonnet again. "My supply of smelling salts is dangerously low, and you know how often I make use of them." I winked at her, and she covered a laugh with her hand.

We were indeed fortunate enough to see Mr. Pike at the apothecary, and I was able to provide him and Lucy with a quarter of an hour's conversation as I spoke with the apothecary and acquired a few items I was nearly certain we already had on hand at Blackwick.

It was only two days before we received a reply from Mr. Russell, but Lucy was too terrified to read it. Instead, she handed it to me and insisted I read it to her.

I smiled at her nervousness, but in truth, I was anxiously impatient for the response as well. I broke the wax seal and unfolded the paper, revealing a one-pound note inside. Mr. Russell's handwriting was as calm and even as his personality and the missive short—also like his personality.

Dear Lucy,

I was pleased to receive your letter. Enclosed you will find enough money, I hope, to pay for both the lime green ribbons and the red ones— were they apple or cherry?—if you decide upon such a course. In matters of fashion, I must trust your taste and Mrs. Westwood's over my own, I am afraid.

Your servant, as ever,

Uncle Duke

"Well?" Lucy said. "What does it say?"

I blinked. I had read the letter silently, leaving Lucy to guess at its contents. "Forgive me." I cleared my throat and read it to her, then handed Lucy the banknote.

Her eyes went wide. "Well, that is very sporting of him, isn't it?"

"Lucy," I said in a censuring voice. "You mustn't allow him to divert you from your goal. Being sent a pound for ribbons, while a welcome surprise, is not our true quest, remember. We wish for his approval for the match."

She blinked quickly, nodding. "Yes, yes. Of course, you are right. You always are, Di." She looked at the bank note in her hands. "Though, I admit I should like to see what ribbons Mrs. Daniels has. It seems only right that I should buy cherry ribbons now."

I took a piece of paper from the escritoire drawer and set it before her. "After you write another letter."

"Another letter?"

I nodded.

"But . . . whatever should it be about?"

I thought for a moment, looking around the room. My eyes settled on the thin stack of paper in the drawer. "Paper. Enough paper and ink to write him a letter a day for an entire year."

Her eyes widened. "A year?"

"If that is what is necessary, then yes."

I dictated another letter, this time having Lucy detail all the reasons she might need paper—correspondence, drawing, keeping a journal, making paper flowers—as well as asking for his opinion regarding the most superior ink recipes, *having so very many more decades' experience than I.*

"He is not so very old, though, Di," Lucy countered as I dictated the line.

"Perhaps not, but if he insists on treating you like a child, he should at least feel some ill effects of it, I think."

We delivered the letter to the postmaster and, as we had begun to make a habit of doing, passed by the apothecary, where we found Mr. Pike just leaving. He accompanied us to purchase ribbons, and again I found myself wondering what Mr. Russell found to dislike in him. He was attentive to both mine and Lucy's comfort, respectful to everyone we passed, and while he was not a man of infinite means, he was kind enough to pay for Lucy's ribbons, insisting she keep the pound note for something else.

———

T wo days later, I pulled on my kid gloves as Tait and I made our way to the front door of Blackwick Hall to make our now-daily visit to the seminary. I had hopes that Mr. Russell's response to our latest letter might be waiting there.

"Di."

I turned and found Valentine looking at me from the doorway of the breakfast room. He generally breakfasted late to avoid my father. Living under the same roof with both of them was a combustible situation. If my father had not been so preoccupied with other matters, though, it would have been far worse, and my own actions would certainly have been under greater scrutiny.

"Where are you going?" Valentine asked.

"Into the village," I said.

His head tilted to the side dubiously. "To arrange a meeting for the Ellis girl and the Pike boy, you mean. Take care, Di."

I shot a glance at Tait, wondering if she had opened her mouth to the other servants. There was no other way Valentine might have caught wind of things. Tait's gaze met mine apologetically, and I turned back to my brother. "Whatever do you mean?" It was the height of hypocrisy for Valentine, of all people, to be urging caution on such a matter—or upon any matter, really.

"I heard you speaking with her guardian at church," he said. "He doesn't approve of the match."

"And since when have you cared the snap of your fingers for obedience?"

"I only meant to warn you," he said. "He does not seem the type of man it would be wise to cross."

I rather thought the problem was that Mr. Russell hadn't been crossed *enough*. "Your warning—and unusual concern for me—is noted, dear brother." I cinched the strings of my reticule and slipped it over my wrist. "I am surprised to see you. I thought you might decide to pay for a room at The Feather and Fawn for the next two weeks." Our father was expecting company—a few of his officers on business.

"Believe me," Valentine replied, "if I had the money, I would. But then again, if I had any money, I wouldn't be here at all, would I? Perhaps we can pool our resources and trade off taking refuge. Your old friend is among our hailed guests, you know."

My brows knit. "Who?"

"Captain Stokes."

My smile evaporated. The last time I had seen Captain Stokes, he had been a lieutenant on the *Dominance*. Hardly a time I cared to be reminded of. "Well," I said, forcing nonchalance, "I see even more trips to the village in the near future, then."

"Mind you do not get in over your head, Di." Valentine turned away, leaving Tait and me to be on our way.

Tait apologized profusely as soon as she closed the door behind us, admitting that she had mentioned Mr. Pike when recounting how she had come by the new tincture she had bought at the apothecary the other day.

"It is of no account," I said. "Valentine is not the sort of person to make any real attempt to stop me. He simply wishes to be disagreeable."

There was indeed a response from Mr. Russell waiting at the seminary. It was still unopened, for Lucy insisted upon my reading it to her.

I forced myself to open it slowly and methodically. There was a ten-pound note within.

Dear Lucy,

Thank you for your letter. It brought to my attention my own alarming ignorance on the subject of ink. It seems clear I have been remiss in providing you with the necessary allowance. Forgive my error and please accept the enclosed note, which I anticipate will be enough for your needs until the next quarter day.

Your servant, as ever,

Uncle Duke

PS Good day to you, Miss Donovan.

My breath caught at the last line. A smile crept over my lips and a thrill through my body as I read them again. He knew my role in this, and I was glad for it.

"Well," said Lucy, holding up the bank note with awe, "we cannot possibly appeal to him for more money *now*. Good heavens. Ten pounds!"

"No, we cannot apply for more money," I agreed. "But there are plenty of other matters over which a guardian can be applied to. In truth, I think him terribly irresponsible."

"Irresponsible?" Lucy asked doubtfully.

"Yes. He sends you a ten-pound note and provides no guidance about what to spend it on or where to keep it. I can tell you, there are a vast number of people who would love to get their hands on that note if given the chance. It puts you at great risk. It also calls into question how he has been handling your expenses up to this point, making so free with money."

Lucy's brow was furrowed. "You think I am in danger of being robbed? Here at the seminary?"

I didn't think anything of the sort. But the more ridiculous Lucy's communications, the more annoying they would be to Mr. Russell, and our goal was to make him eager to hand responsibility for her over to Mr. Pike. He had to be made to think that the only way for him to be an effective guardian was to be involved in the minutiae of Lucy's life, down to telling her where to store her money.

According to Sun Tzu, after all, *Sometimes, you must pretend to be weak*.

At the end of dictating the letter, a concoction full of more ridiculous questions and an urgency for their answers, I paused.

"That will do," I said. "Perhaps before we leave, you can ask your cousin if she has any letters for us to post. I can see to folding the letter."

Lucy replaced the quill in its stand and rose from her seat. "Of course. I shall go straightaway."

When she had left the room, I sat down and took the quill, dipping it in the ink, then putting it to the bottom of the paper under Lucy's signature.

PS An unmarried man who would send an unmarried woman a clandestine message cannot be trusted with a ward of his own.

Smiling, I returned the quill to its place and hurried to sand the ink and fold the letter, addressing it in my own hand, for I knew it would bother him.

Well, I hoped it would. My experience of Mr. Russell told me that little ruffled him. But that was before he had met me.

There was nothing to be done now but post the letter and wait another two days for his response. It was admittedly frustrating to be obliged to kick our heels until then, but there was no helping that. Some warfare had to be waged from a distance.

———

The letter had been posted, and we were in the apothecary shop, waiting for one of Mrs. Pike's concoctions when the door opened. Tait, who had been waiting outside, appeared, looking frazzled, her eyes full of warning. Mrs. Westwood stepped up behind her. She stopped short at the sight of us, and Lucy and Mr. Pike's conversation immediately ceased.

Mrs. Westwood took stock of us, and her nostrils flared. She pushed past Tait. "Miss Ellis, may I please have a word with you outside?"

Lucy nodded slowly, shooting a nervous glance at me.

"You too, Miss Donovan," her cousin added.

I led the way through the door, hoping my placid reaction to being discovered would help calm Lucy. Lucy still had hope of living up to her cousin's expectations of her, a goal I had long since given up striving toward. It was impossible. The woman had some trite phrase to offer for every situation under the sun, it seemed.

Tait shot me an apologetic glance as we passed her to leave the shop, and I put a reassuring hand on her arm. Short of physically detaining Mrs. Westwood, there was nothing she could have done to prevent the situation.

Mrs. Westwood stopped near the side of the apothecary, and I gave Lucy an encouraging smile.

"*The word of a man is his bond, but the word of a woman contains her very soul.*" She let those heavy—and, frankly, ridiculous— words hang in the air for a moment. "I thought we had agreed that you would no longer see Mr. Pike, Lucy. And, Miss Donovan"—she turned to me—"I am surprised at you for allowing such a thing to happen under your care. You certainly know better. I have nothing against Mr. Pike, Lucy, but what sort of woman would I be if I ignored the wishes of your guardian?"

Lucy's eyes were filling with tears, and her cousin was looking harried—hurt, even. I felt a heaviness in my chest.

"May I speak with you privately, Mrs. Westwood?" I asked.

Tight-lipped, she nodded and stepped aside with me.

"You must absolve your cousin of responsibility," I said once we had left Lucy's side. "This is entirely my doing."

Her brow was knit, her eyes full of disappointment as she looked at me. "Why, Miss Donovan? I do not understand."

I hesitated for a moment. *"Marriage is the culmination of a young woman's efforts, the North Star which guides her every choice, the pinnacle of her very existence."* It was only with effort that I managed to finish the phrase she had taught us without shuddering. "I am only trying to help Lucy achieve that, Mrs. Westwood. And, as I knew you did not feel comfortable taking responsibility for continued meetings between Lucy and Mr. Pike, I took it upon myself. I assure you that propriety has not been breached, for I have watched over each and every one."

She looked torn. "I agree that Mr. Pike is an upstanding young gentleman, and if it were up to me, I would be happy to see Lucy marry him. But the fact still remains that her guardian does *not* approve."

"Yes, and he can be quite forbidding, I think. It must be difficult in your position."

She glanced at Lucy and sighed, a little of her anger fleeing. "I feel a great responsibility having her under my care. And yes, Mr. Russell does inspire one with . . . well, I confess I find it difficult to decipher his opinion of my efforts with Lucy."

I put a reassuring hand on her arm, sincerely feeling for her, surprised as I was at her admission of the burden she felt herself under. She was not generally one to express emotion.

But Mr. Russell's severity must be wearing on her, making her feel anxious and unworthy. It was disagreeable of him, for, ridiculous as I sometimes found Mrs. Westwood, she deserved nothing but praise and approval for her years of dedication to forming Lucy into a lady. She had a respite from the rest of the young women during the midsummer holidays, but she had no such thing from taking care of Lucy. It was yet another reason the match was to be applauded and sought after.

But her rigid sense of right and wrong would never allow her to oversee more courting between her charge and Mr. Pike, and if Mr. Russell had his way, she might have charge of Lucy for many years to come.

And that would not do at all.

But perhaps there was something else I could do to help both Mrs. Westwood and Lucy with their troubles.

Chapter Six

When I returned to Blackwick, my father was holed up in his study, where he also took his dinner, and I valued my peace too much to disturb him. My suggestion would have to wait for the morning. My father was an advocate of both arising early and partaking of a substantial meal in the morning, so I timed my own appearance there to coincide with his.

As I entered, he glanced up from the newspaper he was holding, his brows contracting slightly. "What is the special occasion?"

I took a plate and placed some toast upon it, then took a seat beside him. "No occasion. I am simply hungry."

"Out with it, Diana. You never come to breakfast at this hour unless you have something particular to say to me."

I scraped butter onto my toast and gave a little shrug. "Since we are having guests, I only thought I might invite a few other people to come to Blackwick for a week or two."

He lowered his paper slightly. "It is not a house party, Diana. It is business."

"True, but you will not be engaged in business all day every day, surely. You must eat and take respites from time to time. You want your officers to enjoy themselves as much as can be managed, do you not?"

"No," he said flatly. "We are discussing important matters, not hosting a hunting party. I will have no time to play the welcoming host to your friends."

"Neither would I expect you to," I reassured him, slathering preserves over the butter. "I am more than capable of doing that myself."

"You are not in a position to host guests, Diana. If you wish to do such a thing, perhaps you should consider getting married." My father opened the newspaper wider and looked back down at it. I was losing him, losing my chance.

The door opened, and Valentine checked on the threshold as his gaze fell upon the two of us within.

"Valentine can assist," I said before he could close the door and retreat.

My father looked up at him while Valentine stared at me.

"That doesn't sound like me," Valentine said. "Assist with what?" Seeming to accept that he could not disappear at this point, he stepped into the room and began filling a plate.

"I thought you and I could invite a friend or two while Father has his guests here. It has been so long since we had a proper house party. Not that this would be one," I hurried to say at the sight of my father opening his mouth.

I directed my most beseeching gaze at Valentine as he turned from the sideboard to come to the table. He was in my debt, for I had smoothed things over between him and my father more than once over the past few weeks, even convincing my father to pay a few of Valentine's more pressing debts.

"If Valentine is willing to indulge your wishes, I have no argument to make against it," my father said, closing the newspaper and scooting his chair back.

Valentine met my increasingly hopeful and pleading gaze with consternation, setting his plate down and taking his seat.

"What do you say, Val?" I asked.

He held my gaze a long moment, and I recognized exactly what he was communicating to me. He would only be doing this to repay his debt to me. I knew him too well to think he would be any real help hosting. He was not nearly social enough for that, and that suited me perfectly. I liked to be in charge.

"Fine," he said.

My father stopped at the door, looking back at us with his intent and grim gaze. "So be it. But make no mistake, Diana. The priority is my business with the officers. The moment you disturb us or impede that, I shall send everyone packing."

"Of course," I said. "You shall hardly know we are here—unless you wish to, of course."

He gave a curt nod and left the room, shutting the door soundly.

"What is your game, Di?" Valentine asked.

I smiled and gave him an enigmatic look. "Wouldn't you like to know?"

His dark brows knit. "Perhaps not."

I was glad he did not mean to press me, for I thought he might retract his willingness if he knew just whom I meant to invite.

He cut the slab of mutton on his plate. "Is this your attempt to win over Stokes?"

I made a noise of disgust. "Hardly."

He chewed his mutton, then turned to me. "Well, consider yourself in *my* debt now, dear sister." He smiled silkily and pinched my cheek.

Being in my brother's debt would be worth the annoyance if things went according to my plan.

"Take Mr. Pike's things to the Blue Room," I said to the footman.

He picked up the single portmanteau Mr. Pike had brought. Three of my father's four guests had arrived yesterday, while Captain Stokes was expected tomorrow. I wasn't entirely sure how to feel about his coming. Just the thought of him was unpleasant, and I wondered how many other young women he might have manipulated into achieving his current rank. I hated him doubly, for he had used me and torn my character to shreds. Nothing he had criticized about me those years ago had changed, either. Indeed, I was more stubborn and domineering than ever, if anything. That was the inevitable effect of having essentially managed Blackwick since leaving Mrs. Westwood's. But I had been strong-willed even as a child. Between my ability to cajole Father and then his being gone at war, I had become used to having my way. Lieutenant Stokes—or Captain Stokes now—wanted a more docile woman. All men did.

"Have you anything else?" I asked Mr. Pike.

"No," he responded. "I am afraid I shall have to be back and forth between Blackwick and home. My mother is being cared for, but she frets when I am away for too long."

"Of course," I replied. "You are welcome to make use of the carriage or the horses—anything to hasten your return."

He smiled widely. "You are the best of women, Miss Donovan."

"No," I said with a smile. "I simply cannot bear to see Lucy blue-devilled."

Lucy's response to my written invitation to Blackwick had been enthusiastic, evidenced by the effusive gratitude she had expressed to me. I had sent my own maid and the carriage for her just after Mr. Pike's arrival, and I expected to see her within the hour.

Mr. Pike was still in his bedchamber and settling in, though, when I heard carriage wheels on the drive just half an hour later, and I hurried outside to welcome her.

But it was Mrs. Westwood who stepped down from the carriage first, followed by an apologetic and helpless Lucy. Her eyes told me the silent story of failed attempts to curtail her cousin's determination to come. Any hope I had that she simply meant to accompany Lucy to Blackwick were quickly put to rest by the portmanteau she carried in her hand.

"Mrs. Westwood," I said, feeling more than usually annoyed at her. What if we had had no bedchamber to accommodate her? "I had meant for Lucy's visit to provide you with a respite."

"It was very thoughtful of you, Miss Donovan," she replied, "but with all the girls gone for the holidays, I should go mad without anything to occupy me. Besides, I felt it best for me to come. I am Lucy's companion and chaperone, after all, and as you know, *The presence of a trusted woman of good repute, guarding the delicate standing of her young counterparts as a sentinel of virtue, cannot be overstated in importance.*"

Heaven help me. If I was to be subjected to her maxims for the next two weeks, it was *I* who would go mad. I knew precisely what her presence here signified. I would have to occupy her attention if Lucy and Mr. Pike were to have any opportunity to be together.

Perhaps I could foist her onto Valentine from time to time. Just the thought made me quiver with fear for the revenge he would take.

"Quite," I responded with a forced smile. "Let me see to arranging a place for you, if you please." For someone who was so particular about and preoccupied over customs and rules, Mrs. Westwood could be surprisingly thoughtless.

"I should have sent word, of course," she said, "but I didn't wish to delay when Lucy was expected, and I was confident your father would count upon her being accompanied. He has such a robust understanding of what is owed a young woman."

I wanted to turn her away, to find an excuse not to welcome her, but I couldn't find it in myself to do so. Mrs. Westwood had a personality I found difficult in anything but small doses, but I felt for her, and my mother had always taught me to be conscious of and kind to those less privileged than I. Both Lucy and her cousin fell into that category.

Instructing the footmen to take the bags, I led the way inside, only to find Mr. Pike and Valentine coming down the stairs. I considered warning off Mr. Pike, but if Mrs. Westwood was to remain, it was no use delaying the inevitable.

"Mr. Pike," she said, slowing her gait. "I was not aware . . ." She looked to me and then to Lucy, as though to see whether his appearance was as much of a surprise to us as it was to her.

"Mr. Pike is a guest of my brother," I hurried to say. Mrs. Westwood wouldn't hesitate to order her and Lucy's things to be taken back to the seminary if she knew he was my guest. "Valentine and Mr. Pike have been friends since they were children," I improvised.

Valentine's gaze was settled on me, perceptive, as always. Perceptive and warning. Mr. Pike looked surprised, but he managed to cover it, slinging an arm around Valentine's shoulders and smiling.

"Yes, indeed," he said, blissfully unaware that he was in danger of being throttled on the spot.

From my place beside Mrs. Westwood, I sent my brother another one of my most pleading glances.

After a moment, Valentine managed what I imagine he thought was a smile but was much more like a grimace—the expression one might expect if he had eaten rotten eggs but was trying to convince his hostess that he enjoyed them.

"Oh," Mrs. Westwood said, blinking. "Well, in that case . . ."

I let out a relieved breath and turned to the servants

standing by. "Cole, if you could see that the Yellow Room is in order for Mrs. Westwood, Reeve will take Lucy to hers first."

Cole nodded and hurried up the stairs, a valise in one hand and a portmanteau in the other, while Reeve invited Lucy and Mrs. Westwood to follow him. Mr. Pike insisted on taking Lucy's bag and following them, and I silently wished him well in that somewhat perilous decision.

Valentine continued his way down the stairs, saying nothing until he reached me. It was I, not Mr. Pike, who was in danger of being throttled if the unpleasant smile on his face was any indication.

"You will pay for that little trick back there, you know."

"You should be thanking me for the new friend I made for you. Thank you for playing along, dear Val." I leaned over and kissed him on the cheek. He made as if to seem threatening and careless of others, but he had a better heart than he let on. Of all my brothers, I understood him best, for neither of us could abide being told what to do. He merely had the misfortune of being unable to manage Father as I could, which made for a very unhappy relationship between them.

"See to it you don't need anymore saving," he replied. "I am going into the village for a drink and shan't be here to rescue you again. You must have someone else do it going forward, for I assure you, I do not intend to spend the next two weeks with Pike." He started walking away and, without looking back, said, "I mean it about paying for the trick."

***

My father's claim that he would be busy with his naval officers turned out to be surprisingly accurate. They were present at dinner, but once we women left their company, we saw no more of them, as they spent their time in the study. Only Mr. Pike and Phineas made their way to the drawing room to join us after a glass of port. Valentine had, as promised, left to the village and would likely not return until well into the night.

I had hoped Lucy would bring her uncle's most recent response with her to Blackwick, but she informed me that she had not yet had one, something that simultaneously intrigued and disappointed me.

Did Mr. Russell intend to ignore Lucy now? To make her wait longer for a response in hopes of delaying her next letter to him? Either way, I would ensure Lucy continued writing him, response or no.

My other efforts to encourage the match, however, were being frustrated. So far, Mrs. Westwood had stayed by Lucy's side every time Mr. Pike was in her presence, and I was beginning to realize how difficult my own role would be.

Late the next morning, I was in the library with the cook, looking over the menu for the week when I heard the distant rumble of carriage wheels growing louder. Pulling aside the sheer curtain of the window next to me, I peered out at the long, gravel drive that led to Blackwick.

My father had asked me to see that Captain Stokes was properly welcomed, then sent to join the men in the study. Whether he had forgotten my youthful captivation with the captain or merely trusted that I had long outgrown such a thing, I didn't know, but I was eager enough to obey him.

I crossed out a line and scribbled a change above it. "I think roast chicken will be more suitable for Thursday's dinner. On the whole, though, the menu is satisfactory." I blew on the ink and handed the menu to the cook, who took it from me, curtsied, and left.

I kept my actions measured as I set the quill in its stand and rose from my chair. With a quick glance at the looking glass on the wall to my left, I smoothed the front of my dress—a sky blue muslin with a crisp, white chemisette.

I put a hand to my coiffure, twisting one of the ringlets that framed my face around my finger to soften it. When Captain Stokes had known me before, I had just begun to wear my hair up, but the amount of time I spent on the ship decks had hardly been conducive to a neat appearance. My father had often bemoaned how unladylike I was becoming.

I left the library at a brisk pace and made my way outside, paying no heed to the way my heart pattered nervously. Taking the skirt of my dress in hand, I went down the stone steps just as the carriage came to a stop. Two footmen followed behind me, one ready to take Captain Stokes's bags and the other to lead him to the study.

I forced a pleasant expression onto my face, but my mind was full of one of my last memories of him. He had dined with my family that evening—an indisputable honor from an austere man like my father—and I had sought him out afterward to see how he felt it had gone. I had stopped short, though, when I heard myself being discussed among him and the other lieutenants, who were playing cards and drinking in the wardroom.

"She managed to get you dinner with the captain, then? Think he'll promote you now?"

"There is no saying," Lieutenant Stokes said, shuffling the cards.

"Well, you had better take your chance with Miss Donovan, at least, while you have it. Word is the captain is sending her home as soon as we reach port."

Stokes let out a small snort. "I am not fool enough to play games with the captain's daughter. He'd have me hanged for it. Besides, she is too much of a shrew for my taste."

The men laughed.

"Too aggressive for you, is she?" one of the lieutenants offered.

"Too much like her father," another quipped.

"Or does it hurt your pride that she knows as much about sailing as you do?"

"Let us put it this way," Lieutenant Stokes said. "She has all the qual-

ities that would make her a good officer, but none of the sort one wants in a submissive wife."

"A wife? I should think not. She would make a fine mistress, though, wouldn't she? Feisty, domineering, and a pretty armful!"

The men broke out into laughter, and, with fire blazing in my cheeks, I turned and rushed away before more could be said.

Lieutenant Stokes had been promoted to first lieutenant after that, and I had been sent home.

My jaw hardened as the postillion dismounted and went to open the chaise door.

Marmaduke Russell emerged.

Chapter Seven

S urprise gave way to a strange mixture of anger and, if I was being honest with myself, happiness. It was not often that I found myself speechless, but this was one of those moments.

Mr. Russell smiled at me as his feet hit the pavement, his top hat hanging in one of his hands at his side. He swept a bow, then placed the hat on his head, looking far more handsome than I had remembered him—and my memory had not found him at all lacking.

"What are you doing here?" I blurted out. My appearance might be refined enough, but I couldn't hide my tendency toward directness, particularly when caught off guard as I was now.

He raised his brows. "Did you not tell me that my corresponding with an unmarried woman made me an unfit guardian? Behold me repentant. Now, I can converse with you in a manner approved by society and attend to my responsibilities as guardian. I thought you would be pleased—and impressed."

I stared at him stonily, noting the movement of the footman nearby. "Put it down, Reeve." He had just taken Mr. Russell's valise from the box behind the chaise, but he froze, setting down the case slowly. "Mr. Russell is not staying."

"Are you certain of that, Miss Donovan?" Mr. Russell asked.

"More certain than I am of anything, sir."

"Very well," he said. "But if I go, Lucy goes too."

I clenched my teeth together. As her guardian, he certainly had the power to make it so. How had he even come to know she was here? So much for the picture Lucy had painted of a detached guardian.

The door opened behind me, and I looked over my shoulder to see Valentine. Smiles were not a common expression for him, but he wore one now. It was crooked and rakish—likely one of the reasons so many women had fallen victim to a man with such a prickly personality.

"Russell," he said. "So glad you could make it. You can take his bags to the Green Room, Reeve."

Again, I found myself struggling for words, watching in befuddlement as my brother shook hands with Mr. Russell.

"No, Reeve," I managed to say.

He set down the bags once again, looking between Valentine and me with wide, wary eyes.

Valentine's maddeningly victorious smile grew as our gazes met. "You said I could invite someone, did you not?"

"A friend. I said you could invite a friend. You two do not even know one another."

"We do, though," Mr. Russell said. "We met at the church. And then again last night at The Feather and Fawn."

"Thank you for the drink, by the by," Valentine said.

"It was my pleasure." Mr. Russell looked to me. "I feel as though your brother and I have known each other a lifetime."

Valentine clapped him on the back amiably—a gesture as foreign to his retreating personality as it would have been if he had embraced my father.

I stared. This was what it was like to see myself being beaten by the enemy, and I did not like it one bit. But if I insisted upon Mr. Russell's departure, Lucy would have to leave too. And surely it would be easier to have my revenge on Mr. Russell with him in close proximity.

"Very well," I said brightly. "But let us put him in the Red Room. Next to Mrs. Westwood."

Mr. Russell met my gaze, smiling at the tactic, but I thought I saw a glint of promised vengeance in his eyes. "Wherever you see fit, Miss Donovan."

I raised a brow. "The stables, then." I wouldn't let him know that I didn't mind having him here at Blackwick, that it would be much easier to persuade him to approve of Lucy and Mr. Pike if he could observe them together and I could observe *him*.

"Where are your manners, sister?" Valentine said. "Take his bags to the Red Room, as my sister said, Reeve." And with that, he turned, and I watched him disappear through the door. It was just like Valentine to leave so abruptly, without a word. Hardly the actions of a dear friend.

I moved my gaze back to Mr. Russell, and we stared at one another, taking stock of each other. After a moment, though, he smiled slightly. It was subtle and exasperatingly charming.

"How good it is to see you again, Miss Donovan," he said as the postillion mounted his horse and the chaise pulled forward and away from the house.

I ignored his words, meant as they were to get under my skin. I was too interested in his tactics to let myself be distracted by them. "How did you manage to acquire an invitation from Valentine, of all people? I assume it was Mrs. Westwood who alerted you to Lucy's presence here?"

"You assume correctly," he said. "Trustworthy woman."

I raised a brow. If he had meant for that to be an insult to me, he was far off the mark. It was not my responsibility to inform Lucy's guardian of her whereabouts.

"As for the invitation"—he shrugged—"I am simply the sort of man people like to have around for a house party, I suppose."

I glanced beyond him, realizing that, not only was the chaise he had come in leaving, another one was approaching. Captain Stokes, no doubt. What timing.

Mr. Russell turned to see where I was looking. "Ah, more company."

"Yes," I said, "though this carriage happens to be full of the expected sort."

His nose scrunched slightly. "Rather boring, isn't it?"

I pressed my lips together to avoid a little laugh, and Mr. Russell moved toward me in order to make way for the carriage.

The driver stepped down from the box as soon as the carriage was at a stop and hurried to open the door.

Captain Stokes, wearing his full Navy uniform, emerged. I hadn't seen him in nearly a decade, but time had been kind to him. He was handsome as ever, with his sun-touched golden locks, strong jaw, and straight nose. Beyond acknowledging his handsomeness, though, I felt none of the spark that had so consumed me all those years ago. The only spark I felt was one of resentment—a desire to put him in his place and somehow have my revenge upon him.

Captain Stokes' eyes immediately went to me, surveying me from head to foot with the exact sort of appreciation that would have sent my heart into a frenzy at fifteen years old. I sent a sidelong glance at Mr. Russell, whose eyebrow went up at Stokes's slow and conspicuous study of my face and figure.

"Miss Donovan," said the captain. "It has been an eon since we last met."

"It has," I said, infusing my voice with as much geniality as I could muster. Over the years, his voice had been in my mind more than I cared to admit, always with those same words: *She has all the qualities that would make her a good officer, but none of the sort one wants in a submissive wife.*

His gaze shifted to Mr. Russell, and he hesitated a moment. "You *are* Miss Donovan still, I assume? Unmarried?"

"Unmarried, yes," I said, my mouth smiling but my nostrils flared. "You will recall I am not submissive enough for that institution."

Captain Stokes looked at me intently, as though trying to decide whether what I had said was mere coincidence or not. He didn't know that I had overheard his words about me, after all. "Have I interrupted a clandestine encounter, then?" he asked.

I opened my mouth, but before I could respond, Mr. Russell replied. "Yes." His gaze was fixed on the captain, civil but measuring.

I looked at him, my brow furrowing in confused annoyance and my cheeks warming. The last thing I needed was for him to make Captain Stokes think I had resorted to becoming anyone's flirt or ladybird. In any case, who would be ridiculous enough to hold a clandestine encounter in such a place as this, in full view of every front-facing window in the house?

"Captain Stokes," I said, "allow me to present you to Mr. Russell. He is a friend of Valentine's." I shot a glance at Mr. Russell to show him what I thought of such a description.

I watched as the men exchanged bows, wishing they might destroy one another and rid me of the need to do it myself. If one had to win, I would have preferred it to be Mr. Russell, though, which I found somewhat surprising.

But the two of them were not enemies, and their greetings, while appraising, were amiable enough.

I suppressed a sigh. I would have to defeat them myself. And yet, I balked at the idea, hearing Sun Tzu's words in my head. *We can keep our forces concentrated, while the enemy's must be divided.*

Defeating Captain Stokes *and* Mr. Russell would be to divide my forces, and I could not afford to do that.

I looked at Captain Stokes again, an enemy to me from the time I was fifteen. He was handsome, self-assured to the point of arrogance, and more patronizing than ever as a captain. While it would be lovely to humiliate him, though, he held no power over the future, only the past.

I looked at Mr. Russell, a new but formidable foe, who held considerable power over Lucy's future—and who irked me to no end.

If I had to choose to focus my efforts on one of the two men, Mr. Russell was my choice.

Chapter Eight

Once Reeve returned, I instructed him to guide Captain Stokes to the study, hoping I would see as little of the captain as possible during his stay at Blackwick.

But for now, I had a few more things to say to Mr. Russell.

"I hope you will enjoy your stay here at Blackwick, Mr. Russell." By which I meant I intended to make it utter misery.

He held the door open for me to step inside. "I have no doubt at all that I will." The way he looked over at me as he said it left me in doubt about his meaning. Did he anticipate truly enjoying himself? Or did he believe he would rout me and crush the understanding between Mr. Pike and Lucy?

"Did I understand my things were taken to the Red Room? Would you show me the way?"

"Certainly." I hoped Mrs. Westwood would emerge from her neighboring bedchamber just in time to welcome—and annoy—him.

"I would like to change my travel-worn clothing," he explained. "Unless, that is, there are plans to go outside again?"

I raised my brows and looked at him as we reached the

stairs. "I am sure I couldn't say. I haven't any idea what Valentine has planned for *his* friends." It was inevitable that Mr. Russell should spend time with us, but I didn't intend to make it easy for him.

His eyes twinkled appreciatively, but I was deprived of hearing his response by the appearance of the others at the top of the stairs. The dismay in Lucy's eyes at the sight of her uncle would have been comical if I hadn't felt it so keenly myself just a quarter of an hour ago.

"Mr. Russell," Mrs. Westwood said in surprise. "I had no idea you meant to come to Blackwick."

"It rather seems to be the order of this house party, doesn't it?" I said as he and I reached the top of the stairs. It was rich indeed that Mrs. Westwood should make such a comment when she, too, had come unbidden.

"I received your letter," Mr. Russell said, "which I thank you for. As a result, I felt it incumbent upon me to heed Miss Donovan's encouragement and be a more involved guardian. She is so very full of wisdom."

"I might provide a great deal more encouragement for you to heed," I said through clenched teeth.

He put up a hand. "One thing at a time, please, Miss Donovan. My constitution, you know, is rather weak."

I doubted there was a weak thing in Mr. Russell's able person.

He held my gaze, his own so even, yet glinting with amused satisfaction. "*Decrepit,* I believe, was the word someone recently used."

"Well," Mrs. Westwood said, "if your constitution is capable of bearing it, we will be going out for a walk in the woods in a quarter of an hour."

I clenched my teeth more tightly at the unwelcome invitation.

"There is nothing quite like the outdoors," she continued.

"With one's precious complexion safeguarded against the ravages of nature's harsh elements, one can take full advantage of the benefits of fresh air to the lungs."

Mr. Russell glanced at me, and I bit down on the inside of my cheek to keep from smiling. I didn't need Sun Tzu to tell me the unwisdom in sharing amusement with the enemy.

"I shall be certain to cover my complexion," Mr. Russell said humbly.

And, true to his word, he appeared outside a quarter of an hour later with a flat-brimmed beaver hat. His sudden appearance at Blackwick had made us an uneven party, particularly given the fact that Valentine could not be counted upon for adding to our numbers. It made things rather awkward. He took his place beside Lucy, forcing Mr. Pike to fall behind with Mrs. Westwood, while I observed from the back.

Mr. Russell was forcing me to continually change my strategy —the mark of a capable enemy. But I was equal to the task. I had to be.

As we made our way toward the wooded paths with their winding trails, I watched Mr. Russell and Lucy—the wary slant of her brows as she responded to his customarily calm expression. Choosing to walk beside her was strategic, of course. I had no doubt he would be doing it often, trying to keep Mr. Pike and Lucy from pairing off. It must be a relief to Mrs. Westwood, though, not to have her charge's behavior upon her sole conscience.

When we reached the woods, Mr. Russell ceded his place at Lucy's side and, with a brief but meaningful glance at Mrs. Westwood, joined me at the back of the group. Mrs. Westwood seemed to have understood the quick exchange, for she stationed herself just behind Lucy and Mr. Pike on the path— close enough to hear their conversation.

"Intent that Mr. Pike and your niece shall never have a moment of privacy?" I asked as we traded the warmth of the sun on our backs for the chill of the shaded woods. It smelled of dampness and grass under the near-complete cover of the leafy branches overhead.

"Are *you* intent we shall never say a word to one another on a topic other than that of Lucy and Mr. Pike?" he countered.

"It is hardly my fault the subject must be visited so often. You are forever refusing to discuss it for one reason or another."

"Perhaps it is because I have other things I would rather discuss with you, Miss Donovan."

I shot him a dubious look, and he met my gaze unflinchingly. For some reason, it made my heart skitter.

"Here, then," he continued. "What do you say to this? Ten minutes a day of discussion about Lucy and Mr. Pike."

I looked over at him, but the relative dark of the woods made it difficult to see his expression. Not that it would have told me a great deal. I envied his skill at keeping his thoughts hidden.

Ten minutes was not much, certainly, but I could turn ten into twenty if I was skillful, and I could stay away from him the rest of the day easily enough.

"Done," I said.

He held up a hand. "Not too quickly, Miss Donovan. I was not finished. These ten minutes of discussion are at your disposal *only* if we have first conversed on a host of other topics. So, no, you may not avoid me for all but ten minutes of each day."

I pulled my lips in to stop my smile, for he had easily perceived my thoughts.

"Do we still have an accord?" He stopped and turned to me, putting out a hand.

I faced him, looking down at it. I wouldn't shake it until I was certain I was making the right decision, that there were no hidden strategies on his end. "Why? Why do you wish to speak with me on other topics?"

"Because I like you."

His frank response caught me off guard and left me momentarily bereft of words.

"That is impossible," I said. I had been nothing but unpleasant to Mr. Russell. This was merely part of his intent to subdue me, to charm me into thinking of him as something besides my enemy.

He shook his head, his eyes never leaving mine. "I assure you it is not." His hand was still extended, but I made no move to take it, still considering his proposal and stipulations.

Force the enemy to reveal himself, so as to find out his vulnerable spots, Sun Tzu said.

Given my experience with Mr. Russell up to this moment, I had my doubts that he even possessed any vulnerable spots. But that was nonsense, of course. Everyone had vulnerabilities. A good commander made it a point to discover them, and this proposal would allow me to do just that.

"We must quantify things more," I said.

He dropped his hand. "Quantify what exactly?"

I shrugged. "How shall I know when I have met the necessary quota of conversation to allow for discussion of Lucy and Mr. Pike's situation? If it is not a measurable amount, you could easily claim I have not fulfilled your requirement each day."

One corner of his mouth pulled up, giving the hint of a smile a wry quality. "How little you think of me, Miss Donovan. I assure you I shall play fairly. But, to set your mind at ease, let us say that any discussion of Mr. Pike and Lucy shall occur only after dinner, provided we have spent an hour in one another's company during the course of the day."

An hour. An hour in exchange for ten minutes. Part of me wished to rebel at his stipulation, at his attempt to control me, to flatter me into liking him so much that I would not confront him in this battle. But I would make no progress against him until I understood him better. There was no way around that.

I put out my hand decisively, and he took it in a firm shake.

"Have you a pocket watch?" I asked.

His brows went up, but he reached into his coat and pulled one out. He looked at me, and understanding dawned in his eyes. "You wish for me to note the time."

I nodded. I intended to keep Mr. Russell honest and myself protected.

B y the time dinner arrived, I was impatient, itching with unasked questions for Mr. Russell. I had learned a few things about him over the course of the day. He was from northwest Kent and owned an estate called Birchleigh Hall. After the death of his older, half-brother —Lucy's father—he had inherited the estate and a very comfortable fortune. He had two younger siblings, but neither of his parents were living. While we had walked the wooded paths, he had frequently fiddled with the signet ring on his right hand.

None of this information was particularly useful to me.

He had asked me questions, too, of course, something which made me much less comfortable. I hadn't considered how our time together would permit him to come to know *me* better, and that was a dangerous thing to allow an enemy.

But it was a necessary evil, and I determined not to waste a moment in his company. Careful observation would ensure I always had the advantage. But still, I came away from my observations with less ammunition than I had hoped.

His treatment of Mr. Pike was respectful and civil, if somewhat cool, making me all the more curious about his reasons for opposing the match. None of it made any sense.

Such riddles occupying my mind meant I hardly took notice of Captain Stokes at the dinner table, despite the fact that he dominated the conversation and tried to catch my eye a number of times. I merely ignored him, for I was too busy reviewing

how to use the precious ten—or twenty, if all went well—
minutes I would soon have at my disposal. Based on the little
furrow between his brows whenever the captain spoke, it
seemed that Mr. Russell's opinion of the captain was growing
lower and lower, a fact which couldn't help but make me like
him just a bit.

My father addressed himself to Mr. Russell once or twice
during dinner, and he seemed to approve of the responses he
received. This was something, certainly, for he had been predis-
posed not to like Mr. Russell due to understanding him to be a
friend of Valentine's.

We women left the men to their port and took up residence
in the drawing room. It was a warm night, and the two sets of
French doors there had been opened to let in the mere trace of a
breeze the night was offering. Mrs. Westwood left to retrieve a
pair of stockings to darn, and I took advantage of the opportunity to speak with Lucy in private.

"Not quite the house party we had planned for, is it?" I sent
her a sympathetic grimace, for I doubted she and Mr. Pike had
had more than a minute of private conversation today.

"No," she said, "but it is *you* I feel for, Di. My cousin is not
the easiest guest, I know. And my uncle?" She showed a mouth
of clenched teeth.

"You needn't worry about me, Lucy. I can manage and even, I
hope, turn his presence to good account for you and Mr. Pike."

She took my hand up, looking pitifully hopeful. "Do you
truly think so?"

I suddenly felt the weight of her hopes upon my shoulders—
of what it would mean if I could *not* manage to persuade Mr.
Russell he was wrong to deny them their match. "I will certainly
do everything in my power to make it so."

When Mr. Russell, Valentine, Phineas, and Mr. Pike entered
the drawing room some time later, it was all I could do to
remain in my seat instead of rushing over to Mr. Russell and

pelting him with my questions. But he was in the middle of conversing with my brothers, and something he said elicited a laugh from both Phineas and Valentine.

I stared. What sort of comment could achieve such a feat? Of the four children in my family, Phineas and Valentine shared the least in common with one another.

Mr. Russell glanced around the room, and his gaze stopped when it came to me.

I tried to silently communicate to him that it was time to make good on his word.

His eyes shifted to Lucy and the others. In my preoccupation with deciding how to use my time with him, it hadn't occurred to me how impossible it would be for us to discuss things here. It was hardly private.

He had planned this purposefully, of course.

I rose from the settee I had been sitting upon and walked over to him.

"I *will* have my ten minutes, Mr. Russell," I said.

He gave a short bow. "I am flattered by your determination to spend time with me, Miss Donovan. I assure you, I am every bit as anxious to be in yours."

"Shall we play, Russell?" Valentine stood a few feet away, playing cards in hand.

Mr. Russell looked at me as though to gauge my reaction.

I lifted a shoulder. "As long as you understand that you shan't go to sleep tonight until you have made good on your promise."

He smiled slightly. "I shouldn't wish to."

Chapter Nine

Whether Valentine and Mr. Russell were colluding wasn't clear to me—I certainly wouldn't have put it past Valentine to thwart me just for the joy of it—but their card game did not end until Mrs. Westwood, Lucy, and Mr. Pike had all retired for bed. Only Phineas and I were left, both of us with a book in hand. Since beginning to read, I had turned the page twice, while Phineas had done so more times than I could count.

I was distracted with annoyance and impatience, and each laugh from Mr. Russell and Valentine made me grit my teeth. When Valentine emitted a particularly boisterous one just as the clock struck ten, Phineas glanced up and, after a moment's hesitation, shut his book and stood.

He wasn't retiring. I knew him well enough to know that the far west corner of the library was his destination. He had always been one to stay up late reading.

And I? I would stay up until dawn if that was what was required for me to have answers from Mr. Russell. Realizing that my departure from the drawing room might be precisely what was required to end the card game, I followed Phineas from the room.

The wall sconces were lit, making the corridor glow with concentrated spots of light. I paused for a moment outside the drawing room door, then sat on the small window seat that the curtains mostly concealed. The light from the nearest sconce allowed me to continue reading the same three sentences I had spent the last half hour reading.

I only had to wait a few minutes before the door opened and Valentine and Mr. Russell emerged.

"Goodnight, Russell," Valentine said.

"Goodnight."

Retreating footsteps sounded, and I hurried to my feet. I could hardly go knocking on Mr. Russell's door if he reached it before I managed to stop him.

I pushed aside the curtain and rushed out, slamming into Mr. Russell.

"Miss Donovan," he said, his hands bracing my upper arms. "Where are you off to in such a rush? And at this hour of night?"

Regaining my composure, I pulled my arms from his hands. "You know the answer to that very well."

His mouth pulled up at the sides, and the uneven light thrown by the nearest sconces cast his face in dramatic shadows that made him look particularly handsome. "Another clandestine encounter with me? And at midnight, no less. I continue to be flattered by you."

"It is not midnight. It is only ten o'clock. And I was thinking less of a clandestine encounter and more along the lines of wringing your neck while you were asleep in your bed. Still flattered?"

"You are upset," he said, as though I hadn't just threatened to kill him. "I apologize. Last night, I had promised your brother a game of piquet, and he was intent that it should happen this evening. As he was the one who invited me to Blackwick, and since there was no opportunity for you and me to speak privately at the time, I didn't see the purpose of refusing."

Farther down the corridor, a footman holding a silver platter entered the study. Refreshments for my father and his guests, no doubt.

"Do you wish to speak here?" Mr. Russell asked.

"No. We can speak in the library."

A sliver of hesitation crept into Mr. Russell's eyes.

"What is it?" I asked impatiently. "You realize I shan't allow you to go to bed until we have spoken, do you not?"

"I am far less hesitant to spend time with you than you believe me to be, Miss Donovan. It is only . . ."

"You needn't worry; I shan't harm you there."

He chuckled lightly, and the sound produced an unexpected thrill of victory inside me. It was an idiotic reaction. I wasn't here to make him laugh; I was here to gain victory over him. "That was not my concern. It is late, Miss Donovan. And, while the idea of a *tête-à-tête* with you appeals to me more than I should admit, if we were to be happened upon . . ."

I forced myself not to dwell on his comment about the appeal of a *tête-à-tête*. He was concerned for my reputation. Or, perhaps he feared what my father would do if he discovered we had been found alone together late at night. If it was the latter, I couldn't blame him.

"Very gallant of you, Mr. Russell. But I am not so lost to propriety as you assume. Phineas is reading in the library, providing a perfectly respectable guardian against any designs you may have on my virtue. Or would you prefer I rouse Mrs. Westwood to act the chaperone?"

"Good heavens, no," he said, looking mildly horrified.

"That is just as well," I said, leading the way to the library door, "for she would undoubtedly pester us with guilt-inducing maxims, and then we really *would* be obliged to have a clandestine meeting at midnight to conduct this business."

"I have changed my mind," he said, stopping just outside the library door and planting his feet firmly. "Rouse Mrs. Westwood immediately. Or perhaps we can forgo that and simply arrange this midnight meeting you speak of."

He was teasing, I knew, but my mind conjured the image of us out on the terrace in the dark, sending an unfamiliar trickle of shivers up my arms.

I shot him an unamused glance and opened the library door. After a moment of pretended stubbornness belied by the glint of humor in his eyes, he stepped inside. As I had assumed he would be, Phineas was in the far corner, sitting in a wingback chair with an open book obscuring his face. He didn't lower it immediately—finishing reading a sentence, no doubt—but when he did, it was with a quick and indifferent glance through his low-perched, wiry glasses. His sandy hair was slightly askew, as though reading a book required a certain physical stamina.

"You are to play chaperone, Phin," I said.

"Hmm?" he replied, his attention already back on his book.

I smiled at Mr. Russell and took a seat in one of the chairs nearest the fire. "Just ensure Mr. Russell does not try to abduct me. That is all."

The only response Phineas vouchsafed to this was a distracted, "Mmhmm."

"Would he notice if I *did* abduct you?" Mr. Russell asked in an under voice, his curious gaze on Phineas as he took a seat in the chair next to me.

"Likely not."

"Useful information," Mr. Russell said.

"Now," I said, ignoring his attempt to ruffle me, "the time has come for you to uphold your end of the bargain."

He nodded, reaching into his coat and pulling out his pocket watch—a gesture I found annoying in the extreme. "The time is twelve minutes past ten."

"After how long you made me wait, you mean to be particular about the ten minutes?" I said incredulously.

He was looking at the watch. "Nine minutes and fifty-five seconds remaining."

I pursed my lips in frustration, but the longer I argued, the more time I lost. I wouldn't put it past him to simply leave the library when the ten minutes had passed. "Very well. Why do you dislike a match between Lucy and Mr. Pike? Have you something against Mr. Pike?"

He sat back and crossed his ankle over his knee, setting the watch on the arm of the chair beside him. "That is not my business to tell."

I stared at him. "Your own opinion of Mr. Pike is not your business?"

"Offering my opinion requires divulging *information* that is not mine to tell."

I clenched my jaw. "Mr. Russell, you gave me your word we could speak about Lucy and Mr. Pike for ten minutes each day."

"And so we can. You are welcome, for instance, to tell me why you so ardently approve of the match."

"That would hardly qualify as a discussion, would it? Neither is it what I meant, which you well know. You are simply determined to be difficult."

He smiled. "I might point out that you have thwarted *me* on many occasions, going so far as to invite my ward and Mr. Pike to a house party after I gave specific instructions that they not see one another." His level of nonchalance as he said this was almost staggering. I had been certain he would be furious with me.

"Instructions given to Mrs. Westwood," I pointed out. "*You* told me not to meddle in Lucy's guardianship issues, so I specifically ignored your wishes when Mrs. Westwood mentioned them. Besides, both Lucy and Mr. Pike are friends of mine. Why should I not invite my friends to a house party?"

He raised a brow and clasped his hands as he observed me. Perhaps it was the color of his eyes—a light and subtle green— that gave me the sense that he could see through me somehow. It was unnerving, and I didn't like it.

"I thought Mr. Pike was Valentine's guest. Besides, it is a peculiar house party when the invitations only include two young, unmarried people, isn't it?"

"Well, you and Mrs. Westwood both made sure that was not the case, didn't you? And there are five other people here, you know."

"Ah, yes, our dear Captain Stokes."

I held his gaze, not anticipating such a comment. Why did he choose to pinpoint the captain out of all the other guests he had met since arriving earlier today?

But I didn't wish to discuss Captain Stokes with Mr. Russell, for the captain was part of a time in my life when I had been more foolish, and the last thing I needed was for him to know my weaknesses. "Stop changing the subject, Mr. Russell. Why do you dislike the match? Surely, you can speak in generalities."

He frowned pensively. "I have many reasons."

I folded my arms and looked at him expectantly. "I am listening."

His jaw shifted. "I will give you one reason." He smiled, as though taking to the idea even more now that he had said it. "One reason each night."

I gave a little scoff. "Is this your idea of torturing me?"

"On the contrary," he said. "It allows us to thoroughly discuss the reasons and for you to provide a counter argument, supposing you have one."

"And what of Lucy and Mr. Pike? They are to wait until you have expended all three dozen possible reasons for disapproving of the match?"

His brows went up significantly. "So, you admit there are that many reasons to disapprove of it?"

"No," I said flatly. "But I imagine you are capable of delaying that long."

He looked intrigued. "*Would* you allow me to stay at Blackwick for thirty-six days?"

"You should count yourself fortunate if you are still here after three."

"I feel fortunate to be here at all, I assure you. Sadly, this blissful interlude cannot go on forever, however, for I have promised to attend an assembly near my home in a fortnight. But back to the matter at hand, lest you think I am trying to waste your precious"—he picked up his watch—"four minutes and thirty-two seconds. You assume that there is anything for Lucy and Mr. Pike to be waiting *for* while we have these discussions. At present, there is no prospect at all of them marrying."

I said nothing, but he knew that that was exactly what I was assuming—that these daily conversations would lead to him changing his mind. "Tonight's reason, then?"

He rubbed a thumb over the watch face in his hand. "For one, Lucy is too young. She has seen nothing of the world."

I pinched my lips together, wholly unimpressed with his reason. "She is eighteen, a perfectly respectable age for marrying, especially for someone in Lucy's situation, with so few prospects. And as for not having seen anything of the world, how, pray, is she to rectify that? And what makes you think she would choose any differently if she *had* seen more of the world?"

His eyes narrowed slightly. "Are you a romantic, Miss Donovan?"

"Do I seem like a romantic to you, Mr. Russell?"

His head tilted to the side slightly as he looked at me thoughtfully. I had become accustomed to sitting under scrutiny without flinching, but Mr. Russell's gaze did something new to me, making me keenly aware of myself—the position of my arms, the state of my hair, the dress I had chosen to wear.

"More romantic than you let on, I think," he said.

"You *will* insist on changing the subject, won't you? How very aggravating you are." I rose to my feet, feeling too frustrated to sit still any longer. "Seeing the world does not necessarily make a woman better suited for marriage. Believe me."

"Do you offer yourself as an example of that fact?"

I shrugged, pacing before the fireplace. "I am one example, certainly."

"An example to the contrary of your argument, rather. A woman who knows her own mind after seeing much of the world."

"And is unmarried in no small part because of that."

The room went silent, and I stilled. The only sound was of Phineas turning a page. The words had come out before I had considered them. Mr. Russell had that effect upon me, I found—aggravating me to the point that I stopped strategizing and spoke without thinking.

I could feel his penetrating gaze on me, and I instinctively put a hand to my dress, as if to ensure I wasn't as bare as I suddenly felt. "The point is"—I began pacing again—"that your reason—tonight's reason—is a silly one. Lucy is perfectly suited to matrimony, and she adores Mr. Pike."

I met his gaze, expecting to find something like pity there—there was nothing so awful from an enemy as pity—but instead I found his expression inscrutable. Intent but inscrutable.

"Time," he said, eyes still on me. I had never met anyone who could sustain such a long, unblinking, soul-penetrating stare, confound him.

I walked over to his side and snatched the watch from the arm of the chair. He made no move to stop me. Of course he didn't. It would have been entirely out of character for Mr.

Russell to make any movement that wasn't utterly deliberate and calm.

I brought the watch face up and stared at it. My brow furrowed. "This watch does not even work."

Mr. Russell smiled and put out a hand. "Thankfully, I have an impeccable sense of time."

I held his gaze for a moment, debating whether to throttle him or prod him over his insistence on keeping a pocket watch with a cracked face and stationary hands.

I decided to do neither, treasuring up the bit of intriguing information I had just learned about him. What man carried a broken pocket watch with him?

"You are abominable." I handed it back to him. "I demand ten more minutes."

"Not so fast, Miss Donovan." He slipped the watch back into his coat. "I have had my eye on the clock on the mantel." He nodded at it. "Your time is well and truly spent, I am afraid. The rest will have to wait for tomorrow evening. Shall we reconvene then?" He rose from his chair and came before me. Never had I wished more strongly for a few more inches in height so that I could look at him eye-to-eye—or, even better, look down upon him.

"It has been a pleasure spending the evening with you, Miss Donovan." He took my hand in his and placed a kiss upon the back of my glove.

My heart did a flip, and I instinctually glanced over at Phineas. But he was just as absorbed in his reading as ever. I envied him, for he had a book to cover his face, but I had nothing to cover the warmth that filled my cheeks as Mr. Russell left the room.

Chapter Ten

Valentine was proving a better host than I had anticipated. He seemed to genuinely like Mr. Russell, something that both surprised and aggravated me, for I could have used Valentine's ability to put people in their place with the mere lift of a sneering lip.

Instead, I found him making plans at breakfast to go riding with Mr. Russell the next day. It wasn't a terrible thing, really. It meant I needn't split my attention and would be able to engage Mrs. Westwood in conversation, allowing Lucy and Mr. Pike a bit of a reprieve from her vigilance.

As for today, though, we would all be together as we made the walk to the cove as I had promised Lucy. Valentine declined to join us, for he was no lover of the sea—not anymore, at least. I made a point of it to walk beside Mrs. Westwood, but she was a stubborn woman, not to be deterred, for when Lucy and Mr. Pike had outstripped us in pace enough to disappear around the bend in the path down to the cove, she excused herself and hurried forward.

"A valiant effort, Miss Donovan," Mr. Russell said from behind me.

I ignored his comment and focused on ensuring I did not trip on any of the stones that littered the winding dirt path down to the cove.

"You may hold onto my arm if you would like," he said as my boot slipped on a loose patch of dirt. The path had become more treacherous after heavy rains two weeks ago.

"I think not," I said, even as my stomach galloped at my near-fall. In truth, I wouldn't have minded an assisting arm. I had no doubt Mr. Pike was doing just that for Lucy, and even less doubt that Mrs. Westwood would be pinching her lips and trying to decide whether to intervene. Ensuring the safety of her charge while reducing intimacy between the young lovers was a conundrum indeed.

We made it down to the cove without further mishap, thank heaven, for the only thing worse than having to take Mr. Russell's arm would be having to do so after refusing it. Mrs. Westwood and her charges were making their way across the beach at a sedate pace, and I couldn't stop a rueful smile at the sight of her so close behind them.

"Do you think she is contributing to the conversation?" I asked.

"Oh, without question," Mr. Russell said, coming up beside me as we followed in their tracks. "No doubt she has an adage or two to offer about what is and isn't proper at sea."

"Destroying any possibility of the romance Lucy was undoubtedly hoping for in coming here."

"I owe her my gratitude," he said.

I shot him a look, then watched as the others stopped in front of the cave. It was the precise spot where, not long ago, I had come upon my brother Theo and my friend Elena kissing. It was I who had ruined the romance that day, calling out to them as I had. I should have let them be, for they had seemed in their own world and content that it be so.

An image of Mr. Russell and me kissing in the same spot

flashed across my mind suddenly. I blinked in surprise at it and the way it warmed my blood. I didn't thrust it away immediately, for I was too curious at the picture before me. How *would* it be to kiss Mr. Russell? He was so calm and collected, it was difficult to imagine him doing something as passionate as kissing a woman.

Perhaps that was why the image set my heart racing. His ability to stay so levelheaded, no matter what I said or did, made me itch to wrench something more from him, to provoke him into showing more emotion. It was simply another evidence of my wish to dominate him, nothing else.

I glanced at him and found him gazing out at sea. Still fixated on the image I had been inspecting, my focus went to his mouth. The curve of his upper lip reminded me of the rolling waves beside us. Would kissing him feel like the lull of gentle waves? Or would it toss and tug me until I hardly knew which way was up or down?

His brow furrowed. "What is it?"

I looked away, for I hadn't noticed his gaze move to me, and I had been staring at his lips. I had no business focusing on such a thing. I was meant to be discovering his weaknesses so that I could use them against him.

"Is Lucy your only niece, Mr. Russell?" I asked.

He looked at me for a moment before responding, as though he might ignore my question and insist upon dwelling on my strange fixation with his lips. "Yes, she is. My brother and his wife had no other children, and my younger siblings are not yet married."

He referred to Lucy's father as his brother, though they were half-brothers, in reality. An interesting thing, that. "And how old are your younger siblings?"

"How very curious you are today," he commented. "Roger is five-and-twenty and resides in London. Rebecca is one-and-twenty and lives with our grandfather in Northumberland."

"And your parents?"

There was a short pause. "My mother died giving birth to my sister when I was ten, and my father died a few years later."

That made Mr. Russell one-and-thirty—and someone who had experienced a great deal of death from a fairly young age. "And your brother a few years after that?"

He nodded. "Nicholas died in '08." I knew from Lucy that her parents—Mr. Russell's half-brother and his wife—had died in a carriage accident.

I felt a sliver of guilt for asking him such questions with an intent to use the answers against him. He said it all so matter-of-factly, but I knew better than to take such a thing at face value. I did the same thing when I spoke of my mother's death, after all, and there could be nothing less matter-of-fact than the way it had shaken me and left me reeling.

"I am very sorry," I said.

He looked over at me. "I am sorry too. And sorry for *your* loss. Lucy told me of your mother's death."

I felt a little thread of connection bind itself between Mr. Russell and myself, and I resisted it by looking away. "Thank you."

Lucy called out to me just then, and though the wind that often swept through the cove made it impossible to hear, Mrs. Westwood began chastising her for raising her voice—one of the many things forbidden a woman who wished to be considered ladylike.

Obediently, Lucy made her way over to us, and Mr. Russell left my side.

It was just as well. Perhaps the pesky thread that had just fastened itself from me to him would snap with a bit of distance.

Lucy quietly admitted her need for a respite from her cousin's constant company and conversation, and I promised to do my best to better engage her attention.

"No, no," she said. "I understand you are doing what is

needed in order to persuade my uncle to approve of the match. You cannot be expected to do *everything*."

"Well, tomorrow will be better, I hope, for your uncle shall be riding with Valentine, and that will leave me free to keep your cousin occupied."

"You're an angel, Diana," she said with gratitude in her eyes. "How are things with Uncle Duke? Is there any progress, do you think?"

I looked toward him. He was conversing with Mrs. Westwood, leaving Mr. Pike to stare out at the sea pensively. "A little, perhaps. I am afraid it will take time, Lucy. And I know you must be impatient—"

She grabbed my hand, pressing it. "We are simply grateful to you. And in awe of your bravery."

I laughed, for there was no bravery or courage required on my part to speak with Mr. Russell. It was simultaneously maddening and exhilarating to find someone whose ability to engage in a battle of this sort matched my own. Or very nearly matched it, at least. For I had no doubt that I would win in the end.

P hineas had only acknowledged Mr. Russell and me with a subtle nod when we entered the library a few minutes ago. Tonight, he was poring over a book far too large to be held, and he had opted to take a seat in front of the long table of artifacts my father kept in the library from his years on a merchant ship. Among those artifacts were both the original and a French translation of Sun Tzu's *The Art of War*.

"Reason number two?" I looked at Mr. Russell expectantly, and his lip turned up at the corner.

"Straight to business, is it? Very well. Reason number two,

then." He crossed his legs and settled back in the seat. "They hardly know one another."

"Hardly know—" I clamped my mouth shut.

The lines next to Mr. Russell's eyes fanned out in amusement at my reaction.

"Firstly," I said, "they have been in the same parish for years now."

"But admit to taking little notice of one another until quite recently."

"And your solution to this supposed problem is to forbid them from seeing one another?" I retorted.

"An order which has been anything but heeded." He looked at me with an arched brow.

"For which you should be thanking me," I said.

He stared, and I met his gaze unflinchingly. "By all means, please do expound," he said.

"Must I?"

"I am afraid you really must."

I shifted to a more comfortable position in my chair. "Very well. Any but the most obtuse of guardians"—I shot him a significant glance—"knows that the best way to encourage an elopement is to forbid two young people in love from seeing one another."

He smiled. "You needn't worry over that. I successfully struck the fear of God into Mr. Pike on that account."

I scoffed and stood, taking up the poker. The glow of the candles that lit the library, combined with the dusty scent of books, the crackling fire in the fireplace, and the softness of the chairs we sat in made for a very cozy atmosphere. It wouldn't do to get too comfortable.

"And you wonder why Lucy is terrified of you." It was a cooler night, and it was satisfying to prod at the wood in the fireplace given my frustrations with Mr. Russell.

There was unexpected silence following my words, though,

and I looked at him over my shoulder. He had his pocket watch in hand and was staring at its cracked face absently.

I knew a sudden worry that my words had caused him pain. Was he unaware that Lucy regarded him with a bit of fear?

His gaze shifted up to me just then, and the pensive look dispelled. "You may not agree with my reasons for disapproving of the match—indeed, I expected you would not—but I promised to give you one each night, and there you have tonight's specimen."

"No." I shook my head and replaced the poker, rubbing my hands together to rid them of the gritty residue left from the handle. "I am sorry. I refuse to accept such a ridiculous reason. I demand another one—*if* you have one."

He looked at me thoughtfully. "How about a variation on the one I gave you?"

I turned to face him. "I am waiting."

"I have not known *you* very long. What sort of guardian would I be if I offered up my ward's affairs to anyone with a passing interest in them?"

"A passing interest?" I said incredulously. "I am Lucy's dearest friend. And, pray, what designs do you think I might have upon her? What do you anticipate I shall do with the information received from you?"

He lifted his shoulders and wrapped the gold chain around the face of the pocket watch in an absent-minded gesture. "I am sure I couldn't say. You are an enterprising woman, Miss Donovan."

I folded my arms and let out a scoffing laugh. "Very enterprising indeed if you think it profits me personally to see Lucy and Mr. Pike married."

"And, pray," he said, mimicking my own words, "what do *you* think my reasons are for opposing the match? You think me capricious? Eager to destroy young hopes?"

"I think you insufferable," I said, sitting down again. He

watched me, ever-observant, as though taking note of the fact that I could not sit still for long—and paying no heed to my insult. "And reluctant to cede control of the reins, reaching for the silliest of excuses."

"I am far more reluctant to give up our enjoyable evenings together by providing you with every reason in one fell swoop. You wouldn't care to talk with me anymore if I did that."

How did he manage so frequently to render me speechless with unexpected remarks like that one? I hated how effective a strategy it was. "Then perhaps I shall simply stop caring about the fate of Lucy and Mr. Pike, depriving you of the supposed pleasure you take in these ten minutes."

"An hour and ten minutes," he countered. "And there is nothing *supposed* about it, Miss Donovan. I enjoy your company. If I did not, I would not be at Blackwick at all, I assure you."

My absurd heart reacted by beating more quickly. I retaliated against it. "Leaving Lucy to my pernicious influence?"

"Hardly. If I truly thought you a pernicious influence, I would simply send her and Mrs. Westwood home from Blackwick forthwith."

I sat forward, hands clasped in my lap and my expression composed to be full of mild curiosity. "Then how *do* you consider my influence? Ruinous? Objectionable?"

"On the subject of Mr. Pike, of course, I consider you misguided. But on the whole, I would be more than pleased if Lucy became more like you."

Heart still beating double-time, I held his gaze. No one but my mother had ever done anything but bemoan my headstrong personality, my strength of opinion. I forced out a laugh. "You only wish that because if she were more like me, Mr. Pike would no longer wish to marry her."

Mr. Russell slipped his pocket watch back into his coat and rose. "Then he would be a fool." He looked down at me and offered his hand.

I hesitated, then took it, letting him pull me up until we faced each other. He let go of my hand, and I clenched it at my side, grateful for the protection my glove offered against the touch of his skin to mine. He looked into my eyes intently. I had never seen his eyes so close or clearly. There wasn't even a word in my vocabulary to describe the color—a mixture of light blues and greens encircled in a dark gray. Neither was there a word to describe the way his gaze affected me.

"A strong man does not want a mirror of himself in a wife, Miss Donovan," he said. "The man who fears a confident woman is a man whose true fear is his own weakness being challenged."

Captain Stokes's words came, as they so often did, to my mind. Had he been afraid of me challenging his weakness? Why had I never considered it that way? Either way, Mr. Russell's words struck me somewhere deep inside—in a vulnerable place I didn't wish him to know existed.

He held my gaze for a moment before leaving, and I had no response but a skittering heartbeat.

I stared after him, listening to the soft closing of the door behind him. That was how he was—calm and unruffled in every-thing he did. His personality made the smallest of deviations feel so much more pronounced, just as the words he had just said made me feel warm and agitated. Somehow, every compli-ment from him felt like a victory.

But gaining his favor was not the victory I was aiming for.

I glanced over at Phineas and found him to be looking at me. Behind his glasses, his eyes held mine for a moment, then dropped back down to the book he had.

How much had he heard? And what did he make of it? He shouldn't make *anything* of it. I certainly wouldn't. I couldn't afford to if I meant to help Lucy. I needed Mr. Russell to take me seriously as a foe.

Chapter Eleven

M r. Russell and Valentine had already left by the time I went down for breakfast the next morning. I was so focused on whether Mr. Russell would be there that I had already stepped inside the breakfast room before noting Captain Stokes's presence.

He looked up at me from his full plate of mutton, eggs, and toast. "Miss Donovan. Good morning to you."

I wanted to leave and order my breakfast be brought to my bedchamber, but I refused to. Foes needed to be faced, even old and irrelevant ones.

"Good morning, Captain Stokes." I took a plate from the sideboard and set to choosing my meal.

"I regret having hardly spoken to you since arriving," he said. "We have been so taken up with naval matters that there has been little time for socializing."

"Yes, well, that is exactly as my father intended it, I think. He was never one for entertainment." I set my plate down on the opposite side of the table and took my seat.

"I am well aware of that," he said in amusement. His blue eyes sparkled at me from across the table. I had been entranced by those bright eyes at one point, and I met their gaze squarely, curious to see if they still affected me after all these years. But now I found them vapid—flirtatious, perhaps, but still vapid behind the twinkling.

"You provided the little entertainment aboard the *Dominance*," he continued. "I have often wished to thank you for that."

My muscles stiffened with every word, which brought back memories of the little moments between us—a teasing twist of one of my curls, using the narrow passages of the ship to justify brushing up against me, a near-kiss on the quarterdeck—all things which had made my young heart patter violently and given me to hope.

Now, such memories merely made me angry. He had been seven years older than I—old enough to know better than to take advantage of my naivete.

But I was naive no longer, and I would never let him know how low his treatment had brought me. Neither would I let him think I was unaware of what he had been doing. "To thank me for that and your promotion to first lieutenant?"

His smile flickered, and the blue of his eyes turned more flinty, but he was deprived of responding by the entrance of Lucy and Mrs. Westwood. I returned to eating my breakfast, satisfied that he knew that *I* knew what he had done. He had used me for advancement, for his own purposes.

Lucy took her seat beside me, and it wasn't long before Captain Stokes left the breakfast room. In his wake, I could hear Sun Tzu's words. *Hostile armies may face each other for years, striving for the victory which is decided in a single day.* Today felt a bit like that victory.

"Is Mr. Pike still abed?" I asked.

Lucy was looking somber, and she shook her head. "No, he received a note early this morning, informing him that his mother wished to see him. She is becoming more sickly, I think, so he was obliged to leave an hour ago. I think we shan't see him until dinner at least."

"Oh." All my plans to give Lucy and him time together immediately disintegrated. "He is a devoted son, isn't he?"

"He is," Lucy said, admiration filling her eyes.

I made a mental note to point out this admirable quality to Mr. Russell. One could expect a man so devoted to his mother to also be a devoted husband.

Mrs. Westwood was still at the sideboard, and I took advantage of her distance to lean over to Lucy. "Your uncle cannot be *so* very against the match, or he would not let you remain here in Mr. Pike's presence."

And though Mr. Russell had shown no desire to seek Mr. Pike's company of his own volition, he was civil to him. That was something, surely.

I wished I had more hope to offer Lucy this morning, more progress. But it was slow work with only ten minutes a day for persuading her uncle to let me into his mind. If only there was a way to have more than one reason per day from him. Lucy was such a docile young woman and Mr. Pike so amiable that there could not be so very much to say against the match.

Mr. Russell's words from last night came to mind—his expressed wish for Lucy to be more like me. While flattering, I found that simply too large a bouncer to swallow. If he *did* wish that, it was because he didn't know me well enough. I was not simply a determined woman who knew her own mind. I was one set on victory, and he needed to understand that without a doubt. He needed to take me seriously. Then he would know that the last thing he should want was for Lucy to be like me.

"Lucy," I said, my eyes staring ahead at the large case clock that ticked away the seconds in the corner. "What do you know of your uncle's pocket watch?"

"Pocket watch?"

I nodded. "He seems to keep it in his coat at all times, despite the fact that it is broken."

Her brow furrowed. "I do not think I have ever seen it."

It was disappointing, of course, but I was undismayed. A man did not keep a broken watch on his person unless it held some significance to him. And given Mr. Russell's staid personality, it was very difficult indeed to find what mattered to him.

Begin by seizing something which your opponent holds dear; then he will be amenable to your will.

That was what Sun Tzu instructed. Perhaps the pocket watch would be of enough significance to Mr. Russell that he would trade it for two of his ridiculous reasons—or something more. Or perhaps he wouldn't care in the least.

But it was worth a try.

I was playing the piano in the drawing room while Mrs. Westwood saw to some sewing and Lucy perused *La Belle Assemblée* for fashion plates she would never be able to afford.

"Hmm," I said, leaning over the case that held the sheet music and flipping through the different pieces. "I must have left the Pleyel piece in my room. Excuse me."

Lucy and Mrs. Westwood acknowledged this with absent nods, and I left the drawing room to make my way toward the Red Room where Mr. Russell was staying. Even though he was out riding and would be for another two hours at least, my body sizzled with nerves.

It was possible, of course, that he had the pocket watch with him even now, but I rather thought not. If he prized it, which it seemed he did, he would not wish to risk losing it in the chaos of jumping hedges, which was a favorite pastime of Valentine's.

As expected, the door was closed when I reached it. I looked both ways down the corridor and, finding it blessedly empty, put my hand to the handle and turned. It gave way, and I stopped, hesitating.

If the enemy leaves a door open, you must rush in.

This was the door of my enemy, and he had left it open—or at least unlocked. He was too careful to have done such a thing if he truly feared anything within being taken. Besides, this was my house, and I had every right to ensure things within were well. Didn't I?

The sound of footsteps somewhere in the vicinity met my ears, and I pushed the door open, disappearing inside before anyone could note my presence in the corridor.

The Red Room was one of our less frequently used bedchambers. I doubted whether it had been occupied in the last five years. It clearly was now, though, and the sight made me pause for a moment, the persistent, niggling doubt making itself known again by unsettling my stomach. Mr. Russell's valise sat at the base of the bed, and his valet had already lain out the clothing he would change into when he returned from riding—a gray tailcoat, a light green waistcoat, and a pair of black breeches. I wondered absently whether the waistcoat would match his eyes.

But I was not here to inspect his choice of dinner ensemble; I was here to find the pocket watch. I turned to the dressing table that sat against the wall behind me, my gaze running over a pair of silver cuff links and a container of pomade. I picked up the pomade and opened the lid, bringing it to my nose and inhaling softly. It was a familiar and pleasant smell, one that lingered about Mr. Russell, and I put it back down quickly. My gaze moved to the back corner of the dressing table, and I smiled. The pocket watch.

I picked it up, my eyes drawn immediately to the crack that ran across the entirety of the glass front. The hands were motionless, and I turned it over, curious to find any reason Mr.

Russell would choose to keep such an item, or to decide against fixing it. Perhaps the damage was recent, something which had occurred on the journey to Blackwick, and he hadn't yet had time to have it repaired. In that case, it was entirely possible this watch meant nothing more to him than any old pocket watch. What a disappointment that would be.

But, then, why wear it on his person instead of leaving it in his bedchamber or sending it for repair?

The backing was brass, slightly dented, and more than usually plain. Curiously so, in fact. Mr. Russell was not at all ostentatious in his manner of dress, but what he did wear was of obviously fine quality. An old, damaged brass pocket watch didn't particularly fit with what I knew of him.

There was *something* to this watch, then. And I would make the most of that.

Nerves fluttered in my stomach, a small question of whether I was going too far.

Could one go too far in the aid of a dear friend, though?

I dropped the chain into my palm and closed my fingers around it, then left the room.

Chapter Twelve

Valentine and Mr. Russell did not return from riding until it was time to dress for dinner, making me glad I had chosen to take the watch. We hadn't had time to spend the required hour in one another's company, which meant I would need the bargaining chip to have a reason out of him this evening.

As casually as I could manage, I intercepted him in the entry hall upon his return. His eyes were bright and his hair, usually swept toward his face and pomaded, had been tossed by the wind. The dishevelment suited him. But so did the orderly way in which he usually presented himself, devil take him.

He smiled at the sight of me, and I felt an unwelcome niggling of guilt at the warm greeting.

"Missed me, did you, Miss Donovan?" he asked as he shrugged off his riding coat.

I *had* missed him a bit. "I was rather hoping you had decided to ride all the way back to your estate."

"A crushing disappointment," he said with the same subtle smile he always wore. He came up beside me, and we began walking toward the staircase. "Particularly so because Mr. Pike is still away and you have not been able to capitalize on my absence to encourage any misbehavior on his and Lucy's parts."

His ability to perceive precisely what had annoyed me was aggravating in the extreme.

"And *you* are in such a good humor because you think you shan't have to provide your reason tonight on account of staying out of my company the entire day."

We stopped at the foot of the staircase, and he turned to me. "On the contrary. I am hoping you will agree to spend that hour in the library after tea."

The bluntness of his words and gaze, the way he countered my assumption with such ease and frankness, left me stunned for a moment. "Are you making a clandestine assignation with me, Mr. Russell?"

His mouth curled up at the side. "Do you invite your brother to all your clandestine assignations?"

"Only the ones with men I don't trust."

He laughed, and I hoped the flutter of victory I felt was on account of having bested him in this battle of wits and not because I enjoyed hearing him laugh. It was I who would have the last laugh tonight, though.

"After dinner, then?" he said.

"After dinner, then."

Mr. Russell didn't step into the drawing room until just before the bell rang to summon us to the table. He wore the clothing I had seen lain out on his bed, and the waistcoat brought out the color of his eyes just as I had expected it would. I had a feeling that the effect would be mesmerizing if I were any closer, particularly in combination with the scent of the pomade. Better to keep my distance as much as possible.

His expression, though, was somewhat somber, a little wrinkle to his brow that told me he was in a pensive rather than playful humor now. I could wager a guess as to why . . . .

Mr. Pike returned mid-meal, and Lucy's expression transformed at the sight of him. She had been more subdued all day, worried on behalf of Mrs. Pike and eager to see Mr. Pike again. The more I saw of the two of them, the less sense it made to me for Mr. Russell to keep them apart. Like me, he was not of a romantic disposition, but neither was he heartless. And it seemed terribly and unnecessarily heartless to deny Lucy the happiness she felt in Mr. Pike's presence.

When Valentine, Phineas, and Mr. Pike joined us in the drawing room later in the evening, I looked in vain for Mr. Russell to follow behind. But I declined to ask about his absence, for I was wary of Valentine's ability to use everything I said against me and Phineas's knowledge of my visits with Mr. Russell in the library in the evenings. Instead, I played cards with Mrs. Westwood, keeping my eye on the door.

He had said *after dinner.* Had he meant it literally?

I felt impatient and fidgety. Did no one mean to ask after him? Did Lucy have no familial regard? Mrs. Westwood no concern over the unexplained absence of her charge's guardian? Valentine no thought of whether he had perhaps caused his friend to ride too hard? That last one was rather unlikely, perhaps, but certainly someone ought to wonder where Mr. Russell was.

But no one seemed to pay his absence any heed, so when the card game had finished and I was satisfied that Lucy and Mr. Pike had been able to spend some time together, I quietly excused myself.

I made my way to the library and peeked inside, certain I should find it empty and be obliged to assume Mr. Russell had gone to bed with the headache. It did indeed look vacant upon first glance, but a sound caught my attention, followed by a movement. Mr. Russell was on his hands and knees, looking under the chairs by the fireplace.

It was a strange sight, and I smiled at it before clearing my throat loudly.

He glanced up and, finding me looking at him with my face composed in an expression of mild curiosity, he rose to his feet. The small wrinkle in his brow from earlier had deepened, and the smile he had worn upon seeing me earlier was absent.

"Are you looking for something, Mr. Russell?" I asked with studied nonchalance.

He looked at me for a moment, and his brow furrowed even more. I sucked in a small breath at the way his eyes could look so light and so dark at the same time.

"Did you take it?" he asked.

I stared back at him, silent and secretly startled at the unwonted emotion visible in a face that was normally so placid.

"My brother's pocket watch," he said. "Did you take it?"

It belonged to his brother? I felt myself on shaky ground and debated for a moment how to respond. "I thought you might want a working timepiece for our nightly conversations, so I sent it to be fixed."

The intensity in his expression gave way to a widening of the eyes and a sickened look that made my stomach clench and flood with doubt.

"Where?"

I swallowed, tangled in the threads of my deception and this novel territory I was in with Mr. Russell.

He took three long strides toward me, forcing me to stare into those light, fiery eyes. "Where did you send it?"

"I—I—I didn't," I said, faltering. "I didn't send it anywhere."

"Where is it?"

"In my bedchamber," I admitted.

"Go retrieve it." The words were said like an order. He

seemed to recognize this and added, "Please." There was an imploring note to the word that made my heart twist.

I nodded and hurried from the room. My mind was a racing jumble as I hastened to my room and took the pocket watch from my dressing table. I had nearly taken it with me to dinner so that I would have it on hand when the time came to use it, but I knew Mr. Russell enough to guess that he would feel no compunction in prying it from my hands. The image of me backed against one of the bookshelves as he wrested it from me had made my heart race in a way that decided me against such a course.

But my heart was racing now, too, and my hands shaking as I clasped the watch in my hand and left my bedchamber. I was shaking not because of Mr. Russell's anger but because of the realization that he was angry with *me*. Well and truly angry. After all the things I had said and done, I had begun to believe there was nothing I could do that would rattle the man.

But his calm was *not* impenetrable. I had overstepped. I had somehow contravened Sun Tzu's counsel: *There are roads which must not be followed, armies which must be not attacked, towns which must not be besieged, positions which must not be contested.*

I had taken his brother's broken pocket watch; I had followed a road I should not have. I could feel that now.

When I reached the library again, Phineas was still not there, and Mr. Russell was seated on one of the chairs by the fire, his elbows resting on his knees as he stared at the empty fireplace.

He didn't even look up as I entered, and I didn't know which greeting I more disliked: the frown from earlier or the apathy now.

I came up before him and opened my palm, feeling I owed him an explanation. "I thought you might refuse to give me a reason today—or that I might be able to coax two out of you with it." My voice sounded weak and pathetic, but I didn't care.

I wanted him to look up at me so I could gauge how he was feeling.

The watch sat in my open palm, untouched. Finally, he sighed and took it in a slow, steady movement that was much more like him. He rubbed a hand along its cracked face, and I wondered if he had done this so many times he was certain it would not cut him.

"I would have given you a reason without this." He looked up at me, and all the anger was gone from his face, replaced by the calm I had come to expect. "Do you not understand that I enjoy my time with you, Miss Donovan? Or was enjoying it, at least." He looked away, and my chest clenched.

"Forgive me for treating you so ill," he said. "I lost my composure, and I regret that." He turned the watch over, running his thumb along the back, where it was dented. Had he been the one to rub away the polish, doing just as he was now? Or had it been that way when he had received it? "This watch . . . it holds significance to me."

His words rushed over me in a deluge of guilt. It should have occurred to me that the watch had belonged to someone he cared for—one of the people he had lost.

"I am sorry," I said softly.

He shook his head, eyes still fixed on the watch. "You didn't know."

"No, but if I had taken the time to think, I might have guessed."

"It does not excuse my behavior," he said.

"If someone had taken something of my mother's, I imagine I would have reacted in a similar way."

"I as much as dangled this in front of you; I should have anticipated you would see it as an irresistible weapon."

I hated that he was being so forgiving of me. I wanted him to rail at me again, for I didn't know what to do with this mercy. Mercy had no place in war.

I turned to leave.

"Where are you going?" he asked.

I stopped in my tracks, then turned to face him. "To bed, I suppose."

"Surrendering, then." There was the slightest hint of teasing in the words.

I frowned, noting the way the word ignited something in me. "I do not surrender, Mr. Russell."

"And yet you are leaving the battlefield." He was poking the beast, and he knew it. This was his way of showing me he was truly not angry with me for what I had done—that he still intended to fight against me. "I shan't try to dissuade you," he continued, "but I *shall* warn you: do not expect leniency from me."

The little flame he had ignited fanned to a fire. I looked at the clock on the mantel as I walked over to the empty chair across from him. "Fifty minutes left until you give me your reason."

"So be it." He smiled, though there was a bit of a forced quality to it. He might have forgiven me, but he would not forget.

Chapter Thirteen

P hineas had come in and fifty-six minutes had passed before I looked back at the clock that evening, but as Mr. Russell then allowed us seventeen minutes rather than ten, I did not berate myself too much. I enjoyed talking with him, if I was being honest with myself. He had a sharp intellect and even, dared I admit, a dry humor I appreciated. He was a responsible older brother to his younger siblings, and, though it required my reading into his answers, he seemed to harbor a fair amount of guilt over the fact that his younger sister, Rebecca, had been living with their invalid grandfather for so long, deprived of normal society.

The reason he gave for not wishing for a match between his niece and Mr. Pike—an expressed doubt over Mr. Pike's reasons for wishing to marry Lucy—required a surprisingly significant amount of discussion. I had thought the rebuttal to such a ridiculous reason could be successfully encapsulated in one word: love. But Mr. Russell was far from willing to accept it. Sometimes he mystified me.

The discussion had derailed into more of his accusations that I was a romantic, which I had hotly contested, and it was nigh on eleven o'clock when we quit the library for bed, Mr. Russell looking amused and my own expression pinched with annoyance.

I was beginning to doubt the wisdom of these nighttime meetings, for I doubted I was making much progress with Mr. Russell. But I couldn't deny the wisdom of what Sun Tzu had said regarding the importance of timing battles carefully: *A soldier's spirit is keenest in the morning; by noonday it has begun to flag; and in the evening, his mind is bent only on returning to camp.*

If I was to defeat Mr. Russell, persisting in these end-of-day talks might well be a crucial component. But I was not naive enough to think they would be successful all on their own. I needed to try other tactics too. I needed to be observant and watchful for opportunities to wear him down, to take him by surprise. But I would be more circumspect in my choices going forward, for the way he had looked at me when he realized I had taken the watch would not soon leave my mind.

T he stars seemed to align the next morning so that only the people I wished to see at breakfast were in attendance. My father and his guests had gone into Dover for the day, leaving our segment of the strange house party to ourselves—not that we had ever been anything but that.

The weather, too, was cooperating with my plans for a picnic on one of the nearby hills. It was perfectly situated with a view out over the sea, white, towering cliffs to the west, and a copse of trees for shade.

Given the uneven numbers of our party, I begged Valentine to accompany us, arguing that he had hardly been convincing in his role as Mr. Pike's lifelong friend up to this point.

He took the stairs two-by-two with his long legs, forcing me to hurry up beside him. "Perhaps that is because I am *not*, in fact, his lifelong friend," he said.

"You could do with such a friend, you know." I stayed by his side as he purposefully strode down the corridor.

"So that you can more easily have a *tête-à-tête* with Mr. Russell?"

I frowned. "Not a *tête-à-tête*, but I do need to speak with him, and I cannot do so when I am constantly having to hover between whoever happens to be unengaged in conversation at the moment. Five is a terribly awkward number to have."

He stopped in front of his door and faced me. "Six is hardly a more propitious one."

I smiled at him. "Superstitious, are you? Afraid to be the sixth"—I wriggled my fingers and widened my eyes spookily— "in the party?"

"No," he said flatly. "Simply determined not to accompany you on your picnic. I warned you, Di, that I wouldn't rescue you. You are in well over your head now—I hope you know that. In Russell, you have met your match."

I let out a scoffing laugh, but his words rankled. "Time will tell. And you might tip the scales in my favor if you would only do your brotherly duty and come along today."

"Forgive me, but I have no desire to see you and Russell flirting."

I pulled a face, and his half-smile appeared. "Yes, Di, flirting. You are deceiving yourself if you think it is anything else." He held my gaze, raising a brow, then turned and opened the door. "If you need help, ask Phin."

I did ask Phineas, and with a more perceptive gaze than I liked, he agreed.

"You are by far my favorite brother," I said, kissing him on the cheek with such exuberance that he was obliged to set his glasses back on his nose. Sometimes I wondered how someone as good and kind as Phineas managed to be in our family. In many ways, he was more of an oddity than Valentine. But he was simply more like my mother, and I loved him for it.

After Valentine's provoking words, I was feeling more determined than ever to gain an advantage against Mr. Russell, and Phineas coming along on the picnic would make that possible.

If I had hoped for a chance to engage Mr. Russell on the walk to the picnic, however, I was disappointed, for he immediately began a conversation with Phineas, while Mr. Pike sought out my company.

His visit to his mother had done nothing to improve his mood, it seemed, for he wore his worry on his brow.

"You wish for news on my progress," I said sympathetically.

He grimaced. "I do not mean to rush you, Miss Donovan. I suppose my mother's illness is making me think of everything with more urgency. But I also feel that I should be doing more to help. The burden of changing Mr. Russell's mind should not be upon your shoulders, surely."

"I am more than happy to help," I replied. "It must be difficult enough to split your time between the two women you most care for as you are now. The last thing you need is to add the burden of trying to understand Mr. Russell. Perhaps it was wrong of me to have you come to Blackwick."

"No," he hurried to say. "I shall be forever grateful to you for arranging things as you have. It is as you say, though. I cannot be at ease away from my mother *or* Lucy. I wonder if I should simply speak to Mr. Russell myself . . ."

"I do not think he has changed his mind from the last time

you spoke, so I cannot see what good it would do. It might even annoy him." I did not like to admit that my progress was entirely lacking, but I also didn't wish for Mr. Pike to set it back by bothering Mr. Russell. It was a delicate situation.

There was silence as we walked, and I glanced over at Mr. Pike, wondering if I had offended him.

But he merely looked confused. "But I have not spoken to Mr. Russell on the subject."

I slowed my pace until I stopped. "Whatever do you mean? You spoke with him, and he refused to give his consent to the match."

He stopped, too, and shook his head. "I believe you must have misunderstood. He told Lucy that I should not bother applying to him, for he would not give his consent."

I thought back on the conversation Lucy and I had had at the beginning of everything, but it was too faded for me to remember the specifics. "Oh." I began to walk again. "That *does* change things, though I shall have to think on precisely *how* it does." I could see Mr. Russell being very much annoyed if he thought Mr. Pike too cowardly to speak to him directly, instead using Lucy and me as go-betweens. But I was not under any impression that he would agree to the match if Mr. Pike were to ask him at this time, either.

Still a delicate situation.

"Perhaps you could wait to talk to him until I have had a chance to think on things. He is still set against the match, and I am slowly forcing him to tell me his reasons, which are invaluable if you are to persuade him effectively."

He nodded, and I urged him to go keep Lucy company with her cousin. I needed a moment to reflect.

Mr. Russell and Phineas were still ahead of me, and I was momentarily distracted by the way Phin was gesturing as he spoke. It was so rare to see him speaking animatedly. Mr. Russell's hands were clasped behind his back, and he was nodding, his brow furrowed in concentration as he listened. He addressed a remark to Phineas, who nodded vigorously. *Vigorously*. That was not a word I had ever used in the same sentence with my brother's name, and yet it was true just now. Mr. Russell was winning over my family members one at a time, devil take him.

I had barely had time to consider what Mr. Pike had told me when we arrived at the designated place for the picnic. The servants had been before us and were nearly done with the preparations—a few blankets set out under the trees and three baskets of food placed in the middle of them.

For having such a strange group of people, the picnic was surprisingly pleasant, the conversation easy, and the food delicious. Mrs. Westwood, in particular, managed to go the entire hour without uttering a single maxim, something which so surprised me, I felt obliged to comment upon it to Mr. Russell when I found myself near him as we walked along the cliffs afterward.

"I do not know whether to worry or simply revel in the ordinary nature of the conversation," I said.

He smiled. His hands were clasped behind him again, and our arms bumped against each other with each step we took along the breezy path. "The latter, certainly. But I know how difficult it must be for you not to be suspicious of such a thing."

"As would you be if you had spent as much time in her company as I have," I retorted. "Her adages and maxims are as essential to her as breathing."

"Then we should be rendering her aid rather than walking at this leisurely pace." He looked ahead, where Mrs. Westwood and Phineas were walking together just behind Mr. Pike and Lucy. "I think the sayings help put her at ease. It is a comfort, I imagine, to have a guiding phrase for every situation. It gives a semblance of order to life's chaos."

My brow knit. I had never considered it that way, but the

words hit a mark with me. Did I not use Sun Tzu for the same purpose? The only difference was that I did not utter *my* guiding sayings aloud. Perhaps I was more like Mrs. Westwood than I had ever noticed. I wasn't at all sure how to feel about that.

Did Mr. Russell realize the similarity, as well? I looked over at him, but his gaze was still forward. The reflection of the sun on the sea behind him created a sort of halo around his body that I would have found amusing had it not been so aggravating. Mr. Russell was not an angel, even if he was saying intriguing and perceptive things. And we were *not* flirting, despite what Valentine insisted.

This was still war, the battleground yet to be won, and I was meant to be observing him for ideas on other tactics. His defense of Mrs. Westwood's idiosyncrasies was merely a distraction.

Or was it? I looked to Mrs. Westwood and Phineas. Perhaps she should be playing a larger role in this war than I had currently given her, particularly given Mr. Russell's arguments on her behalf.

I smiled as a thought occurred to me, and I treasured it up to be used as soon as the occasion presented itself. *All we need do is to throw something odd and unaccountable in the enemy's way.* I might think little of the maxims Mrs. Westwood had created herself, but Sun Tzu was an indisputable sage.

The servants had taken the baskets and folded the blankets, leaving the grass pressed down where we had been sitting. Lucy and Mr. Pike had already begun to walk down the path toward the road, leaving the rest of us to decide how to configure ourselves. I saw my opportunity.

I was midway between Mrs. Westwood and Phineas, but I gravitated toward the latter. "Ah, yes. Do walk with me, Phin.

For Mr. Russell was just saying how he wished for a chance to converse with you, Mrs. Westwood. He has been lamenting the lack of opportunity to come to know you better, intriguing woman that you are."

Mr. Russell's gaze fixed on me, and a quick glance at him told me that he knew precisely what I was doing.

"You forget, Miss Donovan," he said in a falsely light voice, "that, happy as I am to spend time with Mrs. Westwood, she and I are related."

"Related?" I said, taking Phineas's arm in my own to solidify my plan to walk with him. "Surely not. What is the connection?"

"Lucy," Mr. Russell said. "Lucy is the connection."

"But your relation to Lucy comes through her father, while Mrs. Westwood's is through her mother—and only cousins, at that. Isn't that right, Mrs. Westwood?"

She looked no less pleased with my tactics than Mr. Russell. "Yes, but—"

"There have certainly been matches between closer connections than *that*," I said with an incredulous laugh. It was an outrageous and entirely scandalous thing of me to say, but Mr. Russell's staid disposition required such strategies.

And my strategy succeeded, for I could see the promise of revenge in his eyes.

"Miss Donovan," Mrs. Westwood said in her most censuring voice. "You shock me with such forward talk. *When doubt upon the proper avenue of conversation abounds, a woman should restrict her comments to the weather and the state of the roads.*"

"Such wisdom," Mr. Russell said, staring me down. "You are a veritable fount of it. Miss Donovan was just saying to me a few minutes ago how much she values your counsel. Indeed, she expressed a wish that there was some sort of written record of them—a bound copy, perhaps."

My nostrils flared as I held his gaze and noted the maddening amusement in his expression.

Mrs. Westwood's eyebrows went up. "I had never considered that, for I have no need of such a thing, having them all memorized, of course. But"—she blinked, staring at Mr. Russell as though he had just illuminated something for her—"what a gift that would be for the girls at the seminary."

"Priceless," Mr. Russell confirmed.

I barely heard the last comment, though, for I had tugged Phineas forward to begin our walk. If Mr. Russell chose to defend Mrs. Westwood or encourage her in her silliness, he could do so after spending a more appreciable amount of time in her company. Perhaps then he would understand why Mr. Pike would be preferable to Mrs. Westwood as the person responsible for Lucy's care.

Or perhaps I simply wished to irritate Mr. Russell. That was an acceptable goal too, surely.

Chapter Fourteen

I went to the library earlier than usual, in advance of Mr. Russell's departure from the drawing room. I had seen the hunger for battle in his eyes, the promise of retaliation, and I wanted to be prepared for it. Sun Tzu insisted that, *Whoever is first in the field and awaits the coming of the enemy, will be fresh for the fight; whoever is second in the field and has to hasten to battle will arrive exhausted.*

I would not be second in the field tonight.

The door opened, and from my place staring through the window, I whipped my head around. Phineas was in the doorway, but Mr. Russell followed just after him, his gaze already on me in a way that sent a tremble of anticipatory shivers down my spine.

I smiled urbanely at him and greeted Phineas, who made his way to his usual place in the back corner of the room with nothing but an acknowledging nod at me.

Mr. Russell didn't even pretend to wait for Phineas to become ensconced in his corner before he strode over. He came right up to me, and in my surprise, I took a small step back.

"Six," he said, staring down at me from so near that I could see every lash and every dark fleck in his irises.

Baffled, I wondered for a moment if he was making reference to the number of people who had been at the picnic.

"That is how many maxims I was treated to during the walk home today."

I pulled my lips between my teeth to stifle my smile.

"She must have been storing them up for the duration of the picnic," he said, "for they all tumbled out, one after the other."

I couldn't even pretend not to smile anymore. I could feel it in my eyes and the aching of my cheeks. "And what, pray, did you learn from the fount of wisdom?"

He stared down into my eyes. *Foolish is the woman who goes up against a man stronger than she.*"

I scoffed, still feeling keenly aware of how close we were. He filled my view entirely, making me almost dizzy, as though I might fall backward—or forward—at any moment. "Mrs. Westwood has never said anything of the sort."

"I wish she would have," he said. "She should have drummed it into your skull ten times a day while she had the chance."

I smiled at how the encounter had affected him. My plan had worked in at least one way. "Is it safe to assume you do *not* see a future with her, then?"

He narrowed his eyes, but his lips turned up at the corners, as though he was amused against his will. "You are a brazen little vixen, Miss Donovan."

I reared back, feigning offense. "How can you say such a thing? I was only thinking of your happiness." He let out an incredulous laugh, but I persisted. "I have wondered more than once if you are reluctant to give Lucy her chance at happiness in love because you lack it yourself. Misery loves company, after all."

His brows were raised. "I might say the same of you. You

have been thwarted in love, so you are attempting to live through Lucy. Star-crossed love is an intriguing prospect, isn't it, Miss Donovan?"

I narrowed my eyes as I looked at him wonderingly. "You are determined to think me a romantic."

"Or determined to hope it," he said, holding my gaze in that peculiar way that made me feel translucent.

"What does *that* mean?"

He said nothing for a moment, but the light in his eyes—no longer teasing but . . . ardent was the only way I could describe it—brought a sudden warmth to my cheeks.

"Nothing," he said, turning away and making his way to the chair he always sat in. "Merely that you should not expect for such a move to go unanswered. It may not be right away, but you can be assured that retribution will come."

"Behold me with bated breath," I said dryly as I took my seat. "In the meantime, though, now that you have had a taste of Lucy's life, perhaps you will not be so opposed to a change." I clasped my hands together on my lap and glanced at the clock, noting the time. "And now, the reason for today. A more substantial one than the flimsy excuses you have been heretofore offering, if you please, or I shan't hesitate to employ the sort of stratagems you experienced today. Or worse."

He let out a smiling sigh and stretched his legs before him, looking at me with a measuring gaze. He said nothing, though, and I raised my brows expectantly.

His focus suddenly moved to the rug on the floor. "I have qualms."

"Yes, I rather think we have established that, Mr. Russell. What we have yet to establish is that any of them are reasonable."

"They pertain to Pike's character."

I went silent, for there was a difference in his tone tonight. The reasons he had given up until now had been offered somewhat like a parent offering a child a toy and waiting to see what the child would do with it. This was not like that, though. He was more serious.

"What sort of qualms could you have about his character?" I asked.

His lips compressed. "That, I cannot tell you."

I pressed my palms together and set them in front of my lips to keep from saying anything I might regret. "I should have known," I finally said. "Then allow me to tell you what I have observed of Mr. Pike. You see, *I* can provide actual evidence of his good character, while you expect me to simply accept your unsubstantiated claim."

"I am listening," he said. And he was.

"Firstly," I said, "he is a devoted son. His level of concern over his mother's health cannot but be inspiring. He has been back and forth between his home and Blackwick as few would be willing to do."

Mr. Russell gave a nod of acknowledgement.

"Secondly, he treats Lucy with both respect and solicitude. You are not, perhaps, as well acquainted with Lucy as I am, Mr. Russell, but the truth is that she can be naive and a bit . . ."

"Helpless," he offered.

"Yes. I admit that I have become impatient with her from time to time because of it."

"You shock me," he said with a sliver of amusement.

I shot him a look. "But Mr. Pike does not grow irritated with her. Indeed, he has a seemingly inexhaustible supply of patience for her every anxiety."

He considered my words, mindlessly fiddling with the pocket watch. The sight of it always produced a bit of unease within me, for it was a reminder of how angry he had been with me, how brittle this mutual enjoyment of war truly was.

"Such evidence does not weigh with you," I said, noting how unconvinced he looked.

"On the contrary," he said. "Believe it or not, your assessment of his character holds great weight with me, Miss Donovan. But, as I said, I have reasons for my doubts. I am willing to be proven wrong. If I wasn't, I would not be here."

"And if the evidence I have offered is not sufficient to at least cast doubt upon *your* doubts, what will suffice?"

His brow furrowed, and he tapped the watch with his index finger for a moment, then looked up at me. "Time."

"Time," I repeated.

"Yes. If Pike's inexhaustible supply of patience, as you put it, and his solicitude remain intact, perhaps I shall concede."

I held his gaze, refusing to betray my relief and surprise at this bit of progress. "Intact for how long?"

The corners of his lips turned down at the sides as he considered the question. "Two years."

"Two *years?*"

His brows went up. "You doubt his loyalty?"

I blinked. "I . . . no, I do not doubt him necessarily. But, as we have discussed before, Lucy has very little of substance to offer. I am not acquainted with the particulars of her dowry, but I understand it is far from substantial."

He smiled. "Ah, but love, Miss Donovan. You are forgetting love. It is a force that can overcome such paltry obstacles as time or money."

I pinched my lips together. "Have you told Lucy that you will accept the match in two years?"

"I have not," he said.

"Intent on depriving her of hope?"

"Hardly. I hadn't decided upon the course, but you have helped me see that perhaps I have been too harsh on Mr. Pike. *Perhaps,*" he emphasized as my mouth stretched in a smile. "But, to your point, I shall certainly tell her—when she speaks to me on the matter, which she has not done since my arrival here. Indeed, not since our initial conversation on the subject.

Though, I think I may safely assume that *you* will convey the information to her and Mr. Pike yourself."

His words brought up another point on which I had been meaning to speak to him. "Why did you not tell me that Mr. Pike had not spoken to you formally about his intentions?"

He shrugged. "You simply assumed he had, and I chose not to correct you."

I sighed in annoyance. "And if he *did* apply to you for permission to pay his addresses? Tomorrow, for instance?"

"I would tell him to apply to me again in two years."

"Or," I said, "you could allow them the hope and happiness of an engagement and simply insist that the marriage not occur for two years."

He bent his knees and sat forward with his arms resting on them so that he could look at me more nearly, more intently. My heart sped. "And what sort of a guardian would I be to allow such a thing? Suppose for a moment, difficult as it might be for you, that Mr. Pike's affections for Lucy did *not* survive the two years."

I held his gaze, unable to do anything but silently agree with what he was saying. Raising Lucy's hopes only to have them dashed, engaging her to a man only to be later discarded . . . that would be the height of cruelty and irresponsibility on Mr. Russell's part.

Two years would seem like an eternity to Lucy, though.

"Well," I said, "it seems we are still at an impasse. You will not tell me the qualms you have, and I cannot agree with forcing Lucy to wait two years without knowing those qualms."

"An impasse, indeed." He looked perturbed, and I glanced at the clock on the mantel. It had been well over ten minutes since we had begun this discussion, but he had yet to look at the clock or mention the time.

Perhaps he needed someone with whom to discuss these things. And yet he refused to do so, keeping things cryptic and opaque. I hardly knew what to do with him. The only option was to continue fighting for Lucy and Mr. Pike—to continue these meetings in the library each night and whatever strategies I could manage to concoct outside its walls too.

But we were at an impasse, and the only way to get through an impasse was to try something new.

Chapter Fifteen

P art of me wanted to force Mr. Russell to tell Lucy and
Mr. Pike that they would have to wait two years to
marry. But I hadn't the patience to wait for either of
them to approach him on the subject, particularly when I had
just told Mr. Pike to delay any conversation with Mr. Russell.
Besides, I felt I owed them a report on the progress I had made,
and an agreement from Mr. Russell to say yes in two years was
certainly better than an inflexible no.

We were in the conservatory, for it was the only place I could
think of that we might manage to find a few minutes without
Mrs. Westwood listening to our conversation. I had given her a
pair of scissors and asked her to cut a few of the best blooms to
be put into a vase when we returned to the house, and being an
admirer of flowers and floral arrangements, she had agreed.

Mr. Russell had declined to accompany us, but the look he
had given me as we were leaving the breakfast room made me
wonder whether he knew precisely what I intended to speak
with Lucy and Mr. Pike about, or—even more curiously—if he
had wanted to put the task of telling them upon my shoulders
the entire time.

When I had conveyed the progress I had made, I was met with silence—silent mouths and dismayed expressions.

"Two years?" Mr. Pike said, aghast.

"Good heavens," Lucy whispered.

"It is better than never, surely," I said, feeling a prick of defensiveness. I had been trying valiantly to help them, and though I wished I was able to offer them the prospect of marriage within the month, that was simply not to be. They seemed to underestimate just how stubborn Mr. Russell could be.

"Of course it is," Lucy said, apparently noting my annoyance at their reaction. "And we cannot thank you enough for what you have been doing to help us, Di." She looked to Mr. Pike, as if she expected him to chime in with similar praise.

It took him a moment to respond, for his mind seemed to be elsewhere—somewhere unpleasant, given the look in his eyes. But he blinked and cleared his throat. "Yes, yes. Naturally we are very thankful to you, Miss Donovan." His smile was valiant. "I am afraid today I must make a visit home to my mother."

"Oh," Lucy said. "Yes, of course. I am certain you must be worrying over her."

He nodded, and the concern in his eyes was indeed apparent. "I should be going now. I shall return tonight, I think. Tomorrow morning at the latest."

The decision to leave was all so sudden and rushed, and I couldn't help but think about Mr. Russell's qualms. But it was entirely normal for Mr. Pike to feel crushed at the thought of being unable to marry Lucy for two more years—particularly when his mother was so poorly. What precisely did I suspect him of, after all? I had no reason to suspect anything, save for the unsubstantiated words of Mr. Russell.

Lucy was watching Mr. Pike walk off, her eyes now full of worry. She glanced at me and tried for a smile.

"Is he well?" I asked.

"His mother is not improving, you know, and he is terribly worried on her behalf. I think he was rather hoping we could marry sooner. Then we would all be in the same house, and we could care for his mother together."

I nodded. "Yes, I cannot imagine it is easy for him to leave her—or to leave you."

She sighed, turning her gaze back to him again as he disappeared into the house.

I felt suddenly inadequate, as though I had promised more than I could actually perform. I hated the feeling. But I couldn't stop trying. Neither could I let down my guard, for Mr. Russell had promised retribution for what I had done to him yesterday.

"We shall manage, Lucy," I said, putting a reassuring hand on her arm. "Do not give up hope."

———

Until now, my interaction with my father's guests had been limited to dinners and a few passing encounters in the corridors or at the breakfast table. My father had not been exaggerating when he had told me he would not have time to play the host to anyone else. But perhaps he was tiring of such long days holed up in the study, keeping only the company of naval men, for they all joined us in the drawing room after dinner.

Captain Stokes had not approached me since our encounter at breakfast a few days ago, and I was satisfied knowing he understood that I was no fool. I knew precisely what he had done, what he had thought of me, and I had no intention of playing the fool again. Not that I had any wish for his attentions now. I certainly did not aspire to marry a naval man, and even if I had, my father would have put his foot down. He had lived the life of a married naval man himself, and he had all but said that he regretted marrying. He blamed my mother and her illness for dampening his promising naval career.

The drawing room each evening had been a relaxed affair when I had had charge over it—a quiet card game or two, Mrs. Westwood darning something on the sofa, Phineas reading—but tonight my father was in command.

"The pianoforte, Diana," he said. "Favor us with a song."

I hated it when he spoke in commands like that, and having it done with such an audience was enough to make me tighten my hands into fists.

"With Captain Stokes, perhaps?"

I whipped my head around to look at Mr. Russell, who had made the remark. He was looking innocent as a child.

"Miss Donovan was just commenting to me earlier how much she wished for a duet with the captain," he continued, fabricating yet another imagined conversation between us. Of course, I had done the same when I had said he wished to know Mrs. Westwood better, but this was different.

My jaw tight, I stared at him, willing him to look at me, but he was looking at Captain Stokes.

"Stokes has a lovely baritone," said one of the other captains, smiling in what I could only call an amused way. I had the distinct feeling that I had been discussed between the two of them—and I was under no illusion that I had come off well in that discussion.

"A duet," said Mrs. Westwood, eyes still on her sewing. "How lovely that sounds. *There is nothing more soothing to the ear than the sound of the male and female voice joined in harmony.*"

I needed to say something, to stop this ridiculousness. I was torn between the need to assure the captain that I had not, nor ever would, wish to sing a duet with him, and the need to show Mr. Russell that his attempt at revenge had missed its mark.

"Come, Captain," I said, forcing down my pride and moving to the piano to find a suitable song, preferably one that had a hidden message of hate I could sing while looking straight into Mr. Russell's eyes. And perhaps a refrain for Captain Stokes about how little I cared for him. Why were so few songs written about such emotions?

Captain Stokes didn't move from his place. "You will have to excuse me." He fixed his gaze on me. "I doubt Miss Donovan's voice"—he paused on the word—"and my own would suit. I wager a voice like hers is meant to be enjoyed as a solo."

The other captain chuckled softly, and heat streamed into my cheeks. Everyone in the room knew Captain Stokes was not talking about my voice.

I was normally quick on my feet, ready to parry any thrust sent my way, but I had none now. I was fifteen again, back on the *Dominance. She is too much of a shrew for my taste. . . . She has all the qualities that would make her a good officer, but none of the sort one wants in a submissive wife.*

"I have just the song," I said, mortified to find that my voice was unsteady. "I shall go fetch it."

Captain Stokes had a knowing expression in his eye as he and all the others watched me leave the room.

Blood rushed in my ears as I hurried down the corridor, with no intention at all of fetching the piece in question. It didn't even exist. But I would have to find one all the same, for I couldn't simply disappear for the rest of the evening. I would have to return and sing my solo, if only to spite Captain Stokes.

But for now, I needed air. And to dry the pathetic tears of anger and embarrassment gathering in my eyes.

"Miss Donovan."

I didn't bother looking back at Mr. Russell. The last thing I needed was for him to see my weakness. Somehow that felt like it would be the end.

I picked up my pace as I came closer to the library, then hurried through the door and shut it behind me. Passing the place where Mr. Russell and I had been sitting each night, I opened the door that led outside and onto a small terrace.

"Diana," Mr. Russell said, following behind me. I should have expected as much; he was not a man to give up easily. And how dare he call me by my Christian name at such a moment?

I didn't even bother shutting the terrace door, but before I could hurry down the steps that led to the garden, he grasped my hand.

"Diana."

"What?" I spun around to face him, anger smothering my other emotions for a moment. Why could he not leave me alone for just these few minutes? Was I never permitted a moment of private weakness?

His brows furrowed as he met my gaze, as though he hadn't realized I was near to tears. Maddeningly, this only made my eyes sting all the more. Tears were uncommon for me, but just now, they seemed the most unstoppable force in the world, and I hated them for it. Hated *him* for it.

"Are you happy?" I flung at him, pulling my hand away. I would rather he see my anger than my embarrassment.

He blinked. "Happy?"

"Captain Stokes, at least, must be thrilled. To have such an opportunity handed to him on a platter."

Mr. Russell's confusion only grew. "An opportunity to sing with you?"

I scoffed. "An opportunity to reject me again—to put me in my place."

"He declined to sing a duet," he replied. "I would not call that rejection."

"You are a greater fool than I thought if you believe that is all he was saying."

"Or perhaps you are the fool for assuming he meant more."

My jaw tightened. "You haven't a shred of humility, have you? You assume that you know everything and that what you see is all there is. Well, allow me to disabuse you of such a notion, then. I have known Captain Stokes since I was but fifteen, he a strapping lieutenant of two-and-twenty and I the naive captain's daughter, eager to be noticed and admired. Like the young fool I was, I believed him to be as enamored of me as I was of him." My jaw hardened, and I raised my chin. "Imagine my surprise when I overheard him speaking of me with his friends—how I was too much of a shrew to be the submissive wife he required, but how he hoped my efforts with my father on his behalf would help him achieve first lieutenant."

Mr. Russell stared at me, regret and pity forming in his eyes. "Diana . . ." He reached for my hand, and I took a step back. His arm immediately dropped back to his side.

"For heaven's sake, do not pity me," I said. "That is not why I tell you this. I tell you this to force some humility upon you, to make it clear why I could strangle you. You forced me into a position where Captain Stokes believes he has bested me, has rejected me twice—and this time before an audience."

Mr. Russell's gaze dropped, and the corner of his mouth turned up.

I could hardly believe the reaction. "Is something humorous to you?"

He looked up at me with a wry smile. "I never thought I would be jealous that a woman wished to fight with another man."

I stared at him.

"I didn't mean to hurt you." His voice was soft and low, his eyes striking in their sincerity. "It was a foolish decision, borne half of a need for revenge, half of the need to know what you felt for the captain, for I could feel something between the two of you."

My heart was pounding, my body suddenly alight with tingling. "I feel nothing for him, and there is nothing between us."

"You do not wish to strangle him, then?"

I blinked, caught off guard by the strange comment. "I . . . I hadn't considered it."

"And now that you have?"

"I think it would be a waste of my energy."

He smiled—a more genuine one than I was accustomed to. "I am happy to hear that."

My brow knit. This wasn't the first time I had struggled to follow a conversation with Mr. Russell. "You have such an interest in Captain Stokes's well-being?"

"Something like that, I suppose. I have rarely disliked someone as much as when I believed you held him in particular affection. Now that I know you do not, he may have the world, for all I care."

His words made my pulse race. "I do not understand."

He shrugged lightly. "You have told me on more than one occasion of your desire to strangle me. As I have come to know you, I have come to hope that, for Diana Donovan, that might be a way of saying something else entirely."

My heart beat faster than ever. Somehow, we had drawn close without my intending to. Any thought of tears was long gone. All I could think of, in fact, was the stubble on Mr. Russell's jaw and whether it was as rough as it looked, or his lashes as soft as *they* looked. And his lips . . .

He turned away, leaning his arms on the short stone balustrade. "Perhaps it is just wishful thinking. You are not the only one to dislike me, after all. Lucy never took to me." He looked over at me, his expression rueful again. "She could be entirely at peace as a babe, but the moment she was set in my arms, she would scream and cry. Nicholas told me not to mind it, and I tried not to." He chuckled softly. "I wanted her to love me—I even tried wearing Nick's coat once to trick her into thinking I was him. But she knew. And then she grew older, grew out of crying or being held, but then she avoided me when

I visited. And so, I began to avoid her, as well." He sighed, his gaze fixed on some spot in the distance. "I haven't the temperament to appeal to someone like Lucy."

I swallowed as his words lodged somewhere deep inside me. I knew precisely what he meant. Temperament was not something one could easily overcome. My mother once told me to embrace my spiritedness—to tame it and control it, but not subdue it entirely. But I hadn't listened. I didn't *want* to be a shrew. Yet, every time I had tried to subdue the fire inside me, it had inevitably escaped my efforts, flaming up all the brighter for having been stifled—sometimes burning others as a result of the resulting explosion.

"I am sure her father considered that when he made you her guardian," I replied.

Mr. Russell looked over at me, angling his body slightly so that his weight rested mostly on one elbow. "When I received Nicholas's will, naming me as guardian, I was alone, for he had ordered the will to be read strictly in private." His head shook from side to side slowly, his eyes looking at me but not really seeing me. "I could hardly credit it. I stared at the words for hours, it seemed." His brows knit. "Why me? The one Lucy never liked. Her grandfather—her mother's father—was still alive then, after all, and she had always loved him."

I didn't know why Mr. Russell was telling me all of this. Perhaps it was to make me feel less embarrassed about my own past, about the rejection I had experienced. But I was grateful for it, all the same. "Your brother must have trusted you most."

"Perhaps." He stood up straight, brushing off the elbow of his coat. "But I knew I could never replace him, much less both him and my sister-in-law. It seemed wrong to even try. Lucy had never liked me, so what would she feel thinking I was the one to take her father's place?" He shook his head. "So, I continued to avoid her, certain she would be happier in Mrs. Westwood's care." He met my gaze.

I felt another twinge of compassion for him. Lucy did *not* like him. It saddened me now, seeing the regret in his face and having spent so much time in his company. She had nothing to fear from him, even if he was denying her something she wished for.

"You have given me more time with her." Mr. Russell smiled ruefully. "Forced it upon me, rather. I should be thanking you for that."

I shook my head, eager to disillusion him of the notion that he owed me any such thing. I had seen him as my enemy from the beginning. That was becoming harder to remember—harder and harder the closer we were, with each hour spent in his company. "You have nothing to thank me for. It was not done with your interests in mind, as you well know."

He took a step closer. "I do know. After all, you only want to strangle me." He stared down at me, his striking eyes searching mine, thickening the air around us.

My gaze dropped to his neck, mostly hidden by the folds of his cravat. But it was not my hands I imagined around it. Instead, I pictured what it would be like to touch it, to kiss it. Desire glowed within me.

"Diana?"

My gaze flew up to his. I had been caught admiring the enemy. And what might he do if he knew I admired him? He would have power over me.

But he didn't seem to realize the content of my thoughts. He was staring at me, eyes full of uncertainty, a hint of trepidation, even.

"I want to kiss you," he said.

The words trembled through me, reverberating in my bones, setting my body aflame, as though I had been made entirely of kindling and his confession was a spark. They lit my skin and lips on fire, threatening to consume me if I didn't do something —anything—to stop them. I had to engage them head on.

I wrapped my hand around his neck and pulled his lips down to mine in a clash of enemy forces.

At first, there was no response, no retaliation, like an enemy taken by surprise, scrambling to decide whether to retreat or engage. But I would not accept retreat. This was a battle that had to be fought, and I took the lapel of his coat in hand, pulling him toward me, provoking him to counter my attack.

His resistance crumbled, his mouth responding to mine suddenly and fiercely, taking me captive.

The onrush of a conquering force is like the bursting of pent-up waters into a chasm a thousand fathoms deep, Sun Tzu said.

I was at the bottom of that chasm, waters crashing and cascading over my head until I thought I might drown. I grasped Mr. Russell all the more tightly, for he was both my enemy and my only hope for rescue. His arms wrapped around me, one hand splayed against my back, holding me to him as he kissed me and defeated me. The waters rushed over me without ceasing, and I fought for breath, pulling away for air just long enough to engage again.

And every time, he was there, waiting for me, breaking me down with his kiss until I felt weak, like clay in his hands. And amidst all the chaos and the fire, I realized the truth: This was a battle I could not win, not with all the time in the world. I would be engaged in it until the day I died if I did not pull away now.

So, I did just that. I pulled away, and without a word, I ran.

Chapter Sixteen

I might have physically left Mr. Russell's presence, but mentally, there was no escape from him. I had left mid-kiss, hurried away mid-battle, the work unfinished, the enemy still at large. And my lips . . . they tingled with his lingering touch, demanding resolution. Like a chord progression left unresolved, my mind insisted on imagining what such completion would feel like.

But I wasn't a fool—not entirely, at least—and I had made the right decision to leave.

If equally matched, we can offer battle; if slightly inferior in numbers, we can avoid the enemy; if unequal in every way, we can flee him.

I had been woefully unequal. And worst of all, perhaps, I had enjoyed surrendering to Mr. Russell. I had begun to fall, and the sensation had been exhilarating. But one could not fall forever. At some point, the ground would be waiting, and that realization had been enough to pull me away.

I didn't return to the drawing room. I didn't even care if they were waiting for me, didn't care what Captain Stokes would make of my disappearance. Let him think what he wished; I had more pressing things to worry about.

"What?" Valentine's voice was aggravated, even in its muffled sleepiness from where I stood outside his shut door the next morning.

"Are you dressed?" I asked.

"I am in bed," he said, the annoyance in his voice beginning to overtake the slumber. "Like any normal human at such an hour."

I pushed the door open and stepped into his room in time to see him rip the bed hangings closed.

"I need your help," I said, dragging them open again unceremoniously.

He swore, shielding his eyes from the light. "For heaven's sake, Di. Since when did you become so pathetic and helpless?"

I crossed my arms. "I don't know, Valentine. Perhaps it started when you invited my enemy into our home just to spite me."

He pulled the bedcovers up over his head. "You sound like a fool talking that way. You do not live within the pages of *The Art of War*, much as you might like to think so."

I ignored him and went over to the armoire that sat against the wall behind me. "I need you to take Mr. Russell hunting."

He pulled the covers down to reveal his face. "Hunting?"

"Hunting." I opened the armoire and surveyed its contents.

"And what the devil do you imagine we can hunt in June?"

Pulling out a shirt and a pair of pantaloons, I turned toward him. "I don't know, and I don't particularly care. Hunt sparrows if you must. I simply need him gone."

"And I"—he shut the hangings again, but I stopped him with a hand—"need *you* gone."

"The moment you give me your assurance that you will take Mr. Russell elsewhere today, I shall leave."

"You landed yourself in this mess, Di. Find your own way out. Or"—he looked at me with a manufactured smile—"here's a thought: stop being a chucklehead and accept that you will never find someone as perfect for you as Russell."

I shut the bed hangings and strode toward the door, tight-lipped. "Of all the people I might have had as a brother, how is it that I managed to have the most disobliging one in existence?"

"Sheer, undeserved good luck," he said on a yawn.

I stepped outside and slammed the door behind me.

I had never walked with such trepidation in my own home as I did now, fearful as I turned each corner that I might meet Mr. Russell there. I hadn't the slightest idea how to conduct myself in his company, and it was easier to avoid him than to decide such a thing.

When I reached the door to the breakfast room, I opened it just enough to peek inside. Mr. Russell was not there, so I pulled it the rest of the way open and entered to join the others at the table.

Mr. Pike was notably absent, and Lucy looked a bit wan and pale beside Mrs. Westwood. Her plate of food had been picked at, but nothing had more than one or two bites taken from it. It seemed as though the more time she spent in Mr. Pike's company, the less she was able to bear his absence. Perhaps Mr. Russell would relent when he realized that it was not just Lucy's happiness but her very health which was at stake.

Mercifully, no one mentioned last night's spectacle with Captain Stokes, and I had just sat down with a plate of toast and was pouring my tea when Mr. Russell came through the door. His gaze went directly to me, lingering for only a second longer than was necessary, before he made his way to the sideboard.

I cursed his ability to be everywhere I least wanted him—and with such calm. How was it that his heart wasn't thudding loud enough for everyone in the room to hear, as mine was? This game we were playing, whatever it was, was getting far too complicated for me. It was one thing to face down an enemy in battle, but it was another thing entirely to sit down to breakfast with him and make mundane and civil conversation together when all I wanted was for him to kiss me into oblivion.

I shot up from my seat. "It looks as though we need more sugar. I shall just have a word with Cook."

Mr. Russell had paused at the sideboard and was looking at me with an eyebrow raised. His gaze shifted to the footman standing beside the door.

"I need to speak with her urgently regarding the menu for the week too," I added as an explanation for why I wouldn't have Reeve relay the message on my behalf. Mr. Russell was unconvinced, of course, but I hardly cared. I had not yet recovered from our last encounter, and I needed to recuperate my strength. I was not being a coward; I was following Sun Tzu's advice: *If he is in superior strength, evade him.*

But what came next? I needed to consult Sun Tzu. Somehow, though, I doubted there was any advice in *The Art of War* for what one was to do after kissing the enemy. It was inevitable that I would see Mr. Russell again, and what then? What would he expect of me? Good heavens, would he expect me to kiss him again?

My heart raced.

What if he did *not* expect me to kiss him again?

My heart whined, and I hit a fist against my chest to knock some sense into it.

"What are you doing?"

I looked up at the staircase and found Valentine looking down at me.

I cleared my throat and hit my fist against my chest again.

"I have a bit of a cough." I frowned, remembering how disobliging he had been earlier that morning. "What do you care, anyway?"

He continued down the stairs. "I wouldn't wish to go hunting with Russell if you are falling ill, my dearest sister."

I took note of his attire, riding boots and all. My eyes widened as he reached the bottom of the stairs, and I hurried over to him, wrapping him in a full embrace.

"Saint of a brother!" I planted a full kiss upon his cheek as he tried to pull away. "What have I done to deserve you?"

"Certainly not *that*." He wiped a hand on his cheek with a look of distaste. "This is it, Di. And I mean that. I shan't let you involve me in any more of your games. You cannot hide from him—or yourself—forever." He stared at me intently, then went on his way.

I watched him go, smiling slightly. There was a special place in my heart for Valentine, much as he might try to wriggle out of it.

Feeling much better about the prospects of the day ahead, I abandoned my course to the cook and made my way to the library. I found Phineas there, stationed in his usual corner. Had he noted my and Mr. Russell's absence last night during our normal rendezvous hour?

He glanced up at me and gave a little smile before setting back to reading.

I went directly to the table that housed my father's favorite objects from the Orient, ignoring the trinkets and figurines in favor of the books there. I knew *The Art of War* better than the Bible—it was admittedly much shorter—and yet my mind was foggy, less than usually astute today. I blamed it on that wretched kiss. If I had thought a little smile from Mr. Russell to be all the more powerful for his normally stoic demeanor, now I knew the fire that he could kindle with his arms around me and his lips on mine.

My body warmed at the mere thought, and I hurriedly opened the book, eager for wisdom to douse the flames.

My eyes scoured the words—all in French—looking for anything that might spark a new idea within me. How long would it be until I felt able to face Mr. Russell without wanting to be kissed by him, without thinking of the kiss? Until then, I would have to employ a different kind of strategy, something that allowed me to fight from afar. Such tactics existed. I knew that for certain, and I flipped to the fifth section, smiling as I found the words I was looking for.

Indirect tactics, efficiently applied, are inexhaustible as Heaven and Earth, unending as the flow of rivers and streams; like the sun and moon, they end but to begin anew; like the four seasons, they pass away to return once more.

I sighed, feeling more hopeful that perhaps I could help Lucy and Mr. Pike without being obliged to spend time in Mr. Russell's company.

I flipped through more pages, reading a few lines from each one, hoping for ideas.

There is a proper season for making attacks with fire, and special days for starting a conflagration.

I twisted my mouth to the side and frowned. What might fire represent in this particular situation? And was today the special day and proper season for such a thing? Sometimes it was difficult to translate Sun Tzu's words so that they made sense for my circumstances.

I brushed a few pages aside, placing my index finger to a line.

Gongs and drums, banners and flags, are means whereby the ears and eyes of the host may be focused on one particular point.

I hadn't any gongs, drums, banners, or flags, neither did I know how they would be of use to me if I had.

Impatient, I turned to the next page.

To be well-fed while the enemy is famished—this is the art of husbanding one's strength.

I frowned more deeply. *I* was the one who was famished. I hadn't even eaten breakfast today. But even with an empty stomach, what I truly hungered for was more time with Mr. Russell.

I pinched my lips together and skipped over a swath of pages, my gaze landing on a paragraph in section ten.

If you know the enemy and know yourself, you need not fear the result of a hundred battles. If you know yourself but not the enemy, for every victory gained, you will also suffer a defeat. If you know neither the enemy nor yourself, you will succumb in every battle.

I stared at the words, then read them again. Did I know Mr. Russell? Did I know myself? Or was it Lucy and Mr. Pike I needed to know better?

I hardly knew what I was fighting at this point. It was beginning to feel like I was fighting myself more than anything.

A bit of unease crept into my chest. I was losing sight of things, and I could not afford to do that, not with Lucy looking so despondent, with Mr. Pike weighed down with worry over his mother and set to split his attention for the next two years. I couldn't allow my own growing affinity for Mr. Russell to affect what I had set out to do. He might be a less disagreeable enemy than I had at first suspected, but he was still an enemy in the sense that he was opposed to the goal I had, and I had to find a way to fight him—preferably without allowing myself to kiss him. Unless kissing was somehow an acceptable battle tactic, in which case, I would willingly fight to the death.

I sighed. These indirect tactics Sun Tzu spoke of, supposedly as inexhaustible as Heaven and Earth, were desperately needed.

M r. Pike had still not returned at midday, and Mrs. Westwood and I were left to try to raise Lucy's spirits, to keep her from her building concern over Mrs. Pike. It was exhausting work, and I wished it had been Mr. Russell who was tasked with comforting her. He was responsible, after all, for her lackluster spirits and pale face, not Mrs. Westwood or me.

Mrs. Westwood's influence was not particularly helpful, though. She seemed to agitate Lucy even more sometimes, and I found myself wishing her elsewhere—hunting with Valentine and Mr. Russell, preferably. The thought of her scaring off the little game available for shooting with an ill-timed maxim brought a needed smile to my face.

Valentine and Mr. Russell returned just before dinner, and I was no closer to thinking of any ideas for indirect combat than I had been when they had left. I suspected I was more of a hand-to-hand combat soldier—or lip-to-lip, apparently.

Such insidious thoughts had been my constant companions all day, and I had been annoyed to find myself looking through the window for any sign of the men's return many times in the two hours before they returned to Blackwick.

Mr. Russell sat across from me at the dinner table, and I wasn't blind to his attempts to force my gaze to meet his. Neither was I such a fool that I thought the times when his feet met mine under the table were mere accidents. The third time his foot rested against mine, I looked up at him and found his eyes laughing at me.

I squared my jaw and kicked.

"Ow!" Lucy cried out beside him.

Mr. Russell pulled his lips between his teeth, then covered them with his napkin as he pretended to wipe his mouth.

Lucy looked at me, frowning and confused at the violence she had just experienced at my hands. Or feet, rather.

"Oh, heavens," I said, my cheeks hot. "I am so sorry, Lucy."

She leaned down and reached under the table, rubbing the spot I had kicked.

I stared at Mr. Russell, who had managed to compose himself by now and put a hand on Lucy's shoulder. "Shall we call for a doctor?" he asked.

My eyes widened in embarrassment, but Lucy shook her head. "No, no. It is only bruised."

I spent the remainder of the meal thinking of all the ways I could take revenge on Mr. Russell. If any day was a special day meriting a conflagration, this was surely it.

I stayed away from the library after dinner, remaining in the drawing room and retiring at the same time as Lucy and Mrs. Westwood to avoid any chance that Mr. Russell might catch me in the corridor.

Do not linger in dangerously isolated positions. I meant to heed that advice from Sun Tzu without exception from now on. It was a tricky thing, though, evading one's own houseguest—not that I had invited him, of course, but I had provoked him into gaining an invitation, and that was almost the same thing.

When the next day dawned without any sign of Mr. Pike, I began to feel uneasy. Had I been wrong to inform him that Mr. Russell would require them to wait two years to marry? Had the prospect been too much for him? I was a wretch if that was the case, for I had done nothing but encourage Lucy in her affections for Mr. Pike.

But there was no use fretting over such things until we could know something for certain. In the meantime, I sent one of the maids with a basket to take to the Pikes, hoping she might return with more information.

Perhaps wishing to avoid Mrs. Westwood, Lucy spent the

morning reading in her bedchamber. I made an attempt to coax her from it with the promise of a ride on my mare, but she declined, insisting she didn't wish to be gone when Mr. Pike returned. I gave up and decided to go for a ride myself.

On my way to dress for such an activity, I encountered Valentine in the corridor by his bedchamber. He looked at me warily.

"Don't even think of speaking to me," he said. "Much as I like Russell, I am not spending an entire day hunting sparrows again."

"I wouldn't dream of asking you," I said. "I value my life more than to make such an attempt. I am going out for a ride myself." I could simultaneously make myself absent, clear my head, and come up with a few ideas—all worthy goals. Well, perhaps not worthy ones, but goals, all the same.

"Taking Reeve with you?" Valentine asked.

"Ha! Don't play the propriety card with me, Val. It suits you ill. Besides, I haven't taken a footman riding with me for years."

"Haven't taken one, or couldn't persuade one to go with you?" he quipped.

I didn't dignify his question with an answer, merely sending him an unamused glance and leaving him in the corridor to go dress in my room.

I had never before needed a private ride more than I did now.

Chapter Seventeen

Much as Valentine might imply that I was dead to any sense of propriety, I always kept my rides confined to the area surrounding Blackwick, stopping shy of the line of trees that divided our estate from the Aldridges'. They would have been more than happy to welcome me onto their land, but as it required traipsing through trees with low-lying branches, I never bothered. Blackwick had more than enough dangerous clifftops to suit me.

Being away from everything and shedding my role as hostess for a time was glorious, marred only by the knowledge that I had entered into a battle that I could not escape nor was entirely certain how to emerge victorious from.

I pulled my horse, a sleek bay gelding, to a slow walk at the top of the cliffs on the northern border of the estate. The scene looked out over the sea and the waves rolling in toward shore in relentless rows, crashing on the rocks and cliffs with a force that sent spray into the air. If only I had such an endless supply of assaults. But the truth was I was finding Mr. Russell more like the waves, pulling my feet out from under me only to crash over me again once I thought I had found my footing.

"You cannot avoid me forever, you know."

I whipped around and found Mr. Russell riding toward me, as though my thoughts alone had conjured him. My heart immediately kicked to a gallop.

"Do you always force your company upon people, Mr. Russell?"

"Without exception." He guided his horse straight ahead, as though I was not his target, only to turn at the last moment so that he was approaching me from head-on.

"It is hardly appropriate for you to come in search of me when I am on my own like this," I said. "Any guardian worth his salt would know that."

He smiled slightly. "Is it my fault you are unchaperoned? Or that you try to kiss me the moment we are alone?"

My jaw went slack and my eyes wide. "You . . . you . . ."

His eyebrows went up, and his eyes took on a glint of anticipation. "Go on, then."

"Bounder!" I cried, unable to stop myself.

His lips turned down at the edges, and his brows knit. "Hm. Not familiar with that one. A different insult, perhaps?"

"Gladly," I said, my nostrils flared. "Dirty dish. Ass. Rip. Bell swagger. Wag. Prig. Slubberdegullion." With each word, my frustration with him grew. "You sniveling, sorry, scaly . . . scrub!"

He put his hands together and clapped softly. "Excellent alliteration."

Only with the greatest of effort did I resist the urge to scream. He took so much pleasure in riling me, and he was so very good at it, while I . . . I never seemed to manage doing the same to him.

"Pardon me," he said. "Perhaps you had not finished. I did not mean to interrupt."

I forced a smile. "I could go on indefinitely."

He chuckled. "You were not at the library last night."

I lifted a shoulder, trying to cultivate an attitude of nonchalance, to breathe evenly despite the way the blood pulsed in my veins. On no account would I admit that I was not strong enough to endure more time alone with him or how our kiss had overset me. *Let your enemy know all of your advantages, but hide from him with great care all your losses,* Sun Tzu advised. "I grew tired of listening to your flimsy reasons."

"That itself sounds like a flimsy reason." He brought his horse up against mine so that we faced one another and our knees touched. "I think, Miss Donovan, that you are frightened."

I scoffed, looking away. "And *you*, Mr. Russell, are dreaming."

"I think you are falling in love with me, and it terrifies you." There was less humor in his tone now, and I could feel his gaze on me, taking my measure, noting every shift in my expression and body.

My heart hammered. After a morning of considering indirect tactics—which I had clearly failed to execute, given my tirade— Mr. Russell's direct assault felt particularly jarring. "Acquit me, Mr. Russell. The only person in love with you is yourself."

"Is that so?"

I met his gaze, willing myself to be convincing. "If this is about the other night, I believe you misinterpreted things, particularly if you thought kissing me would mean I would concede my position."

He put up a finger, his eyes pinching. "A slight clarification. You kissed *me*."

I scoffed—scoffed at the truth. I *had* kissed him. And I had never enjoyed thirty seconds more. But he had been the one to suggest it.

"I am certainly not complaining," he continued. "Never has a wish been stated and fulfilled so swiftly, and if I thought you would kiss me again if I expressed the same sentiment now, I would do it."

His gaze was piercing with just a hint of playfulness, and it left me frustratingly breathless. Secretly, my heart wondered what might happen had we both not been atop our horses, making it impossible to grant his wish. Would a second kiss be as heady, as pleasurable as the first? Or had it merely been the novelty of it that had made it so earth-shatteringly intoxicating?

I tightened my grip on the reins. It was a good thing we were on horseback. I was safer here—safer astride a horse at the edge of a cliff two hundred feet tall than in a place where I could give in to the wish to be held and kissed by Mr. Russell again.

"I am more likely to deliver you the kick in the shins you deserve," I said.

He moved his horse away so that our legs were no longer touching, and I smiled at the retreat.

"I'd rather you didn't accidentally kick my horse," he explained. "Or my ward, for that matter."

"And I would rather you didn't terrorize my friend."

"You call it terrorizing; I call it protecting."

My horse sidled beneath me, becoming anxious and impatient at my fluctuating moods. "Protecting her from a happy life with a man who loves her?"

He narrowed his eyes in faux-thoughtfulness. "Ah, yes. This man you speak of . . . where, in fact, *is* he?"

It was true that we hadn't seen Mr. Pike in two days now, neither had Lucy had any word from him, to my knowledge. I couldn't deny, either, that my unease was growing with his absence and silence. But I wouldn't show that to Mr. Russell. "Caring for his ailing mother, as any good son would do."

"So, his absence wouldn't have anything to do with your informing him, as I can only assume you did, that a marriage between him and Lucy would not be countenanced by me for two years?"

"You are determined to believe the worst of him, aren't you? You are wrong to do so, Mr. Russell, just as you are wrong to deny them marriage. And I"—I gathered up the reins more securely in my hands—"am determined that you shall give them your consent—*before* two years have passed."

With a challenging smile, I signaled my horse and set off at a canter, leaving Mr. Russell behind. I forced myself not to look back to see whether he would follow, instead letting the curve of the coast take me to a place where I could see what lay behind me. He had not followed me, and I felt a mixture of relief and disappointment to know it. Why must everything with Mr. Russell be such a conflicting concoction of emotions?

Aggravating, maddening as he was, though, I could feel relief after the encounter. He had not expected any real shift in our interactions after the kiss. Apparently, he anticipated our struggle to continue. He hadn't insisted that we discuss the kiss, aside from his teasing comments, and I was grateful for that, for I didn't know how to discuss it, how to explain why I had done what I had done.

Whether the kiss had been part of a mere flirtation on his end or rather evidence of wanting something more, I couldn't allow myself to repeat the experience. I wouldn't give him the opportunity to reject me. I was not, after all, the sort of woman men wished for in a wife. Thankfully, I had no need to marry, for I could count upon enough of an inheritance from my mother and father to live comfortably until my lonely death.

No. Not lonely. Dignified.

Anyhow, what woman needed a domineering man like Mr. Russell to aggravate and tease and hold and kiss and . . . well, enough of that. The point was that I was not the sort of woman who needed any of it.

What I needed was to win. Winning was the only way to keep myself safe. And to do that, I needed to first discover if Mr. Pike still wished to marry Lucy. I had experienced a small defeat, certainly, but success was still possible. Sun Tzu's reassuring words rang through me: *An army can bring about victory after setbacks.*

Chapter Eighteen

While Lucy was still looking wan and pale, it seemed to be caused by her worry over Mr. Pike and his mother rather than for any concern that he might have changed his mind. The maid had returned with a hastily written note of thanks but no indication of when Mr. Pike meant to return. When I asked Lucy if perhaps she had heard from him and knew when we could expect to see him, she assured me that he would come as soon as he was able, and that his prolonged absence must mean that his mother's health was declining.

Her loyalty to her suitor turned out to be merited, for Mr. Pike rode up to Blackwick in the late afternoon, looking nearly as haggard as Lucy. I silently repented for having doubted him and determined to redouble my efforts to assist the two of them.

I went out with Lucy to meet him, standing aside as they greeted one another, him with a fervent kiss pressed to her gloved hand, her with all the ardor two eyes and a squeeze of the hand could convey.

When I felt that the air around us might combust if they

looked at one another in such a way for even a moment longer, I stepped into the silence. "How is your mother, Mr. Pike?"

His expression darkened, and worry clouded his eyes. "Not as well as I could hope. I meant to return after a short visit the other day, you know, but I could not bring myself to leave her in such a state."

"We would not expect you to," I reassured him. "It does you great credit that you are so attentive to her in her time of need."

"Thank you, Miss Donovan," he said with a tired smile. "Your basket was very much appreciated, and my mother begged me to send her fervent thanks to you. She is too weak, I'm afraid, to deliver or even write those sentiments herself, and all I could manage was that short note. Indeed, part of the reason I have come is due to that very circumstance." His gaze turned to Lucy, grave and intent. "If my mother is to have any hope, the doctor insists she needs more advanced care than she can receive here. He told me I must take her to Harrogate, where she can partake of the healing waters and be seen to."

I glanced at Lucy, whose eyes were wide, stricken.

"Harrogate?" she whispered in a wavering voice.

Mr. Pike nodded slowly.

"Could she not go to Bath?" Lucy said, swallowing. "Surely it would be better to travel somewhere closer."

"I said the same thing," Mr. Pike said, "but with her condition, she requires treatment from a very particular doctor, and he is only to be found in Harrogate. There is something else." He let out a long breath. "As the care she requires will be protracted, it obliges us to relocate there entirely."

I watched with dismay as Lucy began to waver, her knees to shake. I slipped my hand through her arm, hoping to provide an extra bit of stability.

"When must you leave?" I asked Mr. Pike.

He gave a little helpless shrug of the shoulders. "It will take time to prepare everything and arrange for departure. A fortnight? Three weeks at most, as it will depend, of course, upon my mother's health. It is a long journey."

"A fortnight," I repeated, my mind running at a clipping pace. "That should be enough."

"Enough?" Lucy said.

"I am still hopeful of convincing your uncle to approve of the match," I said. "We must adapt, though, and make the most of the time we have left. Lucy, I rather think you should try your best to better acquaint yourself with your uncle."

She looked up at me, confused.

"Give him a chance," I said. "Perhaps he is not so cold-hearted or controlling as you imagine him to be, and if he has the opportunity to see how devoted you are to Mr. Pike, that you are capable of making this decision for yourself, his heart may soften toward the match."

She swallowed but nodded. "I shall try."

I squeezed her arm in mine. "That is your assignment. Mr. Pike, you must focus your efforts on your mother, of course. Leave things with Mr. Russell to me until the time comes. And as for myself . . ." I narrowed my eyes, staring at the window of Mr. Russell's bedchamber. "Do you know the terms of the guardianship, Lucy? Or the wording of your father's will?"

She shook her head. "I do not. I was not at the reading of the will."

Mr. Russell's words from the other night came to mind—*he had ordered the will to be read strictly in private.* I hadn't paid attention to it at the time, but now . . . I had never heard of such a thing, and it piqued my interest.

"Even if I had been," Lucy continued, "I was too distracted with grief to pay anything much heed."

"Of course," I said. She had been so young that it was unlikely she would have understood the will even if she *had* heard it read. But perhaps she hadn't been meant to hear it. "I will see what can be done about discovering that information, as I think it important to know precisely what your obligations are as a ward and his as a guardian. It should be a matter of public record, if I am not mistaken, though I am not certain where one goes about obtaining such a record."

"Doctors' Commons," Mr. Pike said.

Both Lucy and I looked at him.

He lifted a shoulder. "My cousin works at Moorington, Bates, & Higgam. He has told me a great deal about his work. One need only write to the Court of Canterbury to request a copy of the will in question. There is no guarantee, of course, that the request will be granted, but if you explain your relationship to Lucy, they very well might grant it."

"Would my uncle not have a copy of it?" Lucy said.

"I am certain he does," I replied, "but I would rather he not be aware of this. He would only try to thwart me. He takes such joy in doing just that."

"Might I send a request for it?" Lucy asked. "It seems reasonable that I should have a copy of my own father's will."

My mouth twisted to the side in consideration. If the will had been read in private, it was possible that Lucy was not meant to know of its contents. Besides that, she was underage—and a woman. I could have my father sign my request, for he had enough influence and a recognized name that would give us the best opportunity for success.

"I think not," I replied. "There is something about the will that your father wished to keep private. We could make the attempt, of course, but we haven't the time to test various theories. We need to send in the strongest request possible. I am fairly certain I can convince my father to sign it."

Lucy nodded.

"Will you be staying for dinner, Mr. Pike?" I asked.

He glanced at Lucy and nodded. "I would like to. I will have to leave directly after, though, which I wish was not the case."

"I will take care of Lucy in your absence," I said. "You needn't fear on that account. And we will be working toward our common goal while you are away." There was no time to be lost.

Chapter Nineteen

Dinner had become my least favorite part of the day. The formality my father demanded, the stilted conversation if I happened to be seated near him, the constant talk of the war—it all left me itching for the drawing room. Or perhaps it was the library. Either way, every hour I spent at the dinner table with Captain Stokes nearby was another hour I was forced to recall more of the humiliating past, the ill-advised choices I had made in the name of love, and how it had felt when I had discovered how he truly felt about me. Even memories I had forgotten were resurfacing now that I was experiencing those familiar, potent emotions again, this time toward someone else.

I waited in the cramped corridor, anticipation lighting my blood on fire. Lieutenant Stokes would soon pass through, for it was nearly dinner-time, and I hadn't seen him since this morning.

My patience was rewarded when, two minutes later, he appeared, slowing at the sight of me. He was so handsome, with his windswept hair and pink cheeks.

"There you are," I said, moving toward him. "I thought you would never come."

"You shouldn't doubt me, Diana," he said teasingly, taking my hands in his.

"I shan't," I promised, looking up into his eyes, wondering how I ever had doubted him. With a fluttering heart, I went up on my tiptoes, bringing our faces nearer.

He allowed it until the last moment, turning his cheek so that his breath tickled mine. "I cannot kiss you, Di. Not yet. Not until I have more to offer you."

"I do not want more," I said.

"But you deserve more," he replied. There was a pause. "First lieutenant. When I am first lieutenant, I shall kiss you. In celebration of it; in celebration of us."

Such memories sat bitterly on my tongue, reminding me how untrustworthy my heart was, how I could never let it hold sway. For so many years, I had kept that promise to myself. But now, I was finding it more and more difficult.

As we made our way to the dinner table that evening, I hadn't yet decided whether to go to the library when Phineas made his inevitable exit later on.

My father's guests tended to flock toward the end of the table where my father sat, while my guests, as I called them, took their places on the other end. I followed them, choosing a seat opposite Lucy, whose chair was being graciously pulled out for her by Mr. Pike.

"Ah," Mr. Russell said, putting a hand on his niece's chair. "Have a bit of mercy on your shins, Lucy. Why don't you sit here"—he gestured to the chair on his other side—"and I will sit there."

I scowled at him, while Lucy looked at Mr. Pike with uncertainty, reluctant to give up her place next to him in favor of one next to her uncle. He gave her a little nod, and she obeyed Mr. Russell.

"Diana," my father said from the head of the table. "Come sit over here. There is an empty chair here." There was indeed one, and it was next to Captain Stokes.

He didn't even wait to see whether I would obey, and I ground my teeth as I debated whether to make a scene by declining or to subject myself to the captain's company and naval discussions for the duration of the meal. I dearly wanted to kick Mr. Russell in the shins. With his intervention, he had somehow simultaneously managed to aggravate me, separate Lucy and Mr. Pike, and make Lucy nervous.

"Diana," my father said in a tone that promised repercussions if I delayed any longer.

I tried not to betray my annoyance as I obeyed. Vengeance would be mine eventually, but sometimes patience was required. Lucy had characterized her uncle as being controlling, but in comparison to my father . . . well, there *was* no comparison.

Captain Stokes rose to help me into my seat, and I wondered for a moment how he would respond if I kicked *him* in the shins or did half of the things I had subjected Mr. Russell to.

Why my father wished me to sit on this end of the table was a mystery to me. He never welcomed the opinions of women, particularly not when sailing or war were the topics of discussion, and somehow his fellow navy men had apparently not had their fill of such talk over the course of the day—or the past week. But he knew me well enough to realize that I wouldn't sit silent, particularly not now that he had as good as forced me here.

But I found myself distracted by what was happening across the table and a few seats away. Mr. Russell was engaging Lucy in conversation—or attempting to, at least. She would hardly look at him, despite the fact that I had rarely seen him wear such a kind expression.

In the chaos of our kiss and the aftermath, I had largely forgotten our conversation just prior to it, but it came to mind now, his reasons for staying away from Lucy. Was he trying to amend that now? Or was this his attempt to dissuade her from marrying Mr. Pike by increasing his influence with her?

"You seem very intent upon something—or someone—over there."

I turned to Captain Stokes beside me. He wore a smile, the charming sort that had undone me as a young woman. He was objectively handsome, curse him, and somewhere inside me, I felt a little twinge of a wish from a bygone era—to capture his heart in the way I had never managed to do before. It irritated me down to the tips of my toes.

"Should I be jealous?" he asked, one brow quirked.

A little scoffing laugh escaped me, but I could feel the blood racing up to my face, infusing my cheeks with betraying color.

"It didn't escape my notice," he said, "that your sudden disappearance the other night coincided with Mr. Russell retiring for the evening."

"Allow me to congratulate you on your observational skills, Captain. No doubt they have served you well in the Navy."

His smile grew. "You never were shy of pursuing what you wanted. I only wish it was still me."

I couldn't stop my eyes from widening at the brazenness of his remarks, particularly after he had humiliated me the other night. But a quick glance around the table told me that everyone else was engaged in conversation. "What is the promotion?"

His brows contracted. "What?"

"What promotion are you pursuing?" I clarified. "It might be simpler—and faster—if you simply told me. No need to bother with any of *this*." I gestured to the air between us.

"There is no promotion, Miss Donovan," he said, offense written on his knit brow.

I didn't even bother responding. I hadn't any patience for Captain Stokes and his hot and cold treatment of me. Some men simply couldn't abide a woman's affections being directed elsewhere.

Not that mine were . . . .

I glanced at Mr. Russell, whose eyes were on me, slightly narrowed in a way that might as easily have been scrutiny as concern. I had told him of my history with Captain Stokes, and he knew a bit of what it meant for me to be here conversing with him.

He put a hand to his neck and tightened his fingers, as if threatening to strangle himself. He tilted his head slightly in the captain's direction and raised his brows in a question at me.

I bit my lip and hurriedly pulled my gaze away, relieved to find the captain's attention had been taken by the person to his left. It was becoming more difficult to convince myself—and others, if Valentine and the captain were any indication—that there was nothing but enmity between Mr. Russell and me.

I was not fortunate enough to escape my father's insistence upon my performing at the pianoforte again, but this time, Captain Stokes was the one to insist on a duet. I hesitated only a moment before agreeing. To refuse would have made me seem resentful and petty. In any case, it would be good for me to show myself in company other than Mr. Russell's.

We shuffled through the sheets of music near the piano, searching for a piece we both knew.

"I was under the impression you believed our voices would not suit," I said.

"I was wrong," he replied, pulling one out. "Simple as that. You caught me in a bad humor. Besides, how shall we ever know unless we make the attempt?"

I glanced over at him, my lips pinched. How many other women had he coaxed and cajoled as he had me? What other hearts had been touched and then strewn behind him in his quest for position and recognition?

"You have never seen fit to marry, Captain?" I asked, making every effort to conceal my dislike for him as I set the music on the piano and took a seat.

"Not yet," he said. "But it is something I aspire to, certainly." The smile he directed down at me was full of flirtation and implied meaning.

"Yes, well, perhaps the Admiral of the Fleet has a grand-daughter who can help you maneuver your way up the ranks by capitalizing on her father's influence. Shall we begin?" I set out the pages in order and took in a deep breath.

My skill on the pianoforte was nothing spectacular, but it hardly mattered. Indeed, it seemed Captain Stokes had forgotten that we were meant to be singing a duet. His baritone rang out loud and firm, nearly overwhelming my singing. And while I considered attempting to match his volume with my own voice in a sort of battle to be heard, I decided against it. A glance at Mr. Russell's subtle but unpleasant expression made it clear he was not enjoying the performance, and for whatever reason, the need to outdo Captain Stokes was less of a priority to me than the need to make a good account of myself to Mr. Russell.

I had chosen a mercifully short song, thank the heavens, for my ears were left ringing at the end of it. The company clapped politely while I gathered the sheet music together.

"What a pleasure that was, Miss Donovan," Captain Stokes said. "You play and sing very well."

"Oh," I said in mock surprise, rising from my seat and facing him with the music held against my chest. "I was not certain you heard me at all over the sound of your own voice."

He frowned. "I do not know what you mean."

I patted him reassuringly on the arm. "I thought not. But you needn't concern yourself over it. After all, a good captain must be able to shout loudly enough to ensure his authority remains unchallenged. And if you shout even half as loudly as you sing, Captain, I foresee a very successful—if somewhat lonely —career."

I smiled at him and turned away.

M r. Russell caught eyes with me after Phineas retired for the evening. I was still undecided upon my own course, but after a few minutes, Mr. Russell rose and excused himself.

Even if I had been certain of what I meant to do, I couldn't have left just then, for Captain Stokes was watching me, one brow raised and a little quirk to his lip: a challenge.

I was torn between a desire to stare him in the eye as I rose and left, and the reluctance to give anyone reason to believe there was anything between Mr. Russell and me. It was beginning to seem that it was primarily I myself who needed reassurance of such a thing.

Captain Stokes seemed to linger particularly long, and I felt myself becoming more impatient by the minute. The realization that I was letting him determine my actions was simply too much for me to bear, and I excused myself half an hour after Mr. Russell.

I made my way toward the library, certain he would have left by now, if he had ever gone at all. I didn't know if it would be wise for me to enter even if he was still there, but whether the worry was for me or because I doubted it would be a fruitful endeavor on Lucy and Mr. Pike's behalf, I didn't know.

Do not repeat the tactics which have gained you one victory, but let your methods be regulated by the infinite variety of circumstances.

Sun Tzu's words lingered in my mind, telling me to leave, that I was becoming too predictable with these nights in the library. But still I stood before the door, too allured by the thought of being in Mr. Russell's company to heed the wisdom of the ancient general.

"A turning of the handle and a push should do it."

I swiveled around. Mr. Russell was looking at me from a

dozen feet away, his shoulder resting against the wall, the sconce above him accentuating the sheen of his pomaded hair.

"How long have you been there?" I asked.

"Long enough," he said with a smile, coming toward me.

Prickles ruptured over my skin. The last time we had been together in the dark . . .

I pushed open the door decisively. I could not be trusted alone with him.

He followed me into the library, and the sight of Phineas sitting in the corner—ever-loyal Phineas, bless him—acted like a glass of cold water over me. I was not so lost to all sense of propriety that I would kiss Mr. Russell in his presence. Not that I was certain he would notice even if I did.

"I thought you would be in bed by now," I said to Mr. Russell. "You retired early."

He took a seat. "I found my appetite for company . . . depleted, shall we say, after your musical number."

I winced slightly at the insult.

"*Your* playing and singing was thoroughly enjoyed, perhaps I should add. But I think Captain Stokes was correct—your voices do not suit."

I couldn't stop a smile. "Mr. Russell," I said, standing next to my usual chair and looking down at him. "Are you jealous?"

He laughed. "A ridiculous question. Of course I am. I have never wanted to throttle a man so many times in my life as I did during dinner and your duet."

My arrogance evaporated, replaced by a feeling of breathlessness. I scrambled to cover the reaction. "Now you understand how I feel."

His brows shot up. "But you have no one to be jealous of."

"That is not what I—" I pursed my lips. "You are impossible."

"The highest compliment you could give me, I imagine."

"It is not a compliment at all." But that was not entirely true, as I considered it. While it was exasperating, I could appreciate just how skillful Mr. Russell was at parrying my every thrust. What I didn't know was whether this was a game to him or whether there was any truth in what he was saying. Was he truly jealous? And why did that possibility make me feel so . . . so flushed?

I couldn't consider such a possibility. Mr. Russell stood to gain too much by making me think he truly cared for me. If he could woo me, he could subdue me.

He sat forward in his chair so that his elbows rested on his knees. "What *would* a compliment from Diana Donovan sound like?"

I couldn't resist a challenge, so I sat forward, mimicking his body language. "You needn't bother asking, for you are unlikely to ever hear one."

His gaze swept over my face, lingering on my lips so that I instantly regretted my choice to answer his challenging posture by drawing nearer to him. It put our faces twelve inches apart, close enough to feel mesmerized by his eyes, to make me struggle to remember the feel of his lips on mine.

He leaned forward even closer, bringing our knees into contact, and my breathing ceased. I wanted to do what I had done the last time he had been so near, to pull him to me, to keep him from slipping through my grasp as he so often did.

"Humor me," he said, the softness of his voice unnecessary evidence of how close we were.

Lucy. I had to think of Lucy. I couldn't be distracted. "What a fine guardian you are to allow your ward—and niece—to marry the man she loves."

He drew back, breaking the tension. "She was looking unwell tonight."

I followed suit, sitting back in my chair, feeling more mistress of myself with the added distance between us. "She has been looking unwell for days. Ever since she discovered you shall not let her marry for two years. You are making an invalid of her."

I awaited his rejoinder, but it didn't come. Instead, his brow furrowed more deeply, as though I had truly troubled him.

"Are you aware of Mr. Pike's financial difficulties?" he asked.

I didn't respond immediately, for I didn't know what to say. Aside from the short discussion of them when this had all begun, I was largely ignorant of Mr. Pike's finances. His family had the reputation for being well enough off, though. They owned property and had two tenant farmers.

"What sort of financial difficulties?" I asked.

"Gambling debts, among other things."

"The mark of a true gentleman," I said, only half-serious. I wished I had asked a few more questions of Mr. Pike when the topic had come up. I didn't like to be the ignorant one in a conversation with Mr. Russell. But it was hardly irregular for Mr. Pike—or any man—to lose money at cards.

Mr. Russell looked unamused by my quip, and for some reason, it piqued me.

"Not everyone is as flush in the pocket as you are," I said.

I seemed to be more than usually adept at causing him grief tonight, for my words met with a dark somberness. "I do not fault Mr. Pike for being a man of middling means, but I do fault him for being unwise with such means."

"Are his debts so serious?"

He nodded, and I felt a little doubt niggling me. Had I been unwise in encouraging the match? Did Lucy know the extent of the debts?

"Why did you not say something sooner?" I said.

"I have been trying to sort through rumor and reality myself," he replied. "The picture is still not entirely clear to me, I confess. Besides, I have been observing him, and, I must admit, his comportment toward Lucy, while more forward than I might like, has been above reproach."

"Why not simply ask him?"

Mr. Russell settled his gaze on me with an expression that told me he thought little of my thinking abilities at the moment. "What makes you think he would respond truthfully? Besides, he has not asked my permission to pay his addresses to Lucy. That would make it presumptuous, to put it lightly, of me to inquire into his affairs."

"But you told Lucy he should not bother applying to you for such permission," I pointed out.

"I did," he acknowledged. "And perhaps that was unwise of me. When I understood from Mrs. Westwood that there was an affection developing between Lucy and Mr. Pike, I inquired around about him, and what I heard gave me enough doubt to set me against the match."

"And now?"

He twiddled his thumbs, looking down at them with a frown. "I still harbor serious doubts, but I harbor doubts about my doubts, as well. His affection seems genuine."

I let out a little laugh. "Of course it is! Why should it not be?"

He stared at me for a moment but said nothing.

"Are you certain these reports are not overstated?" I asked. "Embellished, perhaps?"

"I am not," he said. "But I would far rather err on the side of caution."

The will came to mind. What was more cautionary than having a will be strictly read in private? I wondered what he would think to know I meant to request a copy of it. I felt a flutter of nerves, an inkling that he would dislike it, much as he had disliked my taking the pocket watch. Perhaps I should rethink the idea.

I pressed my lips together, refocusing on the matter at hand. Would it not be better for Lucy's future to be settled, to know she would be cared for by a man who loved her, even if Mr. Pike did have some unsettled debts? I couldn't tell if Mr. Russell was being a wise guardian or a controlling one.

"Why do you go by Duke?" I asked.

His frown disappeared, replaced by a curious expression.

"Is it meant as some sort of subtle—or not so subtle—statement of your power and influence?"

He laughed more fully than I had yet heard, and he looked more handsome than ever doing so. I had experienced an infectious laugh before, but Duke Russell was the only man whose laugh managed to penetrate to my heart.

I shrugged. "When Lucy told me you had always insisted on being called Uncle Duke, I assumed it was done with a hope that people would come to regard you like a duke and be too terrified to cross you."

"How delightfully imaginative of you."

It did sound a bit ridiculous now that I said it aloud—and now that I knew him better.

"Sadly, the truth is much less nefarious," he said. "My parents thought it wise to name me Marmaduke. *I* thought it wise to take on a variation slightly less ridiculous, particularly when a few people decided to shorten it to Marm." His nose wrinkled slightly.

I smiled. I was always glad for a bit of information to use against him.

"I recognize that smile," he said.

"What smile?"

"When you've had an idea. It is my favorite smile of yours, which puts me in a difficult position."

I frowned. I was becoming thoroughly confused, torn between the desire to keep smiling and to never smile again in his presence.

"I only see it when you believe yourself nearer to defeating me. How does he say it? *When the general's authority is weak . . . the result is utter disorganization.* Your smile, your presence makes me weak, Diana."

I stilled, my smile evaporating.

"You see my predicament now?" he continued. "How can a man win a war when he is falling in love with his foe? When part of him *wants* to be defeated by her?"

I couldn't move, couldn't breathe. The way he was looking at me, the words he was saying were simultaneously crushing me and breathing life into me. They were both victory and defeat, and I didn't know which feeling should concern me more—feeling triumphant to hear that he was supposedly in love with me, or feeling defeated to realize that he knew my guide to this battle we were waging. How long had he known? Had he been using Sun Tzu's tactics against me this whole time?

Behind all of my questions, I felt a deep longing to be loved by him, to embrace what he seemed to be offering. It terrified me.

I couldn't betray how rattled I was, how many questions I had. "I did not know you were a follower of Sun Tzu."

"I am not—or was not, rather. But while I was waiting for you last night, I had nothing to do but peruse the room. That was when I stumbled upon *L'art de la guerre—The Art of War*—and I remembered you quoting Sun Tzu to me once. After rifling through the pages and talking with Phineas, I feel I know you a bit better."

I glanced over at my brother in the corner, but naturally, he was not paying attention. Undoubtedly, he had thought little of telling Mr. Russell about the book or how well-versed we all were in the philosophies it contained. But he had done me a great disservice. The last thing I needed was for Mr. Russell to have yet another advantage over me. Now, he could guess my tactics, or worse, use them against me.

Even now, his telling me that he had fallen in love with me

could well be a strategy, and I knew Sun Tzu's phrase too well to ignore that possibility. *Do not swallow bait offered by the enemy.*

Mr. Russell leaned forward again, his eyes becoming more intent. "But we are not enemies, Diana. We both want the same thing—to see Lucy happy, to ensure she is taken care of."

He gathered up my hands, taking them in his and looking at me steadily with those wretchedly beautiful eyes. "Will you help me? Help me find out if Mr. Pike is truly a man worthy of Lucy?"

My hands gripped his, my body responding to his plea, wanting to give him precisely what he was asking for. His own hold became more firm, more sure, reminding me of how he had responded when I had kissed him. It was just two days ago, but it felt like an eon. I liked the warmth, the security of it, and I wished he would take all of me into such a hold.

I looked down at our hands, at the way his covered mine almost entirely. Captain Stokes had once held my hands in such a way. It had charmed me at the time, having them so enveloped, but I was different now, not so young, not so naïve. I didn't want my hands or my spirit surrounded by a man's. I didn't want to be used by one, to be a puppet working for him, as Captain Stokes had once made me.

I looked up at Mr. Russell again. Why was it so difficult for my heart to tell the difference between a man who truly cared for me and one who only wanted something from me?

I wouldn't be used again, though. I couldn't take that chance. "I shan't be your spy."

His brows pulled together slightly, and I pulled my hands away.

He sat back slowly, looking disappointed. "You insist on seeing this as war. On seeing me as your enemy."

"I insist on achieving what I set out to do, Mr. Russell. And *you* insist on standing in the way of that, which makes you an enemy, yes."

He didn't respond immediately, searching my face for a moment before rising to his feet. "I hope to change your mind with time, for I do not wish to be your enemy. Quite the opposite. But I know you better than you think, Diana Donovan. You would never love a man you could defeat, and that is why I shall never let you defeat me."

Chapter Twenty

I wanted to be loved by Mr. Russell, and I hated that realization. I didn't want him as my enemy, but the moment I agreed to be his ally would be the moment I lost my ability to keep myself at a safe distance from him. It would mean trusting him, and I couldn't trust a man who might be using me to have his way. I couldn't trust a man who might change his mind about me the moment I gave him what he wanted.

Despite what he had said, he didn't know me—not really. Just like he didn't know Mr. Pike well enough to judge him as unworthy of Lucy. Certainly, he didn't know me enough to love me. Perhaps he thought so now, but I would inevitably do something to give him a distaste for me, to make him realize that I was not the sort of woman a man took for a wife. I had already done that when I had taken the pocket watch, and his anger then haunted me, an omen of how I would inspire him with anger and frustration in the future too.

The sooner he realized that regret awaited both of us, and the sooner I stopped allowing myself to see him as anything but my adversary, the better.

I sat at the desk in my bedchamber, a place I was not often found, and the state of the ink there betrayed that fact. It was clumpy as I put my quill to the paper. I detested letter-writing and correspondence, but today I would make an exception, despite the way my hands shook. We had very little time before Mr. Pike was obliged to journey with his mother to Harrogate, and I could only hope that requesting the will would lead to some actionable information, some snippet I had not yet considered.

It would anger Mr. Russell—I was almost certain of that. But that was necessary. I had foolishly let my affection for him weaken my resolve and shorten the list of strategies I would use against him. That was not the approach of a woman serious about winning. No longer could I walk the unstable and untenable tightrope between pleasing him and keeping my word to Lucy. Once he knew the extent of my determination to achieve what I had promised to do, whatever he thought he felt for me would inevitably dissolve.

I tightened my jaw and finished my task.

As I came to the point of signing the request, though, I left the space blank. It was time to seek out my father.

———

I rested my back against the wall outside the study door, listening to the muted voices within as I clutched the request in my hand behind me. Chair legs scraped against the wooden floor, signaling the moment I had been awaiting the past ten minutes. The men were taking a short morning respite for a drink and some food, as had become their custom.

Most of the men paid me no heed, continuing in conversation as they filed out of the study, but Captain Stokes glanced at me, then stopped, eyebrows raised.

"Miss Donovan."

"I am not here for you, Captain," I said, brushing past him and into the study. I had no patience for him at the moment—or for any man who wanted something from me.

My father was gathering up the papers in front of him on the desk, but he looked up at my entrance. "Diana," he said with surprise.

I had been avoiding him as much as possible for the last week and a half, so his reaction was not without merit.

"I was hoping you might be willing to sign this for me." I held up the paper in my hand.

"What is it?" he asked again.

"A request," I said, trying to sound nonchalant. "Lucy never received a copy of her father's will, and she wishes to have one. I told her I would write the request and send it to Doctors' Commons on her behalf."

"Why not have her uncle do it? He is her guardian, is he not?"

This was the question I had been fearing. "He is, yes. But I understand the court is quite overloaded with work and are prone to ignore requests that come from unrecognized names. I thought your signature might help . . . facilitate the request, shall we say?"

My father was hardly insusceptible to flattery. While he would always be waiting for the next opportunity of advancement, he took great pride in his position as an admiral and the doors his position could open for him.

"Ah," he said, "I see." He reached for the quill in the inkstand on the desk and motioned for me to bring the paper over.

I set it before him and watched as his hand flew across the bottom. "Is Miss Ellis ill?" he asked. "She was not looking well last night."

"Just tired and worried, I think. Mr. Pike's mother is ill, and

Lucy has such a kind heart, she cannot help but be as concerned as though it were her own mother."

He handed the paper to me. "She is very taken with him, isn't she?"

"She is. And she will be very grateful to you for doing this. Thank you, Father." Rarely had I experienced such an easy interaction with him. I checked that the ink was dry and began folding the paper.

"And you," he said, looking at me intently now. "You are equally taken with Mr. Russell, it seems."

My eyes flew to his. "You have misinterpreted things, Father. There is nothing between myself and Mr. Russell, I assure you." That was not entirely true, but the last thing I intended was to tell him of the kiss we had shared. I clenched my jaw at the memory of it, strengthening my determination to put all thought of Mr. Russell out of my mind. "Neither have I any desire for such a thing."

"Oh." He frowned again, as he so often did. "Well, I cannot pretend not to be disappointed. I like him very well. But it was a foolish thought. I am quite resigned to the fact that you will never marry, my dear, stubborn woman that you are."

My heart plunged to the pit of my stomach, stirring up a sick feeling there. I forced a smile. "Very wise of you, Father." I held up the folded letter, eager to be gone. "I should go address this and see that it is sent off right away."

I went to the nearby library and scribbled the London address of the court. My father's comment reinforced what I was doing. Those who knew me best knew I was not destined for marriage.

I hesitated only for the briefest of moments before giving it to one of the servants to be posted.

I was doing this for Lucy. The less I focused on what Mr. Russell thought of me, the happier I would be. My father had resigned himself to the fact that I would not marry, and I needed to do the same. I had done it before; I could do it again.

I f Lucy had been looking ill at dinner last night, she was looking even worse today. Mr. Pike had returned home again, and his absence showed on Lucy's face.

She sat at the breakfast table, pale face and glassy eyes, her food untouched. I was not the only one who took notice of her state this morning. Mrs. Westwood was looking at her with concern.

"I think we should return home, my dear," Mrs. Westwood said. "I have preparations to see to before the girls arrive in a few days."

If she thought Lucy would take to the idea, she was horribly wrong. Lucy's eyes widened, filling with panic. The prospect of being unable to see Mr. Pike would likely undo her. Things were becoming more and more urgent.

I put a hand on her arm. "Why don't you go lie down for a while? See if you can get some rest?" I hoped that, by then, Mr. Pike might be able to return for a few hours and liven her spirits. Besides, I had a few questions I wished to ask Lucy. I had refused to help Mr. Russell discover Mr. Pike's true intentions, but my own curiosity was roused. I needed to know if there was anything that should give me pause in continuing to promote the match.

"Here," I said, pushing my chair out and offering my hand to her. "We can have this food brought to your bedchamber. Perhaps you will have more of an appetite after a rest."

Lucy didn't even bother resisting. I imagined she was simply relieved she was not being taken back to her cousin's immediately, cut off from Mr. Pike. She followed me into the corridor and up the stairs, her arm looped through mine, feeble and flimsy. I grimaced. At this rate, it would be a death, not a marriage, that Mr. Russell would have to manage.

I helped Lucy out of her dress and into the wrap she used as a dressing gown, then pulled back the bedcovers for her to slip into bed.

"I cannot possibly sleep right now," she said in agitation. "I am too restless. Edwin shall be leaving soon, and"—her chin quivered—"I shall never see him again. I just know it."

"Hush, love," I said, tucking her hair behind her ear. I wondered how Mr. Russell would feel to see her like this—so undone by something he could so easily rectify. "You mustn't work yourself up. It is essential that you rest. There is still hope, you know, and that is what I wish to speak to you of." I nodded, coaxing her into the bed, and she conceded.

I pulled the covers over her and sat down on the edge of the bed, my body turned toward her. "I must ask you something, Lucy."

She nodded, waiting.

"What exactly is Mr. Pike's financial situation?"

Her brows drew together. "Why do you ask?"

I observed her for a moment. I didn't want to set up her back, but I needed to know this. "Mr. Russell has again expressed concern over whether Mr. Pike is in a position to take care of you."

Lucy's expression grew almost angry, a rare sight for someone so sunny-tempered as she was. "Of course he can! And he *will*. It is a terrible thing for my uncle to insinuate that he would not. Edwin's circumstances are necessarily straitened due to the care his mother requires and some unfortunate past debts, but that fact only makes me love him all the more. He will do anything for her, and I shan't want for anything if I have Edwin by my side, either. But that is something my uncle cannot possibly comprehend, for he is intent on hating Edwin."

I felt an impulse to defend Mr. Russell, but I resisted it. This conversation was hardly conducive to Lucy resting. But I needed to be certain that there was transparency in their relationship.

"So, you have discussed the matter of how you shall live and what money you shall live upon?"

"Of course," she said, looking surprised that I would even ask such a question. "Edwin has promised me that all shall be well. Besides, I would rather marry for love than have all the finery in the world. Money may come and go, but love endures."

"Well said," I hurried to say, hoping to ward off any more bursts of frustration from her. "I think you should rest now."

She took hold of my hand, looking at me intently. "You will wake me if Edwin comes, will you not?"

"Of course," I replied reassuringly. "And I will come and check on you in an hour or two."

Lucy did not sound as though she was ignorant of Mr. Pike's circumstances, a fact which relieved me, for it meant Mr. Pike was not trying to take advantage of her. Now, to convince Mr. Russell of that fact.

Chapter Twenty-One

Despite Lucy's protestations that she could not sleep, she stayed abed the greater part of the day, undoubtedly making up for the rest she had been losing, worrying over the future.

The future preoccupied me too. Mrs. Westwood's comment about returning to the seminary, Mr. Pike's upcoming removal to Harrogate, and the impending departure of my father's guests were constant reminders of the changes afoot. Soon, Blackwick would again be empty, and then what would I do?

Mr. Russell would leave, and the thought gripped me, filling me with regret when it should have elated me. It terrified me to realize how attached I had become to the man I had determined would be my enemy.

You would never love a man you could defeat, and that is why I shall never let you defeat me.

The memory of the words sent chills across my skin, and I chafed them away. He would have me think he wished for me to love him, and I feared I was more than halfway there, much against my will as it was. But it was as much his love of me and

179

his trustworthiness as it was my worthiness of being an object of such love which were in doubt.

There was no avoiding the fact that, as things stood, I was an obstacle to him, and I couldn't allow him to have victory over me. He was right, after all. I didn't want a man I could defeat, and Mr. Russell was proving a very difficult foe indeed. But if I *could* defeat him, perhaps my inclination to admire him, to wish for his company, would disappear.

Lucy asked to have dinner brought to her room, leaving the company far thinner than it had been since Mr. Russell's arrival nearly two weeks ago. Mr. Pike had not yet returned, and given the time of day, I did not anticipate he would do so until tomorrow.

When a letter was brought by Reeve as we gathered for dinner, I thought it might be from him, but it was addressed to Mrs. Westwood, who took it with a blinking frown.

Her eyes widened as she read it. "Oh, dear."

"What is it?" I asked, trying to ignore the way my arm and Mr. Russell's rested against one another as the covers were cleared for the next course.

"One of the girls was obliged to return earlier than anticipated. She went to the seminary, expecting me to be there and is now at The Feather and Fawn. I must go to her immediately." She folded the letter up again quickly, then paused. "I cannot leave Lucy here."

"Of course you can," I said. "What she needs most is rest, and you will have enough on your hands without seeing to her, I imagine. I am more than happy to take care of her."

"And, more to the point, I am here, as well," Mr. Russell said drily. "Her guardian."

I stilled as a thought occurred to me. I had told Lucy at the beginning of everything that she needed to become more of a nuisance as a ward. Perhaps we had not been doing enough to pursue that avenue. Mr. Russell should not be enjoying a house party at Blackwick. That was one of Sun Tzu's philosophies, after all: *If he is taking his ease, give him no rest.* He had had nothing but ease since arriving as far as his guardian duties were concerned.

"Yes, Mr. Russell will see that she is well cared for." I glanced over at him, holding his gaze, forcing him to understand that I had been entirely serious when I told him I still considered him an enemy.

He met my eyes, the little quirk at the edge of his mouth evidence that he understood exactly what I was doing. He looked over to Mrs. Westwood. "You needn't worry over her tonight, Mrs. Westwood. I can accompany her to the seminary myself tomorrow."

I pinched my lips together. Lucy would not be returning to the seminary tomorrow if I had anything to say about it. Having her here at Blackwick without Mrs. Westwood's constant watch would be a relief, and with the amount of rest she had managed today, I hoped Lucy would be able to enjoy more time with Mr. Pike tomorrow. I, of course, would see to it that Mr. Russell was distracted during it.

The prospect left me feeling a shameful amount of anticipation.

"At the latest," Mr. Russell continued, "I will ensure she returns by Wednesday, for that is when I must leave if I intend to keep my promise to attend the assembly near my estate. Not that I anticipate she will still be unwell in six days."

Six days. He would be leaving, for better or worse, in six days. I didn't at all know how to feel about that.

Mrs. Westwood gave an uncertain nod, fiddling with the letter in her hands. "It is very kind of you. I can confidently leave her reputation in your hands, after all, whereas leaving Miss Wilde at The Feather and Fawn a second longer than necessary would be an atrocity her parents are not likely to forgive—and rightly so."

Instinctively, I shot a glance at Mr. Russell, who was already looking at me, ready to appreciate the drama with which Mrs. Westwood insisted on regarding life. I pulled my gaze away. Sharing such moments with Mr. Russell was not conducive to any of my goals.

Neither was sitting beside him at dinner, but he had hardly given me a choice in that matter. "If you think that sitting with me at mealtimes will keep you safe," I said in a low voice only he could hear, "allow me to disabuse you of that notion."

"Oh, I haven't been safe from you since the moment I met you, Miss Donovan."

I glanced over at him quickly, annoyed that, no matter how many times he said such things, they always managed to make my heart flutter. Most of the flirts I had known, Captain Stokes included, would have been wearing a sort of smirk and looking at me to see how I was reacting to their dalliance. But not Mr. Russell. He was unfolding his napkin, setting it on his lap with all the calm of someone who had just made a comment on the weather. It was that very restraint that both drew me to him and made me doubt him. Surely someone who felt the things for me that Mr. Russell implied he felt would not be able to speak of them so coolly. But Mr. Russell was not like any person I had met.

"Though," he said, "I am admittedly curious what sort of tactics you intend to use during a meal. Should I protect myself from another kick in the shins? If so, perhaps you should warn your brother on your left, as your faulty aim puts everyone in the vicinity in danger."

I pulled at the fingertips of my gloves with studied calm. "I couldn't very well call myself a student of Sun Tzu if I only had one mealtime strategy in my arsenal, could I?"

"No, but then, I cannot say I found any mention at all of shin kicking during my study of his words today."

I glanced over at him again. Was that where he had been today? Studying in the library?

"Allow me to pour you a drink, Miss Donovan." Without waiting for a response, he took the bottle of champagne and began pouring it into my empty glass. He didn't stop when the liquid had reached three-quarters of the way to the top, though.

I looked at him to see whether he had perhaps become distracted while pouring, but it was not so. He was watching what he was doing, certainly, and the liquid continued to rise until I was sure it would spill over. He tipped the nose of the bottle back at the last possible moment, leaving my glass brimming so that the champagne formed a bubble at the top. The veriest hint of movement would cause it to spill.

I smiled at him, my teeth clenched. "Thank you, *Marmaduke*."

His own lip turned up at the edge as he looked me in the eye. "Fascinating."

I frowned. "What is?"

"I have always detested that name, but I find I don't dislike it nearly as much when you are the one using it." He took the bowl of potatoes *au gratin* in front of him and began to serve me, putting a generous helping on my plate. Perhaps generous was the wrong word. It was far more than I would ever be able to eat, so there was nothing generous about it.

"Perhaps you could leave some room for the venison," I said with tight cheerfulness. "I find I have quite an appetite for game tonight. Something about a vanquished wild animal is simply irresistible." I held his gaze meaningfully.

He met my significant look with an amused one of his own, then reached for the platter of venison. "Of course. Someone like you must content yourself with another man's spoils. Personally, I prefer the taste of the meat I myself have hunted."

He kept his eyes on me as he served me an exceedingly small portion of meat—indeed, it might easily be overlooked amongst all the potatoes—then set the platter back in the center of the table.

I gritted my teeth together, clenching the gloves sitting on my lap. Being tasked with serving me, he had an infuriating advantage over me in this situation. It was all I could do not to betray how desperately I hated it and yet how reluctantly I admired his ingenuity.

Our attention was soon taken by my father, who took the opportunity to speak to the table, expressing his gratitude to the officers who had spent the last ten days at Blackwick and his regret at their impending departure.

He raised his glass, looking around at his officers. "To His Majesty's Royal Navy. May our recent victory be but one of many to come."

The table rumbled with repetitions of the stated toast as a few glasses clinked together. My own glass was far too full to be used for such a purpose, but as the focus was on the officers, no one took notice of my lack of participation. Except for Mr. Russell, of course, who looked at me with barely concealed amusement as he raised his glass, pretended to clink it against my imaginary one, and took a drink.

My throat was feeling particularly parched, and I tried not to envy him as the champagne washed down his throat. I also tried not to mind the bit of bare neck that showed above his cravat as he tipped his head back slightly. Or perhaps it was not wrong of me to admire Mr. Russell's finer points. It was important, after all, to be well-acquainted with the enemy's abilities and strengths. Mr. Russell seemed to have an overabundance of them.

He moved to set his glass down, then paused with his hand still wrapped around the stem. He rose to his feet.

"Might I be so bold as to propose a toast, as well, Admiral?"

"By all means," my father said with a nod as he took his seat.

Mr. Russell raised his glass and looked down at me, his eyes twinkling with impish amusement. "To Miss Donovan, then, for being such an excellent hostess."

Glasses around the table were taken in hand and raised up, all eyes moving to me.

I clenched my jaw, setting a tight-lipped gaze on Mr. Russell as everyone waited for me to take up my own glass.

"Will you not drink, Miss Donovan?" he asked.

"Diana," my father's censuring voice met my ears.

I forced a smile and reached for my overflowing glass, taking it and ignoring how its contents spilled down over my hand and trickled down toward my elbow.

"To Miss Donovan," Mr. Russell said.

"To Miss Donovan," echoed around the table, Captain Stokes's voice standing out with its volume.

I brought my glass to my lips and kept it there, drinking its entire contents and finishing well after everyone else had already set their glasses down.

Mr. Russell had his lips between his teeth, struggling to hide his amusement at my improper behavior. If Mrs. Westwood had been here, she would certainly have taken me aside at the soonest opportunity to state one of her adages about precisely what and how much it was proper for a young woman to drink.

The table soon filled with conversation, and I turned to my right. "You *will* pay, you know." I could feel the liquid on my arm, but I refused to dry it.

"I have no doubt you will attempt to make me do so," he said. "But first"—he took his fork in hand and, of all things, pierced its prongs into the small piece of venison he had served me earlier.

I watched in stupefaction as he brought it to his mouth and ate it. A piece of food from *my* plate.

I stared at him as he chewed, his brow puckered in appreciation as he gave a few *mm*'s. "So tender. My compliments to your talented cook, Miss Donovan." He looked at me and smiled, leaning in toward me so that our shoulders touched. *"One cart-load of the enemy's provisions is equivalent to twenty of one's own. Is that not what Sun Tzu says?"*

By the time I retired to the drawing room—for, I was the only woman present—both my body and my temper were on fire. Everything Mr. Russell did was calculated to ruffle me. How could I be so angry with him and yet so preoccupied with kissing him again? How could I simultaneously wish to defeat him and be defeated by him? To both humiliate him in front of an audience and find a way to be alone with him?

It was not a fair battle. I was realizing that now. Every day, I was obliged to rack my brain to determine how to gain an advantage over him, to find some new tactic to use against him. But for Mr. Russell, gaining such an advantage over me was as simple as placing himself beside me. His very presence threatened me, weakening my resistance, for all I could do when he was near was think of how much nearer I wished him, how near I had once had him.

My susceptibility to his charm, my admiration for his character were alarming.

Rather than linger in the drawing room, I made my way to Lucy's bedchamber. She was sitting up in bed, not looking nearly as rested as I had expected after how long she had been sleeping.

I sat on the side of the bed. "How are you, my dear?"

She smiled wanly at me. "Well enough, I suppose. I am afraid I shall be up all night, though, for I slept much of the day."

"Yes, I rather wondered if that might happen. I should have woken you, but you looked so peaceful whenever I came that I could not bring myself to."

"Have you had any word from Edwin?" she asked.

I shook my head. "Nothing as of yet. I am sure he is much occupied with his mother and all the arrangements."

Lucy swallowed, and I could have hit myself for reminding her of his impending departure.

"No doubt." She looked away.

I watched her, chewing my lip. While the rest of us slept soundly, she would be up all night, with nothing to keep her occupied but the dismal prospect of the future. She was not looking well, despite all the rest she'd had.

A thought occurred to me, and I scooted closer to her on the bed. "Do you truly think you shall be up all night, Lucy?"

She lifted her shoulders. "I feel weak but not at all tired. I think I shall just read."

"You could certainly do that," I said. "Or . . . I have another idea."

She looked at me, frowning, and I smiled at her, feeling the anticipation of the new tactic flood through my veins. Lucy needed attention to her health, and Mr. Russell had offered himself to do just that.

Chapter Twenty-Two

I*f he is taking his ease, give him no rest.*

The phrase repeated in my mind as I sat before my mirror in my dressing gown, candlestick in hand, staring at myself, vacillating. Normally, I wore my hair tied up in ribbons as I slept, but tonight, I had chosen a simple plait, which rested in front of my shoulder. I had done it with the prospect of seeing Mr. Russell. A silly thing.

It was past the time I had told Lucy I would return with Mr. Russell in tow, but I couldn't dispel the uneasiness about what we had agreed upon. *Agreed upon* might be a generous way of putting it. Lucy had resisted my idea, and though I had made every effort to convince her that it would be a humorous thing to wake her uncle and insist he see to his sick ward, the truth was that I had my own hesitations about it all. And the longer I had sat in my room, waiting for the appointed hour, the more those hesitations had taken hold.

I blew out a decisive breath and stood with the candle in hand, opening my door softly and going out into the corridor. It was entirely dark, all the sconces hanging on the wall devoid of flame, for it was nigh on one o'clock in the morning, and the servants had all been abed for hours. Everyone had. That had been rather the point of my plan.

But I didn't feel right about it, worrying Mr. Russell needlessly, particularly when I remembered our conversation about Lucy the night we had kissed. His concern for her went deeper than any of us recognized, I surmised, and I didn't wish to do anything to make him look at me the way he had when I had taken the watch.

I kept my footsteps light as I approached Lucy's room. It was entirely possible that she had fallen asleep while waiting for our little game, so I knocked softly, then entered. She looked to be asleep, lying on her back under the blankets.

"Lucy," I whispered. "Lucy, I have changed my mind." I went over to the bed and set a hand on her arm to rouse her gently. At the light of the candle in my hand, her brow furrowed, and she turned away.

"Lucy?" I said, worry creeping into my chest. I put my hand to her forehead. She didn't react to my touch or my voice, but her skin burned like a furnace.

Panic settled inside me as the light of the candle illuminated her red cheeks. She had a raging fever, so hot it reminded me of the one my mother had had just before she died. Without another thought, I left her bedchamber, making my way to the door of the Red Room.

I rapped on the door three times firmly, listening intently, impatiently.

After a moment, muffled movement sounded within, becoming more defined as footsteps pattered and drew near.

The door opened, and a disheveled Mr. Russell appeared. His dressing gown had been hastily thrown on, lying unevenly on his shoulders so that one sleeve draped lower than the other. Beneath its hurriedly secured tie, his shirt gaped open, providing me a view of his bare chest.

"Diana?" He blinked and ran a hand through his dark hair, his eyes sleepy. "What is it?"

"It is Lucy," I replied, my voice uneven. "She needs you."

Mr. Russell's eyes narrowed slightly, a bit of the slumber dispelling from them as he stifled a yawn. "Is this your idea of revenge for what happened at dinner? Perhaps it can wait until breakfast."

I shook my head, thinking how near he was to the truth, though. How stupid I had been to suggest such a trick to poor Lucy. *"Please*, Mr. Russell. She has a terrible fever."

His eyes widened slightly at my tone, and he put a hand on my arm, nodding quickly. "Of course. Only give me a moment."

I stepped away from the door, and he shut it softly, leaving me in the corridor with my lone candle, worrying more with each second Lucy was left alone.

When the door opened again, Mr. Russell stepped out, his shirt hastily tucked into his breeches and his hair still ruffled from sleep.

"Is she in her bedchamber?" he asked as he finished the top button.

"Yes," I said, turning and leading the way.

I opened Lucy's door, and Mr. Russell hurried into the room, taking the candle for me and placing it on the escritoire. He walked back over to the bed, coming up beside me and putting a hand to Lucy's arm, which she had wrested from under the blanket.

"Lucy," he said in a quiet but urgent whisper. Even in the dim light of one candle, I could see the concern on his face. He released her arm and put a hand to her forehead, letting it rest there for a moment, until Lucy turned her head away.

"She is burning." He looked at me.

"I know," I said, swallowing. "I left her just a few hours ago, tired and with a headache, but nothing else."

"How did you come to know of her fever?" Mr. Russell

asked.

I bit my lip, but I wouldn't lie. "We had planned a little trick on you together, and I came to speak with her about it, only to find her . . . like this."

"So, when you left her, you didn't know she was truly ill?" Mr. Russell said, clearly confused.

"No," I admitted, pulling the bell to call for a maid. "But I should have seen the signs." I had been so caught up in my feud with Mr. Russell that I had neglected to truly see what was happening to Lucy.

Well, I could not help the past, but I could certainly do what lay in my power to help her now. The room was hot, and I hurried to the window, lifting the latch and breaking it open so that a little breeze came in. It was a pleasant night, cool enough to lower the temperature in the room without freezing us.

"Should we call for a doctor?" Mr. Russell asked, his eyes on Lucy as she made a tangled mess of the bedcovers.

"No," I said flatly. "Dr. Helms will only insist on bleeding her."

"Then what do you suggest?"

"Following Dr. Buchan's advice," I replied. "*Not* further weakening her with all sorts of powders and bloodletting and what have you."

There was a hesitant knock on the door, and I went to it. The maid wore a cap, but the hair underneath was disordered, evidence of the fact that she, too, had recently been asleep.

"Anne," I said quickly, "Miss Ellis is very unwell. I need you to listen carefully. First, I need you to bring me a large bowl of warm water and a dry cloth along with it. Then, use the recipe in Dr. Buchan's book in the section on fevers—something with cream of tartar and oranges, if I remember correctly. Can you do that?"

Anne nodded quickly. "Of course, miss." She disappeared, and I closed the door again, going over to sit on the bed.

"Lucy," I said, taking her hand in mine. "Lucy, can you hear me?" Her hand was clammy, and while her brow furrowed at the sound of my voice, she made no other response.

"She is delirious," Mr. Russell said. His voice was almost blank, as listless as Lucy had been before taking the day to rest.

I rose to my feet, feeling too anxious to sit while we waited for the maid to bring what I had requested. Instead, I paced the floor while Mr. Russell took the place I had vacated on the bed. After a moment, he gently took Lucy's hand in his, staring down at it. The small gesture—and the hesitation in it—brought a lump to my throat, making me glad I had not tricked him as I had intended. It would have been cruel.

Anne returned shortly, holding a large, heavy bowl of water with a dry cloth draped over the side. Mr. Russell relieved her of her burden, and she excused herself to make the drink I had instructed.

"Where do you want this?" Mr. Russell asked.

"Over here," I said, gesturing to the trunk at the foot of the bed. "We must bathe her feet."

He followed my instructions without a word, setting the bowl down carefully on the large trunk as I pulled the bottom of the bedcovers away to reveal Lucy's feet. At first, she resisted our efforts, her tossing and turning making it nearly impossible to place her feet in the water.

I tried to keep my grip on her legs firm but gentle, but she pulled and squirmed until Mr. Russell took the cloth, dipped it in the water, and pressed it to one of her ankles. Her muscles stiffened for a moment, then relaxed enough for us to set her feet in the bowl.

We looked at one another, acknowledging our shared relief. Both of us had been splashed generously in the small struggle.

When Anne returned, it was with the requested drink, a cordial, and a bowl of thin gruel. Mr. Russell helped raise Lucy up so that I could press the drink to her lips.

Her agitation was lessening, though her temperature was still high enough that I could feel the heat emanating from her. Her cheeks were flushed and her brow covered in beads of sweat.

"I can stay with her, miss," said Anne.

"No," I said. Realizing my tone was harsher than necessary given the thoughtfulness of the suggestion, I took in a breath. "Thank you, but I shall stay with her. I wish for her to see a familiar face when she wakes."

"I will stay, as well," Mr. Russell said from his place supporting her.

I looked at him, and he held my gaze until I nodded once.

"Very well," Anne said. "Can I bring anything else, miss?"

I looked around the room, trying to think what might be needed, but I could think of nothing at the moment. We were doing everything Dr. Buchan suggested. "I will call you if I think of anything."

She nodded, gave a little curtsy, and left, shutting the door behind her.

I pressed the cordial to Lucy's lips, managing to get only a few drops into her mouth before she turned her head away. Sighing, I set the glass on the table and rose, beginning to pace the room as I brushed my forefinger nervously against my lips.

"You must rest," Mr. Russell said. "You have done everything you can for now. She is more peaceful, at least."

I nodded, but I knew how quickly a fever could return. It was what had finally carried my mother off. Her body had already been so weak, though; I could only hope Lucy was young and robust enough to fight off whatever she was combatting.

"Can you help me lay her back down?" he asked. Her back rested against his body, forcing him to twist in a way I could imagine was uncomfortable.

Happy for something to do, I hurried over and carefully wrapped my arms around her shoulders, letting her weight rest on me while Mr. Russell extricated himself. Slowly and carefully, he slipped out from behind her, helping me to ease her back down onto her pillow.

Both of us breathed out a sigh of relief when the task was done, and I glanced at Mr. Russell, smiling wanly at the coincidence as I sat down on the bed again. His shirt clung to his body, darker in some spots where Lucy's hot back and head had rested against him for the past twenty minutes.

Noticing the direction of my gaze, he glanced down. Putting a hand to his shirt, he tugged it away from his chest again and again, airing it out but saying nothing. In other circumstances, I had no doubt he would have teased me for staring, and I almost wished he would. This more somber situation carried an intensity and intimacy that made me feel strange. Afraid, even.

"You needn't stay," I said suddenly. Half of me feared he would agree, while the other half hoped for just that.

"I want to." He went over and took the chair from the escritoire, carrying it over and setting it next to the bed. He took a seat in it, leaning forward and clasping his hands as he watched Lucy.

Her hair was pressed against her forehead, her cheeks still flushed pink, but her body was finally still, hopefully allowing her more rest. Silence reigned in the room as we both watched her, lost in our own thoughts. My own were full of unease, on Lucy's behalf and my own. Her sickness had stripped away the protection my enmity with Mr. Russell had provided, making the battle between us seem silly and leaving me with no safeguard against him.

"Is this my fault?" Mr. Russell's voice was a low whisper.

I looked up in surprise, meeting his gaze. His eyes were full of distress, almost pleading with me to soothe his conscience.

"Tell me truthfully, Diana," he said. "I can always rely on you for the truth. Have I driven Lucy to this?"

I swallowed. How was I to answer such a question?

Chapter Twenty-Three

This was my opportunity for victory over Mr. Russell. He was, as I had said upon one of our first meetings, providing that very opportunity for me: *The opportunity of defeating the enemy is provided by the enemy himself.* I could tell him now that it was indeed his fault that Lucy was laying in bed with fever, that he had driven her to such great despair over the impossibility of a future with the man she loved. Mr. Russell was holding a stake to his chest and giving me the opportunity to drive it into his heart.

But I couldn't do it. For all my talk of victory, I couldn't say the words. Indeed, I wanted to take him by the hand and soothe him with assurances that he had done nothing wrong. But I *wasn't* certain that Lucy's illness had nothing to do with what was happening between her and Mr. Pike.

"I don't know," I said, giving him the truth he was asking me for.

His eyes held mine, and he nodded, directing his gaze back at Lucy. There was silence as he reached a hand to her forehead, brushing the drying hair away from her face.

It was an affectionate gesture, that of a concerned uncle.

Often as Lucy referred to him as Uncle Duke, it had been easy for me to forget the close relationship they shared. He was her nearest family in the world, nearer even than Mrs. Westwood. They had shared a deep loss, one that couldn't help but connect them.

"I am terrified of failing her," he suddenly said, his voice a whisper as he clasped his hands, resting them on the bed. "Afraid of making a mistake and dooming her to unhappiness. She is so young, so trusting that the world means her well. Trust like that is a treasure."

My heart quickened, for his words pierced me—the vulnerability of them, but also the words themselves. *Trust like that is a treasure.* I couldn't remember the last time I had trusted someone, had offered them the treasure he spoke of. I certainly didn't believe that the world meant me well.

"I am paralyzed with the thought that her trust might be taken advantage of by someone," he continued.

"By Mr. Pike," I said.

He nodded slowly, and suddenly I felt terribly selfish for refusing to help him determine Mr. Pike's sincerity. He *did* want the best for Lucy, but I had accepted Lucy's characterization of him as an enemy to her happiness and encouraged her to see him that way. If she *was* ill on account of his refusal to let her marry Mr. Pike, I, too, bore some responsibility for it.

"In case it matters at all," I said, "Lucy seems aware of his financial situation. She cares not at all for it. She is certain he will take care of her, has assured me that he has promised to do so."

Mr. Russell's lips pinched together, and he shut his eyes. "She cannot know that."

"But you can?" I asked.

"She doesn't know—" He clamped his lips shut, looking away. His jaw clenched and unclenched.

"Doesn't know what? How to tell if a man loves her truly?" If that was what he meant, I supposed I could understand. Perhaps he thought she was much like I had been with Lieutenant Stokes —naive and so eager to be loved that her mind was muddled. In more ways than I cared to admit, I still felt like that too.

He stared at me intently, then glanced at Lucy before returning his eyes to me again. When he spoke, his voice was nearly a whisper. "She is set to inherit a great deal of money."

I gave a small laugh, but it faltered as the intensity in his eyes continued. "What do you mean?"

"Precisely what I said."

There was a pause as I looked for any indication that he was joking. There was no such sign. "Lucy has never mentioned anything."

"That is because she knows nothing of it. No one does. No one except me—and now you. That is how her parents wished it to be."

My eyebrows drew together as I tried to understand, to comprehend this news. "How much money?"

He glanced at Lucy again, as though afraid she might be listening. She was peaceful, still, but Mr. Russell jerked his head toward the far wall and rose quietly from his chair.

Still feeling puzzled and wary, I moved my weight gently from the bed and followed him to the corner near the escritoire and window, where the light breeze blew in.

He leaned against the wall, folding his arms across his chest as he watched Lucy with a furrowed brow. His hair was still slightly disheveled, the slit in his shirt still open enough to distract me for a brief moment.

I faced him, forcing my eyes to his, waiting for an explanation.

"Five thousand pounds."

My eyes widened. Surely, he was having a laugh at my

expense. Lucy inheriting five thousand pounds? Lucy, who had spent the better part of her life living at a seminary?

"My brother made a number of investments over the years. On the whole, he experienced an inordinate amount of bad luck in those investments. We made one together a year before his death, which turned out to be a very wise one indeed. And as Lucy was their only child . . ."

I couldn't take my eyes from his. He was serious. Entirely serious. Lucy was an heiress.

"But . . . but," I sputtered, "I don't at all understand. Why would they wish for her to be ignorant of such a thing?"

"You know Lucy, Diana. She believes the best of everyone." He paused, a slight frown on his brow. "Or most everyone. My brother had the greatest fear that she would become the target of fortune hunters, that with her kind heart, she would be an easy victim, eager to help the first man who expressed a need for the money or an affection for her."

I looked over at Lucy. An *heiress*. An ignorant heiress, no less. A young woman without parents but with more money than she could comprehend. The memory of watching her with a ten-pound note in her hand flashed across my mind. She had been in awe of that amount—what would she think of five hundred times that? What would Mr. Pike think of it, for that matter?

"So, you suspect Mr. Pike of having designs upon her fortune? Even though you admit that you are the only one who knows of it?" Him and me. He had told *me*, of all people. I hadn't the mental wherewithal to address *that* fact at the moment, to think what it meant, but the secrecy of the will suddenly made sense.

He sighed. "It is not beyond the realm of possibility that he could be aware of it. The will was read in strict confidence, but there were necessarily people involved in the business of it."

I nodded, but I thought the likelihood was very small that Mr. Pike, of all people, was aware of the secret. If he had been impatient or trying to persuade Lucy to elope, perhaps I would have been more likely to consider such a possibility, but as things stood, it was looking to me more and more as though Mr. Russell was being an overly apprehensive guardian—and for reasons I could understand. It was a great weight to put upon a man's shoulders, particularly when he knew that Lucy did not care for him. It would be too easy for her to blame things on him if things took an ill turn on his watch.

"It looks as though she has come through the worst of it," he said.

I glanced at the bed, where Lucy lay fast asleep. "I certainly hope so."

"You think not?"

I lifted a shoulder. "My mother was like this before—" I stopped. I hadn't spoken of my mother's death with anyone, not even my brothers, except for in the most practical of terms. Nothing about the suffering that I watched her endure. Emotions that were more powerful than me were better kept inside, for their strength frightened me, much like Mr. Russell's kiss had.

I charged forward, hoping to cover my lapse in judgment. "You should return to your bed. I will stay in case the feverishness returns."

He looked reluctant, and I wished I knew if the hesitation was on Lucy's behalf or mine. "If she takes a turn for the worse, I will come fetch you myself," I added.

"Thank you. I am glad you came the first time"—he smiled slightly—"even if it was originally planned with the worst of intentions."

"The worst of intentions would have entailed far more than knocking upon your door," I countered.

"Still dreaming about strangling me in my bed?"

My cheeks warmed, for I had had more than one dream about Mr. Russell in the past week, and none of them had entailed strangling him. "Well, it would serve you right after dinner this evening, wouldn't it?"

His smile grew, and I felt suddenly short of breath—the way he was looking at me, the relative darkness in which we found ourselves. What had happened to my resolve never to find myself alone with him again?

"On the contrary," he said. "I was being the most attentive of dinner companions."

"By forcing me to spill champagne all over myself?" I touched my fingers to my arms, for I could almost feel a lingering stickiness there, despite having washed it away.

He noted the gesture with amusement. "I thought I saw a drip or two make their way down your arm."

"More of a deluge," I said drily.

He took in a breath, his smile fading. "Do you promise you will fetch me if she takes a turn for the worse?"

I hesitated. *Would* I fetch him? I had already seen enough of Mr. Russell's chest, already had enough opportunity to imagine kissing him in the most unlikely of situations—a sickroom. I hardly needed more time with him.

"I shall just remain here, then," he said after my momentary pause.

"I shall fetch you," I said hurriedly. Better to bet on the hope that Lucy would continue sleeping for the rest of the night than to have Mr. Russell remain here with me now. I had a sneaking suspicion that if he did, I would end up doing something I might regret—or worse, something I should regret but would not.

Chapter Twenty-Four

L ight had begun to creep through the gaps in the window hangings when I finally heard Lucy stir in the morning. As far as I could judge the situation, Mr. Russell had left the bedchamber somewhere around two-thirty. I had begun the night in the chair he had brought over from the desk and ended it on the floor. I hurried up from the rug and went over to Lucy's side, ignoring my body's protests after a night of unrestful sleep.

Lucy was tossing and turning, trying to make herself comfortable.

"Lucy, my dear," I said as I sat on the edge of the bed. "It is me, Diana." A quick hand to her forehead told me that she was once again feverish.

Should I fetch Mr. Russell? Suddenly, I wasn't certain whether my promise to him had referred only to the nighttime hours, or if he would expect me to come fetch him now, as well.

I went over to the bell pull and, after a moment of hesitation, tugged it. Sitting beside Lucy and trying yet again to fathom that she was not the poor orphan I had always thought her, I waited for Anne to appear.

Anne and I discussed Lucy's condition for a few minutes before I sent her away with the things she had brought during the night and instructions for what to return with.

Together, we cared for Lucy, bathing her forehead and feet, trying to encourage her to drink. More than once, I wished Mr. Russell was the one with me, for we had worked well together during the night, seeming to understand what to do without even speaking. His strength, too, had been an asset when Lucy needed to be raised to a sitting position.

Her fever seemed immune to all our efforts to force it to break, though, and she traded off between states of delirium and unrestful dozing. My own body was feeling sluggish and tired, my right shoulder achy from my weight pressing it into the floor during the night.

There was a soft rapping on the door, and, with a glance at me, Anne went to open it. Mr. Russell stood in the doorway, and his gaze took in the room, lingering upon me for a moment before it moved to Lucy.

He frowned and stepped into the room, going over to the side of the bed and touching the back of his hand to Lucy's brow. "How long has she been like this?"

"Two hours or so," I replied.

"Why did you not fetch me?" He looked sincerely put out, and I soaked the rag in the water near Lucy's feet again.

"She slept until morning." It was a pathetic response, but it was certainly better than *I am afraid that I shan't be able to control what I do if I am too much in your presence.*

"And you have not had any respite from this room?" He came over to me and put out a hand for the rag. "You need a rest."

I ignored his hand and set the rag to Lucy's feet. "I am perfectly fine."

"Your appearance would say otherwise."

My jaw went slack, and I looked at Mr. Russell with affront. "Aren't *you* charming in the morning?" I turned back to my task, ignoring an impulse to check my reflection or see to my hair.

"What? Because I say you look tired?" He reached and set his hand over mine, stopping me. He held it there until I looked up at him mulishly. His gaze was intent, though. "The last thing I want is for you *and* Lucy to be ill, Diana."

I swallowed, feeling as though some of the warmth from Lucy's body had suddenly transferred into mine.

"Lucy being ill may be your concern," I said, "but if I fall ill, rest easy knowing that it shan't fall to you to care for me, Marmaduke."

His eyes squinted slightly as our gazes warred. "If you refuse to go willingly, I will be forced to carry you to your bedchamber myself."

My nostrils flared. "You wouldn't dare."

"On the contrary," he replied, his hand still covering mine, "it would be a pleasure."

My cheeks warmed, and I glanced at Anne, whose eyes were slightly wide and her attendance to straightening Lucy's pillow a mite too studious.

Mr. Russell followed my gaze. "Her presence shall not deter me."

"She's calmed a bit, miss," said Anne with a quick look at me and then away, as though she felt herself intruding on an intimate moment.

I contemplated my options, part of me curious whether Mr. Russell would truly follow through with his threat, the other part fearing whether my heart would survive such a thing intact. Being carried in Mr. Russell's arms? To my own bed? It was far too much like one of the dreams I'd had.

I *was* tired, though. Everything in me drooped with the desire for sleep.

He watched me as I debated. "So be it, then." He took his hand that had been resting over mine and reached it around my waist. The other hand looked as though it would soon wrap under my legs. My whole body tightened.

I hurried to a stand, dropping the rag in the water. "Very well." I pulled his arm from about my waist. "I shall rest. But not because you are ordering me to. Only because I need my strength to help here the rest of the day."

Mr. Russell stepped back from me and nodded. "A wise decision."

I narrowed my eyes at him, wishing it wouldn't have been childish for me to stick out my tongue. "I shall return in an hour, Anne."

"Two hours," Mr. Russell said.

I paid him no heed, leaving the room and shutting the door behind me. Once in the corridor, though, I paused. I was still in my dressing gown, or else I would have gone anywhere but my bedchamber just to spite Mr. Russell.

But I had a shred of propriety left to me somewhere. Someone should congratulate Mrs. Westwood on that success, surely.

The door opened behind me, and Mr. Russell peeked out. "Just as I suspected. Have you forgotten in which direction your bedchamber lies?"

"*Actually*, I was just contemplating whether to send a note to Mrs. Westwood and Mr. Pike. They should know of Lucy's state, I rather think, don't you?"

"I agree. And I will write them. Your only task is, as agreed upon, to rest. For two hours."

I raised my brows. "How dictatorial of you. Do you intend to stand by my bed to ensure I comply?"

"If that is required. Or you could simply give me your word that you will, indeed, sleep. Not that your word means much, as we have seen." He cocked an eyebrow, referencing the fact that I had not called for him when I found Lucy's fever had returned.

I was too tired to argue further. It was difficult to fight someone who demanded you do the very thing you most wished to. "Two hours, then."

The side of his mouth drew up in a small smile. "You are a sensible woman, Miss Donovan. Most of the time."

Chapter Twenty-Five

I slept three hours. When I woke, I hardly knew where I was or what had happened, for I rarely napped. Evidently, I had needed it. Confound Mr. Russell for being right again.

I dressed in a hurry and went to Lucy's bedchamber, but only Anne was there keeping watch over her slumber. Lucy had woken for a time during my absence, and she had been conscious enough to partake of a bit of broth, which Anne had fed her.

"Mr. Russell left until she fell back asleep," Anne explained, "for he worried Miss Ellis would be agitated by the sight of him."

I frowned. Lucy was unaware, then, how much time he had spent caring for her in the past twenty-four hours, the sleep he had sacrificed, the worry he felt on her behalf. Lucy was ignorant of a great deal, in fact, for she had no idea that she was an heiress, either.

"Where is Mr. Russell now?" I asked.

"He left a few minutes ago to send for the doctor."

I felt a flash of annoyance. I had made it clear to him last night that I did not wish for Dr. Helms' intervention. Perhaps I was merely eager to blame someone for my mother's death, but I had felt ever since then that he bore some responsibility for it.

I gritted my teeth and made a mental note to address Mr. Russell's presumption and disobedience with him later. Never mind that he was Lucy' guardian. This was my house. Or my father's. But that was a paltry distinction. "Thank you, Anne. And now it is *your* turn to rest."

She balked a bit but obeyed when I insisted. I did not resort to threats, as Mr. Russell had. I wasn't a beast, after all.

When Mr. Russell returned, he had hardly stepped in the door when I accosted him with his sin.

"You called for the doctor?" I hissed at him, trying to strike a balance that would keep the room quiet but convey my annoyance. The annoyance won out, unfortunately, and Mr. Russell glanced at the bed as Lucy's head tipped from side to side.

"I did," he said softly as he shut the door.

"And who gave you permission to make such a decision as a guest in this house?"

He opened his mouth, but I rushed to speak. "If you say Valentine, I shall scream."

"Then, for Lucy's sake, I shan't say it."

I pinched my lips together. "I would have thought you would at least pay some heed to my opinion. Valentine did not have to sit and watch as Dr. Helms leeched and bled my mother to death."

Mr. Russell's smile faded. "I am so very sorry, Diana. But I assure you, I—"

"It hardly matters now," I interrupted, annoyed at the way I seemed unable to keep from speaking of my mother's death in front of him. "What is done is done. But if you think I intend to stand by while he does the same to Lucy, you are very much mistaken."

"Oh, I would never think you would stand by while *anything* was happening." He smiled and brushed past me, moving to the chair by Lucy's bed. She was still for the moment. "I will sit with her a while. I imagine you haven't eaten much today."

He was correct. I had only had a bit of bread and butter that Anne had brought that morning, and I was famished.

"I imagine the same is true of you." I always had to be difficult. It was something I was coming to regret more and more about myself. For some time, it had seemed like a strength. But with Mr. Russell's presence over the last two weeks, it had come to feel like a petty weakness masquerading as a strength.

"Yes," he replied, "but my temper can withstand a bit of hunger. I do not think the same is true of yours." The way he smiled at me told me he was waiting for me to counter with my own insult. So, naturally, I refrained.

In fact, I left for the kitchen and ordered two plates of food to be prepared, which I took with me to Lucy's room.

Mr. Russell was sitting in the same chair as he had been when I had left him, leaning his arms on the edge of the bed and watching Lucy with a thoughtful frown. He looked up at my entrance, his gaze going immediately to the plates of food. The look of surprise on his face was deeply satisfying to me, for I had not truly succeeded in surprising him—without angering him, at least—since meeting him. It was unfortunate, of course, that I had been reduced to performing an act of kindness to achieve it.

We ate together while Lucy slept, only to be interrupted by the sudden arrival of Mr. Pike. He was all worry and concern over Lucy, lamenting the fact that he had not been by her side during the worst of her fever.

Perhaps it was merely coincidence, but Lucy improved drastically during his visit, waking presently and gaining enough energy to sit and eat a bit of gruel. Mr. Russell and I shared surprised glances, and neither of us made to chastise the two of them when they held hands for a time. We were both too satisfied to see Lucy feeling better to say anything. I couldn't help but wonder as I watched them, though, about what Mr. Russell had said. Did Mr. Pike know of the fortune? Was he simply wooing Lucy for her five thousand pounds? His loyalty to her, the way he attended to her now, adjusting her pillows and helping to feed her made it impossible for me to believe such a thing of him.

Mr. Russell, too, was observing carefully, and I wondered what he made of it all.

Mr. Pike's visit was necessarily short, given everything happening at home, and Lucy was visibly tired once he left, her eyes drooping and her posture becoming less energetic.

"We shall leave you to rest, my dear," I said.

"No, no," she said urgently, sitting up. Her cheeks grew pink, as though she hadn't intended the outburst. "That is, if you wouldn't mind, I feel so much better having someone I know near my side."

"Of course," I replied with a glance at Mr. Russell. "I quite understand."

Lucy calmed enough to doze off soon after her outburst, and it was not long before we heard the footsteps and the subsequent knock that notified us of the doctor's arrival. I shot Mr. Russell a look that told him I was prepared to combat the doctor. He met my aggravated expression with a smile as he rose to open the door.

"Dr. Chisholm," he said, shaking hands with a man I had never before seen. "Thank you very much for coming so far and on such short notice."

"Of course, of course," the doctor said. "Your family have been loyal patients of mine for years. Where is she? Ah, there."

I looked to Mr. Russell, who met my gaze with a little smile that told me he knew exactly how I was feeling at this moment. I had assumed that he had gone against my wishes in calling for Dr. Helms. He had not.

Mr. Russell left the room to give Lucy privacy while the doctor made his evaluation and I looked on. I was prepared to dislike the doctor, to disagree with his assessment and his suggestions for treatment, but I was finding it difficult to justify any such sentiment. He was thorough in his exam as he was with his questions, and aside from suggesting a tonic and a slight adjustment to her diet, he was very complimentary of the approach we had taken.

At the end of the visit, he took his traveling bag in hand as I opened the door for him, revealing Mr. Russell waiting outside, hands clasped behind his back patiently.

"I suspect she may experience more fever again tonight," said Dr. Chisholm, "so she should be watched closely. I will return tomorrow morning to see how she is getting along."

"Shall we take turns by her side?" I asked once Mr. Russell returned from seeing the doctor out. "She expressed a wish to have someone she knows here, after all."

"I am positive she was not referring to me when she said that."

"She should know of your attendance to her in her time of need," I countered. "And if she *does* begin to scream at the sight of you, you may ring the bell and send for me."

"Very reassuring," he said drily.

I insisted on taking the first spell, which fell during the dinner hour. With Lucy asleep, however, I found myself restless. Not just restless, though. I found myself missing Mr. Russell.

Almost since meeting him, I had looked forward to Mr. Russell's company, relishing the banter we enjoyed together, in the knowledge that I had met a worthy opponent who could challenge me. But this was different. We had worked as a team for the past twenty-four hours, and it had forced me to realize that it was not just battling I took pleasure in with him. I simply enjoyed his company—and enjoyed it enough that, even though he had only left ten minutes ago, I was anxious to see him again.

The more I tried to see him as an enemy, the more my heart rebelled, whispering to me the very thing I had been attempting to drown out: I was falling in love with Marmaduke Russell.

I stood in front of the window, watching the hedges in the garden shift from being haloed in gold light to bathed in twilight blues. The door opened, and I turned. Mr. Russell held a tray in his hand, and the candle upon it illuminated the plate of food and the glass full of what appeared to be claret.

My heart fluttered at the sight I had been wishing for the past two hours. It was too dim for me to see his features clearly, but I knew them well enough to fill in the shadows—the arresting contrast between his light eyes and his dark lashes and brows, the suggestion of a beard that was always present on his jaw by this time of day, the way his hair came to a peak in the middle, like an arrow pointing the way. It was almost like seeing him for the first time—seeing him and feeling him without trying to restrain what I felt.

Oblivious to what was happening within me, he glanced to where Lucy lay asleep, then closed the door carefully behind him.

"The servants were cleaning up dinner," he whispered as he came over to me, "so I thought I would bring this to you myself. Note the generous helping of meat on your plate and the very appropriate amount of liquid in your glass." From our hour-long, daily conversations, he had come to know of my secret liking for claret.

I smiled weakly, feeling both overwhelmed and fearful at the way things suddenly felt more right in my world with him here. His thoughtfulness on my behalf too—it frightened me how badly I wanted to interpret it as evidence of his regard for me. "I congratulate you on managing the barest of civility, Marm."

He chuckled softly and set the tray down on the escritoire. "How has she been?"

"Quiet mostly," I said. "Dreaming of Mr. Pike, I assume."

As though she knew we were speaking of her, she shifted under the covers. Mr. Russell went over and put the back of his hand to her forehead.

"She is hot again," he said, disappointment in his face.

I hurried over. He was right. Her cheeks were flushed, her brow hot, and she tossed away from my hand, as though my touch alone was causing her discomfort. Her eyelids fluttered, and she gave a little moan, pulling one of her hands from beneath the covers and plunking it down beside her.

We glanced at one another as Lucy turned back toward us, reaching for Mr. Russell's nearby hand and grasping it. Her eyelids fluttered again, opening enough to fix on him languidly.

Tension filled the air as we waited for her reaction. If she believed herself to be holding Mr. Pike's hand, seeing her uncle in his place would undoubtedly be a rude awakening indeed.

But Lucy's mouth pulled up into a weak smile as she regarded him. "Father."

Mr. Russell tensed.

"I have missed you," she said in a scratchy, weak voice.

Mr. Russell was stricken, and he opened his mouth. I put a hand on his arm and shook my head, warning him against setting her right.

He gripped his lips together but kept silent.

Lucy's eyelids drooped, then finally closed, her hold on his hand slackening.

He waited a moment, then slowly pulled his hand away from the bed. The silence in the room was heavy as he stepped back.

I watched him, wishing I knew exactly what he was feeling. "I apologize for stopping you," I said softly. "I just . . ."

"No. You were right to do so. It would not have helped her for me to correct her." He seemed to shake off what was distracting him, and he turned to me. "In any case, you are free to go now."

I nodded, but I made no move to go. I didn't want to.

At my hesitation, his brow furrowed ever so slightly, his eyes focused on me. The frown slowly dissipated, and his gaze grew more intent, as though he realized exactly what was keeping me where I was—a reluctance to leave his company.

"Perhaps it would be better if you stayed a while," he said. "Just until we can be certain the delirium does not return. You can eat here in peace too."

I swallowed and nodded, wondering if I had misjudged the recognition in his eyes or if he was merely being kind enough to give me an excuse to stay. He offered me the seat in the chair by the escritoire, and I took it as he seated himself on the trunk at the end of the bed.

"Do you and Nicholas look alike?" I asked softly, curious but simultaneously hesitant to bring up a sore subject. My food sat untouched in front of me. I didn't have the appetite for it after what had just passed.

"Very much so for only being half-brothers." He reached into his coat and withdrew something. The pocket watch glinted in the candlelight as he grasped it in his hand. He smiled slightly. "Nicholas loved this pocket watch. He was a frugal man, but *this* . . . this was an exception. He was so proud of it, constantly taking it out and telling the time even though no one had asked for it. He wound it every night just after dinner. 'We wouldn't want time to stop,' he would always say." Mr. Russell's smile slowly faded, and his lips turned down at the edges as he stared at the timepiece. "Seven-fifteen. That was the moment that time stopped for Nicholas, the moment my own life changed. Lucy's life too."

I swallowed. The pocket watch had broken in the carriage accident that had killed Lucy's parents. And I had used it in my war against Mr. Russell.

"I had no idea when I took it," I said.

He shook his head. "I know. I didn't tell you that to make you feel guilty. I told you because . . ." He looked at me, and the end of the sentence hovered in the space between us, making it difficult for me to breathe properly.

He sighed and looked over at Lucy. "I may look like Nick, but I am not him. I felt that keenly, and I preferred to stay away rather than pretend. But now she has no trust at all in me. My wishes, my opinion carry no weight with her. To her, I am a monster."

"Anyone who stands between her and the man she loves would be viewed that way," I replied.

He didn't respond, which told me he didn't entirely believe me. "You wouldn't."

"I wouldn't what?"

He met my gaze. "Lucy would never see you as a monster. She adores you, idolizes you."

I shook my head.

"It is true, Diana. She listens to you more than anyone but Mr. Pike." There was a pause. "She would listen to you if you told her to wait, not to despair."

I sucked in a breath. He was asking me to help him again, to ally myself with him. I had paced the room for nearly two hours, thinking of how much I wished to end this war, but now that he was giving me the opportunity, I felt sickness wash over me. He didn't want to end the war; he wanted me to change to his side. Sun Tzu's words flashed into my mind: *Peace proposals unaccompanied by a sworn covenant indicate a plot.*

Was this what he had been hoping for all along? Tease and flirt with me until I lowered my defenses enough to do his bidding? Or was I so accustomed to seeing life as a battle that I mistrusted everything instinctively?

I didn't know what to say. My heart felt like it was shriveling inside me, just as it had done the night I had overheard Lieutenant Stokes. I rose to my feet.

"Diana," he said in an urgent whisper as I made my way to the door.

I ignored him, pulling open the door swiftly and slipping into the corridor. Picking up my skirts, I hurried toward my own door, reaching for the handle just as Mr. Russell stopped me with a hold on my hand.

"Diana, wait," he said breathlessly.

I could feel the ominous lump rising in my throat and the burning at the back of my eyes. I was going to cry. There was no avoiding it.

Well, I might not be able to control my tears, but I could control my mouth. I had spent a lifetime making certain of that.

I wrenched my hand from his grasp. "You think you can come here uninvited, unannounced, that you can annoy and badger and torment and woo me until I give in to your wishes. But if you think to defeat me by turning me into a traitor, you have gravely miscalculated your enemy." Realizing how near we were under the shelter of the doorway, I pressed my back against the wall.

"Defeat you? My enemy?" His brows knit tightly. "Diana . . . I do not wish to defeat you. I wish to love you. I *do* love you."

"You do not even know me." I thrust away his words before I could let them do me any harm or admit my own feelings.

"Do I not?" He searched my eyes, taking a small step toward me. "I know you are strong, that you know your mind, that you care for Lucy as the sister I always wished she had."

I wanted to move away, to put greater distance between us, but there was nowhere to go. I didn't believe Mr. Russell could love me, but neither could I pretend I did not wish to know what in the world he thought there *was* to love about me. I was a cactus amongst fields of flowers.

"I know that when I am with you, I never want to be

anywhere else. I feel alive as never before." His eyes shifted to my mouth, and slowly, he lifted his hand until his thumb brushed my lips. I trembled.

His voice grew softer. "I know that I have not stopped thinking about the night you kissed me, have not stopped wishing to repeat it."

I had fortified myself every way I knew how against Mr. Russell, but my walls crumbled like sand with each word he said. I wanted to be loved by him. Could I not just try?

He drew nearer, and his gaze shifted to my eyes again, his hand cradling my cheek. "If I know anything, though, Diana, it is that I would rather play at war with you than to love anyone else."

He was watching me, waiting, as though trying to gauge my wishes. He would not kiss me without a signal from me that I wished for it too. I knew that, though I did not know how I knew it.

My heart sped erratically, and my knees quaked under my dress. The last time I had kissed Mr. Russell, it had been a fierce battle, a fight to the death. This time, I felt timid, and the time stretched long as he waited for me to give him some sign. I was paralyzed, though, the enormity of what it would mean for me to do such a thing making my limbs leaden.

He gave a rueful attempt at a smile and dropped his hand from my cheek. After a gentle nod, his eyes full of sadness and sympathy, he turned away.

"Duke," I said, his name pulled from my chest almost without my consent.

He stopped just out of my reach, turning his head slightly to hear whatever I had to say.

I sucked in a large, quivering breath and stepped toward him. I looked down at the hand which had been cradling my cheek until just moments ago. Reaching out slowly, I took it, lacing my fingers through his as the rhythm of my racing heart rushed in my ears.

I was tired of fighting—of fighting him, of fighting myself. Just for a moment even, I wanted it to stop.

Gathering what was left of my courage, I looked up at him. His eyes were alert, fixed on my face, but after a moment, they dropped to our hands. His hold tightened, and he turned his body fully toward me, his focus still on our joined hands.

He let out a breath that quivered as much as my body was, then brought his other hand up to the hollow of my neck, resting it there so gently, I doubted it was even there. He looked at me, his eyes searching mine, then dipped his head and shut his eyes.

I closed my own, waiting for the feel of his lips on mine. But it was upon my right cheek I first felt their soft warmth. I sucked in a small breath of surprise. He pressed a kiss on my cheek, his hand still holding mine, gripping it again more tightly. Somehow, the urgency of his hold on my hand, the softness of the kiss on my cheek . . . they felt more intimate than the last kiss we had shared, in all its passion.

His lips brushed the skin of my cheek, moving over to the edge of my lips as the tips of our noses brushed. Finally, his mouth met mine squarely.

It was as gentle as our last had been harried, tender and slow, intentional in a way that left no room for me to doubt what he felt. I was not just being kissed, I was being cherished. Cherished by Duke Russell.

Chapter Twenty-Six

I knew the rush of victory, but it paled in comparison with what I felt in Duke's arms, with his lips pressed to mine. Was this what I had been fighting for the past three weeks? Who knew surrender could be so sweet?

I pulled my lips from his, letting them hover close enough that I could easily change my mind, pressing them to his again. "Lucy," I whispered, my body still trembling.

"Lucy," Duke said, as though trying to remember the name. "Yes, Lucy. I should be with her."

I nodded, feeling reluctant to be away from him. Was this what I had become? A woman who could not bear to be away from a man for a few hours? It was pathetic, and I could absolutely not allow myself to exhibit such—

"I will come with you," I said.

He smiled and nodded, visibly pleased with my insistence.

Lucy passed another difficult night, just as Doctor Chisholm had feared. After calling for Anne to bring a few things, Duke and I spent the next two hours seeing to her needs until the fever abated enough for her to sleep again.

"And now," Duke whispered to me as we cleaned up a few of the things Anne had brought, "it is time for you to go to sleep, as well."

"But it is the end of *your* spell," I countered.

He laughed softly and kissed me on the forehead, sending a bevy of butterflies fluttering in my stomach. "Must you fight me on everything?"

I put a hand to his cravat and straightened the folds, which had become crushed and limp. "You would worry about me if I did not."

"Very true." He shooed me toward the door, and I secretly delighted in the feel of his hands on my back, pushing me firmly but gently forward.

"I shall return in three hours," I whispered as he opened the door.

He swept me into his arms, pressing a kiss upon my lips, and I grasped the lapels of his coat as dizziness came over me. For so long, I had sneered at the swooning misses of London ballrooms, and in an instant, I had become just like them.

"And I shall do *that* again in three hours," he said as we broke apart.

I pulled my lips in to stop a smile. "And if Anne is with me?"

"Then she will return to the servant quarters with a great deal of gossip to share." He kissed me again, and I pulled away half-heartedly.

If anyone asked me how I arrived at my bedchamber, I might have been tempted to tell them I had floated rather than walked. I didn't wish to ring for Tait, given the lateness of the hour, but I needed to ensure she woke me to take Duke's place in Lucy's room in three hours. I was eager to relieve him of duty and to claim the kiss he had promised.

The last thing I remembered before falling asleep was touching a finger to my lips, trying to capture the memory of the night's kisses.

I sat at the writing desk in my room, scribbling the final words of a letter to Mrs. Westwood. Her students would soon be arriving, and I wanted to reassure her that Lucy was being well cared for here at Blackwick. The second half of the night had passed without incident, and I had left Lucy with Duke and the tray of food. The doctor had come first thing in the morning and had been pleased with her progress, instructing that she not overexert herself but expressing his hope that she could begin to go about as normal within two days.

Whether it was weakness from the fever or something else, though, her spirits had been very low upon waking, and I hoped they would raise with a bit of food.

I sprinkled sand on the ink, then folded the letter and addressed it to Mrs. Westwood. I had yet to speak to Lucy about what had transpired between Duke and myself. Indeed, I hadn't any idea what to say or whether I *should* say something about it. And as for her fortune . . . well, that was another matter entirely. Part of me felt strongly that she deserved to know of it. But I understood her parents' hesitation to tell her, young and naïve as she was, and even if I had not, I could not violate Duke's trust by divulging the information.

I took the completed letter downstairs myself, handing it off to one of the servants. I slowed at the sound of carriage wheels outside. Most of my father's guests had left yesterday, but Captain Stokes and one of the other officers stood in the entry hall, their valises and portmanteaux collected on the floor around them.

Captain Stokes looked up, and his gaze fixed on me.

"Miss Donovan," he said, coming over. "I am happy to see you. I was worried I would not have the opportunity to say goodbye. You were not at dinner last night."

"No. I have been caring for Miss Ellis." And kissing her uncle.

"Yes, you and Mr. Russell have been quite occupied with her." The way he let his eyes rest on me made it clear what he thought of this observation.

"He is her uncle and guardian," I said, "and I am her friend." I hated how defensive I sounded.

"How kind of you to be so helpful to Mr. Russell. You certainly were to *me* all those years ago." There was a maddening glint in his eyes that made me itch to slap him. Somewhere inside, I recognized this spurt of malevolence for what it was: the last struggles of a man defeated. But his words still rankled.

I smiled, though my teeth clenched. "I wish you a safe journey, Captain."

I turned and left, trusting I would never have occasion to see him again. But he had planted a seed all those years ago that had since flourished, and despite my trying to hack away its branches, the roots still ran deep.

I had fallen asleep on a bed of clouds, but since waking, I had been fighting off creeping unease. Everything that had occurred with Duke yesterday had happened so suddenly. It had been too easy, too perfect, and my interaction with Captain Stokes was an unwanted reminder of the reality that not everything was as it seemed. I had been thoroughly convinced last night that Duke loved me, but I had been just as convinced of Lieutenant Stokes' regard for me when I was fifteen. Perhaps I was not so different from that young girl after all.

Or perhaps Captain Stokes was merely trying to ruin something perfectly good.

"Miss Donovan!"

I turned and found Mr. Pike walking swiftly toward me on the stairs. He was looking more haggard than I had yet seen him, and I felt a surge of sympathy for him. He looked like a man brought to the brink. It couldn't be easy to have his mother and the woman he loved in such states, with an impending departure bound to separate him from the latter, likely forever. Yorkshire and Kent were very far apart indeed.

"I have come to see Lucy," he said. "How is she?"

"Better," I said, hoping to reassure him quickly as we made our way toward her bedchamber. "She was able to eat a bit this morning, though it is her spirits that now keep her from recovering quickly, I suspect, and your arrival is bound to help with that."

He smiled, but it was somewhat strained. Once he came abreast of me, I turned to walk with him to Lucy's bedchamber. "How is your mother?"

"She is . . ." He sighed. "She is doing better, in fact."

"Well, that is welcome news," I said with a smile.

I received another weak one in return. "Yes, in some ways it is. The doctor has informed me, though, that this is often the case—a short reprieve from symptoms before they again worsen."

"Oh," I said.

He nodded with a sigh as we reached the door to Lucy's room. "It is a difficult reminder that she will need more robust care shortly."

The door opened, and Duke looked out at us from the doorway. His eyes settled on me, warming considerably as his mouth drew up into a smile that sent my heart into a frenzy. I sent a glance at Mr. Pike, whose brows were slightly furrowed, though whether due to the silent exchange between me and Duke or because he was preoccupied, I couldn't tell.

"We thought we heard voices," Duke said, finally letting his gaze move to Mr. Pike.

"Edwin?" Lucy's voice came from inside the bedchamber, and Duke moved aside, making way for Mr. Pike to pass through.

"You mustn't look at me like that," I said once Mr. Pike was out of earshot.

Duke reared back slightly. "Like what?"

"As though . . ."

"As though I had been waiting all morning to do this?" He slipped out of the room and closed the door behind him, then wrapped his arms about me.

My eyes widened. "Duke," I said in a scandalized voice, searching the corridor for any servants. But my heart was pounding, and it was all I could do to keep a smile from my lips as he kissed the place just below my ear.

I pulled away as one of the maids came into view at the top of the servant staircase at the end of the corridor. Duke let me escape, but the way he looked at me told me he wouldn't have bothered stopping if I hadn't forced him to.

"You truly mean to leave them alone in there?" I jerked my head in the direction of Lucy and Mr. Pike.

He lifted a shoulder. "Perhaps you have been more persuasive than you think. I thought you would be glad I am truly considering your evaluation of Mr. Pike's character."

"I am," I said. "I am merely surprised." And suddenly unsure of myself. What if Duke was trusting me and I was wrong about Mr. Pike?

We stayed in the corridor, standing next to one another with our backs resting on the wall. Out of sight, our hands touched, his pinkie overlapping mine against the wall. My heart raced as though we had been kissing again.

After a few minutes, I opened the door, feeling that Lucy and Mr. Pike had had more than enough time alone together. What was I becoming? Before I knew it, I would be spouting Mrs. Westwood's maxims about unmarried men and women spending time alone together.

Mr. Pike was seated on the edge of the bed, holding Lucy's hand. Lucy looked more energetic than when I had left her that morning, but there was bewilderment in her eyes as she looked at me.

I pinched my lips together. Mr. Pike must have told her about his mother's improved health. But once Mr. Pike left, Lucy's mood did not falter as I had expected it to. Indeed, she seemed so much improved that, when she assured us she was well enough not to require our attendance at her bed, I made no move to counter her. Indeed, I was feeling anxious to do something besides sit in the uncomfortable chair.

Duke and I left her with Anne and a tray of a few foods she had expressed interest in.

"And now," Duke said as we made our way down the corridor, "what must I do to persuade you to take a walk with me outside?" Our arms bumped against each other, and his fingers brushed mine, one hooking around my pinky for the briefest of moments before letting go. How had I ever thought to defeat Duke Russell when he was capable of making my heart and stomach flip in such a way?

"You must simply agree to hold the flowers I cut for Lucy's bedroom," I replied.

"A tall order," he complained. "Though, there are a few things you could bestow upon me as recompense, I wager." He sent me a teasing glance, dropping his gaze to my lips in a gesture dripping with implication.

"Are we transforming Lucy's bedchamber into a conservatory?" Duke asked as I placed another stem in his hands. They were already brimful of a rainbow of blooms.

"No," I replied, looking around in case any other flowers caught my eye. "Merely trying to support her improved mood."

He frowned as he looked at the bouquet. "If her humor is dependent upon cut plants, what happens when they inevitably wilt?"

I shot him an unamused look, then led the way out of the conservatory. He pulled on my hand before I could pass through the door, though, drawing me up against him and looking down into my face.

"I believe you have forgotten something, Miss Donovan."

I studiously avoided his gaze, looking around us at the flowers. "No, I think that is everything." When I looked back at him, he was smiling at me, and I couldn't have resisted him a moment more if I had wanted to. I pulled his mouth toward mine and kissed him the way I had been wanting to since our last opportunity.

When we broke apart, he blinked a few times in succession, his chest rising and falling as quickly as mine. "Perhaps we *should* stay a bit longer—another few blooms couldn't hurt. We owe it to Lucy's mood, I think." His eyes pled with me, half-sincere, half-humorous.

I hesitated, equally reluctant to leave. "I suppose we might cut a few flowers for the parlor while we are here."

His mouth stretched in a smile, and I turned back to the blossoms, considering which ones would look best with the pale yellow walls of the room.

The door to the conservatory opened suddenly, and the footman, Reeve, appeared.

"A letter for you, miss," said Reeve.

I opened the shears and set them to the base of a lily. "That will be Mrs. Westwood. You can give it to Mr. Russell."

"Very good, miss." He handed it to Duke and made his way out of the conservatory as soon as he had come.

"What does it say?" I snipped the lily stem at an angle.

"I am not skilled enough to open a letter with one hand, I'm afraid."

I laughed. "You may set down the bouquet. I will have to rearrange it once they are in the vase, in any case."

The crinkling of unfolding paper sounded, and I cut a few stems of white roses, placing them beside the lily. When the silence continued, I looked over at Duke.

His brow was knit tightly.

"What is it?" I asked, my stomach clenching with worry.

Duke looked up at me, and the way his gaze rested on me made the unsettled feeling grow. "You requested a copy of Nicholas's will?"

I froze. I had all but forgotten about the request.

My reaction seemed to be confirmation enough for him, though. Betrayal and disappointment filled his eyes. "When I told you that it was read in the greatest secrecy?"

I swallowed, not responding. My conscience writhed inside me as the silence continued.

"I confided in you, Diana," he finally said.

The disappointment in his voice tore at me. It was everything I had feared—I had done something to give him disgust for me, and it had worked. Lieutenant Stokes had been right all those years ago, and he was right now: I was too forward, too aggressive, too much of a shrew, even for Duke Russell.

"Perhaps you should not have," I said, hoping my words would keep the growing desire to cry at bay.

His forehead knit even more deeply. "Is there nothing you won't use as a weapon?"

I swallowed, torn between a desire to apologize and the need to defend myself.

He held my gaze, then looked down at the letter. "You applied to the Court of Canterbury."

I maintained my silence, unsure what to make of his remark.

"When did you make this request?" he pursued.

I shrugged, trying to remember. "A few days ago." These last days ran together with the lack of sleep and variation in activity.

"Before I told you of Lucy's fortune, then."

I nodded, wondering if that fact would give him more or less disgust of me.

"Why did you not request it from the diocese?"

I didn't respond immediately, caught off guard by his focus on such a detail. "Should I have?"

"The diocese handles the wills of lesser estates."

I stared at him, trying to comprehend what he was trying to convey.

"If you were unaware of Lucy's fortune," he continued, "everything you knew of her should lead you to believe that her father's will would have been handled by the diocese."

"I hadn't any idea of the distinction. Mr. Pike mentioned only the Court of Canterbury."

Duke's gaze grew more intent. "Mr. Pike?" There was suspicion in his eyes, and I hurried to allay it.

"He has a cousin who works in the office of a solicitor. When I stated my wish to know the contents of the will, he mentioned that the Court keeps them as matters of public record."

If I had expected Duke to relax at my explanation, I was disappointed.

"Do you know the name of the solicitor?"

I shook my head, trying to remember the conversation. I had been too focused on planning how to go about the request to pay any heed to such an inconsequential detail. I did, however, remember what Duke had said about the possibility of Mr. Pike knowing of the fortune. "You think his cousin told him of the fortune?"

His jaw tightened, and he handed me the letter. "I don't know. I need to go."

I took the letter, opening my mouth to say something—anything to keep him from leaving—but words escaped me.

"Take care of Lucy," he said. "Please." The difference between how he was looking at me now and a few minutes ago had my heart plunging into the pit of my stomach. There was no warmth there, only somberness.

"I will," I said weakly.

Jaw tight, he held my eyes a moment longer, then turned and left.

Chapter Twenty-Seven

Duke was gone by the time I returned to the house with the flowers, and I felt his absence everywhere. One moment, I had been wrapped up in a floral euphoria, and the next, I wasn't sure if or when I would see him again. To forgive me for the pocket watch incident was one thing; but now he must see my behavior as a pattern, and that was a different matter entirely.

With all the guests gone, the house was eerily silent. I was desperate not to be alone with my thoughts and worries, so I threw myself into household duties, thrusting meetings upon the cook, housekeeper, and gardener without warning.

I led the way out of the library with one of the young maids, having just instructed her on how I preferred the cleaning to be accomplished in that room, when Valentine approached. I had never been so happy to see my grumpy brother—anyone to occupy my time.

I excused the maid as Valentine slowed, his gaze following her for a moment as she curtsied and walked away.

"Have you nothing better to do than terrify the young maids?" he said.

"Better terrified with me than in danger with you," I quipped. "Besides, I was not terrifying her; I was telling her how to do her work."

"A distinction without a difference."

I pinched my lips together.

"By the by," he said, "where is Russell? I thought I saw his carriage being pulled around earlier."

I tried not to react, but Valentine was cursedly astute under those dark and lazy eyes. "He had some business or other to attend to," I said, aiming for nonchalance.

Valentine raised a brow, his lip curling up at the edge. "Finally drove him away, did you?"

I prided myself on being master of my emotions, but Valentine's words pierced my already weakened armor, hitting me squarely in my greatest apprehension.

His amused smile flickered, and his eyes searched my face. "Di . . ."

I shook my head hurriedly, forcing out a laugh. It came out as weak and unconvincing as any laugh ever did.

He put a hand on my arm, looking me in the eye. "If ever I saw a man in love with a woman, Russell is in love with you."

"Curse you," I said, brushing away a determined tear. I turned my gaze elsewhere, hoping to conceal my emotion. "I am not the sort of woman a man falls in love with—or stays in love with."

Valentine let out a pithy curse to show me what he thought of my assessment. "An uncommon woman requires an uncommon man. And if Russell does not see that, he is not the man I thought him." He held my gaze a moment longer, then, in a gesture as foreign to him as fainting would have been for me, he placed a kiss upon my cheek.

And then he left.

Mrs. Westwood's reply came later, a hastily composed note of gratitude and concern for Lucy, sprinkled with references to how occupied she was with making ready for the return of all the other girls from midsummer holiday. Despite that, she expressed that Lucy should feel at liberty to return whenever she was able.

When I went to read Lucy the letter, though, she showed a clear reluctance to return to the seminary. I couldn't blame her. Her visits with Mr. Pike and the freedom she had enjoyed at Blackwick would immediately come to an end upon her return to her cousin's.

Her reluctance took the form of an insistence that she was still not feeling well enough to make the journey, even the short one to the village. I let the excuse pass, content for Lucy to remain under my watch as Duke had pled with me to do. I wasn't entirely confident, either, that a journey *wouldn't* bring on the fever again.

My sincerest hope was that Duke would return, and that when he did, it would be with an assurance that he had been wrong in his assumptions about Mr. Pike. I couldn't bear to think of Lucy's despair if the alternative proved to be true. If the thought of delaying marriage with Mr. Pike was enough to make her fall ill, what would happen if she discovered he was insincere in his affections, nothing but a fortune hunter?

"What news have you from Mr. Pike?" I asked as we partook of a small nuncheon in her bedchamber. I was hesitant to bring up the difficult subject, but in all honesty, I had expected Lucy to do so, particularly after his earlier visit.

She glanced up at me as she picked up a small sandwich. "The same as usual. He is very much occupied with preparations for Harrogate."

I watched her carefully. Lucy was not generally adept at hiding her emotion, but she stated it in such a colorless tone.

"Have I understood correctly that he and his mother hope to leave in a sennight?"

Lucy nodded. "I believe so."

There was silence as she chewed her sandwich.

"And have you made any plans to see one another at some future date? Shall he return to Kent once his mother is settled and her health better in hand?"

"That is the hope, I think."

I frowned. "Lucy, you are being terribly opaque. I am certain this cannot be at all easy, and I feel badly that I have not been successful in achieving what we had hoped for."

Her lips pinched together, and the sandwich in her hand hovered before her. "Do you?"

I paused with my hand over the sandwiches, and my brows went up. "Do I what?"

She met my gaze. "*Do* you feel terrible about that?"

I blinked. "Whatever do you mean? Of course I do."

She looked away. "I rather thought you had changed your opinion to conform with that of my uncle."

I stared at her.

"Edwin believes you have a *tendre* for Uncle Duke."

To my consternation, my cheeks were immediately consumed with heat. "I certainly have developed a healthy dose of respect for him. And, in truth, I think you would, too, if you gave him a chance. But that does not mean I share his opinion, Lucy."

"He is determined to tear Edwin and me apart," she said.

"He is trying to protect you."

"Protect me from what?"

I pressed my lips together, wishing I could make her understand exactly what her uncle feared, just how deeply he felt responsible for her well-being and future. But I couldn't. It was not my place to tell her of her fortune, of the reality that there were men in the world who might wish to marry her for no better reason than to commandeer such an amount of money, for the moment she did marry, the money would no longer be hers.

I let out a frustrated sigh and reached for her hand. She retracted it, and I looked at her in surprise.

She avoided my gaze.

I pulled my hand back. "He merely wishes you to wait, Lucy," I said softly. "He is not saying *never;* he is merely asking you to prove the endurance of your affections for one another." I smiled ruefully. "Some of us survive unmarried past the age of twenty and still live to tell the tale, you know."

"I do not wish to become you."

My gaze snapped to her, my heart twinging. Never had I heard such unkind words from Lucy's mouth. "No, I suppose not."

I paused for a moment, then rose from the bed, brushing down my skirts. "I have a few matters to discuss with Tait. If you will excuse me." I managed a small smile at Lucy, who looked at me with eyes half-stricken, half-obdurate as I turned to leave.

I was not one to dwell on unpleasantness, but I found myself feeling more blue and hopeless than I could ever remember. Between Lucy's words, the confrontation with Duke, and his continuing absence, I was unsure what to do with myself.

When Mr. Pike arrived for his daily visit, I found myself in a dilemma. I wanted to ensure Lucy knew I was not her enemy, for nothing good could come of that, but I also felt the need to watch over her. Neither Mrs. Westwood nor Duke was here to take responsibility for her.

Sun Tzu's words came to me, as they so often did. *But when the army is restless and distrustful, trouble is sure to come.* I needed Lucy's trust if I was to ensure her well-being, so I allowed her time with Mr. Pike alone, well-aware that Mrs. Westwood would have chastised me soundly had she been aware of it.

I sighed. I seemed to be failing everyone.

But this time with Mr. Pike was my peace offering to Lucy, and I hoped dearly that she would see it for that and place her trust in me again. I hoped she would see me as her ally.

Mr. Pike only stayed a quarter of an hour, a fact which reassured me yet again of his character. It took a Herculean effort for me to humble myself enough to go to Lucy's bedchamber when it came time for dinner. She had wounded my pride in such a way that it still smarted to remember her words. *I do not wish to become you.* So much for Duke's assertion that she admired me.

After a fortifying breath and a reminder that my pride was the least important thing at the moment, I knocked on the door softly. "Lucy, it is Diana. Are you coming for dinner?" I pushed on the handle, but it resisted. She had locked the door.

"I do not wish to be bothered," came her muffled voice from within. "Please."

I sighed, hesitating as I tried to decide what to do. Mr. Pike's visit must not have gone as well as the prior one.

"You must eat, Lucy, or you shall never return to full health."

"I am not hungry. Please leave me be."

I let out a frustrated sigh. I would send something up for her and hope that she might change her mind about eating once there was food before her.

A similar encounter happened the next morning, with Lucy informing me from her locked bedchamber that she did not wish to see anyone all day. That was certainly not true. When Mr. Pike inevitably came, she would wish to see him.

I made my way to the conservatory to cut flowers for a new bouquet, hoping they would provide a bit of cheer to Lucy until Mr. Pike's visit. Whether the blooms would exercise the hoped effect was a matter of grave doubt, but what was not in doubt was the lowering effect the activity had upon me. I could not help but be reminded of the last time I had come to the conservatory.

Since Duke's sudden departure, I had dithered to and fro between an intention to apologize profusely to him in the hopes that he would have mercy upon my cursedly willful disposition, and a determination to protect myself from the likelihood of rejection when he returned.

But Duke Russell was a gentleman, and he would undoubtedly think his actions toward me bound him to offer for me. And that I could not abide. I could think of nothing worse than a man who did not wish to marry me feeling beholden to do so.

I gave the vase of cut flowers to Anne and asked her to see that Lucy received it. I would give her a few hours before making another attempt to see her.

It was late in the afternoon when I noted the vase sitting upon the table in the entry hall.

"Reeve," I said with a frown as I caught sight of the footman at the bottom of the staircase. "This was meant to be put in Miss Ellis's bedchamber. Have you any idea why it is here?"

"I believe, miss, that Anne made the attempt and was rebuffed by Miss Ellis. Would you like me to try again?"

I pinched my lips together. "Thank you, but no."

He bowed and continued on his way.

My patience, never a very robust trait of mine, was wearing thin. Lucy was being, to be frank, more stubborn and more petty than I would expect of someone so good-natured. After all, what had I done to merit such treatment from her? I had gone out of my way to help her and Mr. Pike.

I took the vase in hand and made my way upstairs, determined that she should know that I thought her childish behavior one of the reasons Duke was wary of trusting her choice in a husband.

I knocked soundly upon the door. "Lucy."

There was no response, so I knocked harder. "Lucy, I know you do not wish to see me, but this is becoming ridiculous."

Silence.

I pushed on the handle, but again was met with resistance. "You cannot hide in there forever, Lucy."

Silence.

I glanced down the corridor as Anne emerged from one of the bedchambers, an armful of linens in hand. She and some of the other maids had been busy cleaning the rooms that had been occupied by the naval officers.

"Anne," I called out.

She hurried over to me, her brows raised expectantly.

"What did Lucy say when you brought the bouquet earlier?"

"Nothing, miss," she said, wide-eyed. "She didn't answer my knock, so I thought she might be sleeping, and given her recent illness, I thought I would wait to take the flowers until she'd had a chance to rest."

I frowned as an uneasiness began to creep its way into my chest. So, she had *not* refused the bouquet. Reeve must have assumed that. "We need to open this door."

Anne's eyes widened even more, but she nodded hurriedly. "I'll go fetch the key from Mrs. Groves right away, miss."

I paced back and forth as I waited, each moment making me more anxious. Was Lucy sleeping soundly, or was she so angry, so stubborn that she refused to speak with anyone? Or—I swallowed—was she gone?

Finally, Anne returned, and I exchanged the vase in my hand

for the key in hers, setting it in the lock and turning it hurriedly. I pushed open the door, my eyes darting immediately to the bed.

My shoulders relaxed, and I breathed out a sigh of relief at the sight of Lucy's form, turned away from me and covered in blankets. She must have slept enough in the last week to last her an entire month.

"Lucy," I said, going over and setting my hand gently on her shoulder. My fingers gripped at nothing but blankets, though, and I stilled. Reaching for the edge of the covers, I ripped them back.

A pile of pillows sat where Lucy's body should have been. My stomach filled with dread as my gaze flicked to the escritoire against the windowed wall and the lone paper sitting upon it.

I rushed over, not bothering to be gentle as I unfolded it and devoured its contents.

Dear Diana,

I am a wretch. I know you shall never be able to forgive me for serving you such a trick, and for that, I shall be forever sorry. Nothing but the strength of my affection for Edwin could persuade me to use you so ill as I have, to say the things I said. I needed you to leave me be, and you are so kind and true a friend that it obliged me to do things I am not proud of.

But I am not like you, strong enough to stand alone, to face the world with no one beside me. I need Edwin as much as my lungs need air. I know I shall be happy with him and he with me, and I hope that someday, you shall be happy for us, as well.

If you should wish to see us once we have returned from Scotland, we will gladly welcome you into our home in Harrogate. If you can forgive me.

Your friend forever and always,
Lucy Ellis (Pike)

Chapter Twenty-Eight

I let out a string of curses, tossing the letter back onto the table and turning back to Anne, who was staring at me with eyes round as dinner plates.

"Anne," I said as calmly as my racing heart would allow, "I need to question the servants immediately until I know as precisely as I can when Miss Ellis left."

She gave a hurried nod, and I followed her from the room. Time was of the essence.

But behind my urgency and impatience bubbled uneasiness and a terribly sick feeling. I had failed in every way imaginable. I had failed Lucy. I had failed myself. I had failed Duke.

I could not let Lucy do this to her uncle, to any of us. I had given Duke my word to watch over her, and I had every intention of looking him squarely in the eye when he returned—if he returned—and being able to say I had done just that, even if that meant traveling to Gretna Green myself.

After piecing things together with a few of the servants, it became clear that Lucy and Mr. Pike could not have left more than an hour and a half ago, two hours at the most.

I hurried to my bedchamber to retrieve my reticule and

bonnet. There was no time for changing. Holding my skirts in one hand and my bonnet and gloves in the other, I rushed back toward the stairs.

"Where are you going?" Valentine's voice came from behind me, but I didn't stop.

"Out," I replied as I went down the steps.

"With whom?" His quick footsteps sounded behind me, drawing nearer.

"Four horses and a postilion."

"Di." He took me by the arm, forcing me to stop at the bottom of the staircase.

I pulled it away, but Valentine was far stronger than I. "Let me go, Valentine. I haven't a moment to waste."

He made no move to release me. "Then you had better talk quickly."

I glanced around us, on the watch for any servants. I had told them that Lucy had been delirious from fever and that I suspected she had walked in the direction of the village. It would serve her right if talk made its way around the area and followed her for some time. "Lucy and Mr. Pike eloped."

Valentine's grip slackened slightly, and he swore. "And what? You think you are going after them?"

"I know I am."

His grip tightened again. "Do not be a fool, Diana. It will be dark soon."

"All the more reason for you to release me so that I can make use of the little light left—and the small head start they have."

His eyes became more intent. "How much of a head start?"

"An hour and a half," I said.

His jaw tightened, his gaze pensive, and I used his distraction to wrench my arm free, hurrying toward the entry hall. Valentine swore again, his footsteps pattering after me on the marble floor. I picked up my pace as I slipped through the front door, slamming it behind me.

Lit by the glowing sunset, the chaise and postilion were waiting in the courtyard, and the latter helped me up into the equipage.

"Toward Scotland," I said. "As fast as you can manage. And do not, on any account, stop for my brother."

He gave a curt nod and shut the door. I expected to hear Valentine calling my name or ordering the carriage to stop, but fortune must have finally smiled upon me, for I heard nothing as wheels and hooves crunched on the gravel and the chaise pulled forward with a jerk. The tree-lined drive came into view through my window, and I prayed I would be seeing it soon again, with Lucy by my side. Then I could wring her neck in peace.

I let out a breath through rounded lips. It was time to set my mind to—

The chaise door opened, and Valentine slipped inside as though it was the easiest thing in the world to enter a moving equipage.

I let out a sound of disbelief as he simultaneously pulled the door closed and took a seat, hair disheveled and devoid of the hat he normally wore when traveling.

I pursed my lips in annoyance. "If only you possessed a shred of the regard for your own reputation that you seem to have for mine."

He slid down to a more comfortable position against the squabs, stretching a boot onto the seat next to me as though we were on a leisurely ride to town rather than attempting to catch eloping lovers. He wore the annoyed expression that was so common for him. "If only you expended a fraction of the thought you put into your insults toward the devilish inconvenience you are causing me."

"I didn't force you into this carriage, Val."

He let out a caustic laugh. "And what do you think would have happened when the Admiral discovered I let you go on a wild goose chase at night. *Alone?*"

I said nothing. I had no doubt my father would blame Valentine every bit as much as he would blame me. Valentine was an easy scapegoat, in many ways, for he never tried to defend himself against our father's accusations. He merely listened to them with a snarling lip and, once my father had expended his anger and lecturing, lost himself in rebellious dissipation.

We sat in silence as the chaise bumped and jolted us; traveling at a quick pace was anything but comfortable.

When we stopped for the first change of horses, Valentine insisted on stepping down to ask for any news of Lucy and Mr. Pike. I hated sitting useless in the carriage, but I couldn't deny that it made more sense—and less of a stir—for him to carry out the business.

I watched through the window, though, craning my neck for a better view of the bustling inn yard, but with the dimming light and the smallness of the pane, I was largely unrewarded for my troubles.

I jumped when the door opened suddenly.

I made an irritated noise to show Valentine what I thought of the unceremonious and unnecessarily abrupt gesture.

"What news?" I asked impatiently.

He wore a strange, half-smiling expression. "You will never guess who I stumbled upon."

My heart soared as he stepped aside, only to flip and plummet at the sight of Duke behind him.

Chapter Twenty-Nine

Duke was attired for travel, his shoulders enveloped in an olive green coat with three capes, his hat in hand as the light on the chaise shone on him. His eyes, looking more vividly green thanks to his coat, held mine, impassive and inscrutable. In all my urgency to go after Lucy, it hadn't occurred to me that Duke might be traveling the same roads as us but in the opposite direction.

Swallowing down the blooming of nerves spreading throughout me, I looked to Valentine.

"No," he said to the silent question in my eyes. "I thought I would leave the honor of informing him of our destination to you."

Duke's brow knit, a presage of the disappointment and anger he would feel with me when he discovered what had happened under my care of Lucy. My annoyance with Valentine fanned to life for a moment, but I smothered it. Perhaps this was for the best. Nothing could more surely cure him of whatever regard might still linger within him than yet another glaring mistake of mine.

"They eloped," I said before I could lose my nerve.

He stood stock still. "What?"

"Lucy and Mr. Pike," I replied flatly. There was no use trying to soften the blow or temper his frustration with me.

"Surely not," he replied.

His reluctance to believe what I was saying aggravated me. Did he think I was accustomed to making hasty evening journeys toward Scotland for no reason at all? "I would love to take the time to convince you of the facts, Mr. Russell, but I am rather occupied in chasing them down at the moment." I turned my focus to my brother. "What news?"

"They passed through an hour ago," he replied.

I leaned toward the door, peeking my head out enough to verify that the horses had been changed. "Let us be on our way, Leigh."

The driver nodded and swung up onto the horse.

I reached for the door handle and looked to Duke again. "Perhaps you can convey Valentine to Blackwick for me. If you care to verify the elopement, there is a letter in Lucy's room I think you will find rather persuasive."

I pulled on the door, but Valentine stopped it unceremoniously with a firm hand. Both of the men stared at me, and I pinched my lips together. They would have no trouble at all stopping my departure if they had a mind to do it.

"Get in, or get out of the way," I said through clenched teeth.

"After you," Duke said, putting out a hand to invite Valentine to precede him.

As Valentine stepped up into the chaise, Duke turned his head and called out a few commands to his own coachman before pulling himself up and into the chaise.

Valentine seated himself across from me, but before Duke could take the place beside him, he stretched himself out, resting a leg in the vacant space there. "If you wouldn't mind, Russell, I have a knee that could use a bit of stretching."

Duke looked at him for a moment but said nothing, then

took the seat beside me. The chaise was really only meant for two people, and I was obliged to scoot into the wall to accommodate his broad shoulders.

Looking at Valentine's thinly veiled amusement, I stared at him with disfavor and hit my fist against the ceiling, picturing him in its place, for I would have dearly loved to hit him.

The chaise lurched forward, and we were on our way.

"It makes no sense at all," Mr. Russell said as our bodies jostled one another. "Are you certain you did not misunderstand the note?"

I tried to scoot closer into the wall of the chaise, for Mr. Russell smelled of horses and wind and amber, but there was no escaping it—or him. "Unless you can think of another reason for Lucy and Mr. Pike to journey to Scotland together without informing anyone of the fact, then no."

"I cannot, but neither can I understand where they might have come upon the means to do so, nor how Mr. Pike would leave his mother for such a length of time, nor what Mr. Pike—"

My hand shot out as an idea occurred to me.

Duke went utterly silent, and Valentine cocked a brow. I glanced over at my hand and found that I had placed it upon Duke's leg. Cheeks flooding with heat, I wrenched my hand back.

"What is it?" he said, as though nothing had happened.

"The money you sent Lucy," I said, hoping the subject would distract him from my wildly inappropriate gesture. "The eleven pounds. She never spent it. They could be using that to fund at least some of this journey."

Duke swore under his breath. "No doubt you are right. But still, why elope? I do not understand it at all."

I scoffed. "Why elope? Because we drove them to it, of course! They felt they had no other option."

He shook his head. "You do not understand, Diana. I confirmed that Mr. Pike's cousin works in the office that handled my brother's will. It seems the clause in the will requiring secrecy over Lucy's fortune was the subject of lengthy discussion there—discussion that Pike's cousin admitted had carried beyond the office walls on one occasion. But if Pike knew the will, he would understand that marrying Lucy out of hand would put the fortune beyond their reach forever."

I turned my head, fixing my gaze on his face.

He met it and nodded. "The inheritance is contingent upon Lucy marrying with my blessing."

"I had no notion," I said, mystified.

"Not for lack of trying, certainly," he said.

The reference to my requesting the will was a swift reminder of where things stood between us, and I looked away, but the sting in my heart made me want to ensure that he understood his own role in this. "I warned you of the potential for this to happen, and you assured me that you had, as you put it, *struck the fear of God into Mr. Pike.*"

"Apparently Mr. Pike fears neither God nor poverty."

I shook my head, unwilling to believe such a thing. "A man in Mr. Pike's financial situation would not willingly forgo five thousand pounds."

"Five thousand pounds?" Valentine repeated.

I shot him a look and ignored his question, while Duke smiled down at me in a way that almost made me believe his regard for me could still be intact. "What happened to your obstinate assurances that Pike was motivated only by love?"

The carriage jolted over a large bump, sending me careening into Duke, who caught me deftly. I pushed myself up and back into my place. How was a woman supposed to keep her composure or pretend her heart was unaffected when fate insisted upon thrusting her—quite literally—into the arms of the man she loved?

I straightened my ruffled skirts and readjusted my bonnet. "Perhaps if you had seen fit to provide me with the necessary information about Lucy's fortune, I wouldn't have given such assurances."

"Well," he replied, "if Pike is under the impression that he will soon be coming into a large sum of money, I have every intention of being present to see the look on his face when he discovers that he has put that money forever out of his grasp."

"Yes," I replied caustically, "surely your satisfaction at Mr. Pike's dismay merits forcing your niece and ward to forgo a secret fortune of thousands of pounds."

Duke looked down at me, the edges of his lips turning down thoughtfully. "No, of course it does not. I do not imagine that is what my brother intended when he instructed the will be kept secret."

We were gaining on them and far more quickly than I had anticipated we would. Whatever money they were using to fund their elopement, it seemed sufficient that they took refreshment wherever they stopped—more often, even, than their horses required changing—an odd luxury for a couple on the run.

And yet, despite our progress, the journey felt interminable, surrounded as I was by inflexible carriage walls on one side and Duke's body on the other. Each jolt of the carriage forced me closer to him or him closer to me, as though I wasn't already conscious of every point of contact between our bodies or how nice it would be to relax my muscles and surrender to our proximity, leaning into him.

On our next change of horses, when I could hardly bear it a moment longer, I moved to get up before the carriage had even come to a full stop. But Duke took me by the hand, keeping me in place and sending my heart into a fever of activity.

"Perhaps you would be so good as to inquire after Lucy and Pike, Donovan," he said to Valentine.

My brother shot me a devilish smile and rubbed his knee. "Certainly. My knee needs a good stretch, after all."

"Or a good kick," I replied as he disappeared through the

door, leaving me alone with Duke. I should have expected as much from him—abandonment when I needed him most. He was the only weapon in my arsenal at this point. Being alone with Duke had never been a position of strength for me, and the quarters were closer than ever. I didn't trust myself for a second.

"You look like a rabbit caught in a trap," he said, releasing my hand.

I moved to the seat across from him, taking my first full breath since I had seen him at the last inn. "I set off on this journey alone; now I find myself surrounded by uninvited companions."

"I remember a time when you begged for ten minutes of my company."

My jaw dropped at his ability to say such a ridiculously teasing thing—and in such circumstances. "I never *begged*, and you know full well why I was anxious for those ten minutes."

His mouth turned up in a smile at my reaction. "I know what excuse you gave, certainly." A clatter in the inn yard somewhere made his gaze shift to the door, and he scooted toward the edge of his seat, his expression growing more serious. "Diana, I wanted to speak with you—"

"There is no need," I interrupted.

He watched me, searching my face. "For me, there is."

I pressed myself farther back into the squabs, desperate for some distance, to be somewhere where his eyes didn't draw me in, where his scent didn't invite me nearer, where his lips didn't tempt and call to me.

"I have been kicking myself for how I left things the other day," he said. "I was angry and panicked." His brow furrowed. "No, I was hurt—hurt to discover you used my confidences against me."

Hearing how I had disappointed and caused him pain twisted and wrung me inside. But he needed to understand me, to see me the way I *should* be seen—not some rosy, glossed over version of me. "I warned you from the beginning that I meant to win." The words tasted bitter and cold in my mouth, an utter misrepresentation of how I now felt.

"You did."

"And you said the same thing to me."

"I did." He searched my face again, though what he hoped to find, I couldn't tell. "But it wasn't long before I knew that it was your heart I truly wanted to win. And I began to hope that perhaps you had begun to wish for the same thing. Was I wrong?"

I couldn't move, could hardly breathe. He wasn't wrong. He was entirely and exactly right. At some point, my wish to defeat him had changed into a desperate wish to be loved by him—and my fear of losing him or trusting him without good reason.

But even once I had begun to surrender to my wish to love Duke and be loved by him, I had disappointed him. How could I trust his love to withstand the inevitable disappointments I would cause him in the future? For cause them, I would. I had no doubt about that. I was volatile of temper, headstrong, and sharp-tongued. How could anyone wish for such qualities in a wife?

I couldn't bear a future where Duke grew to regret his decision to marry me.

"I cannot give you what you want, Duke," I said, my voice sounding strangled even to my own ears.

The door opened, and Valentine climbed up. "If we hurry, I think we might catch them at the next—" He stopped in the doorway, looking between me and Duke. "Ah, are we to enjoy the rest of the journey in awkward silence? Fantastic." He ducked inside, and the postilion closed the door behind him.

Valentine turned to us again, waiting expectantly. "You will recall I require my own seat—for my knee." He touched a hand to it and, after a long delay, sucked in a breath and winced.

"For your sake," Duke said, rising from his seat, "I hope you are never obliged to make a living on the stage, Donovan." He sounded so composed, as though my words had had no effect upon him.

The realization simultaneously squeezed my heart and reassured me that, though my own heart might not recover, Duke was not the sort of man to be crushed by a loss. He was too cool and collected. He would recover easily enough, and he would see the sense in finding a proper wife.

I scooted over against the wall again as far as I could, wishing for the tenth time that I could have done the journey alone. With an obnoxious smile at us, Valentine slammed his fist against the roof of the carriage, sending us on our way again.

Duke and I had been sitting beside one another the entire journey, and the proximity had been difficult from the start, but now . . . now that I had given him to believe he and I could never be, it was torture of the worst kind. Every touch was a reminder of what I would not have but wanted more than anything.

When we reached The White Hart at West Kingsdown, full dark had long since fallen, but the lamps in the yard showed us just what we were looking for: a carriage matching the description of the one Lucy and Mr. Pike had taken.

As our own chaise came to a stop, both Duke and I made for the door. Valentine merely smiled as he watched the awkward moment as we decided who should go first. That seemed to be all my brother had done the entire journey—smile knowingly at us in a way that made me want to slap him. I would have my revenge on him someday.

Duke not only exited the chaise first, but he left behind his intoxicating amber scent before turning to provide me his hand. It was childish not to take it, but after nearly two hours of nearly sitting in his lap and wishing I had not been born with the temper of a shrew, I was desperate to distance myself from him.

I hopped down from the carriage and rushed over to the one standing stationary in the yard. I was not entirely certain that it was Lucy and Mr. Pike's, but at this point, I cared little for the spectacle I would create by opening the door of a stranger's equipage.

I yanked the door open and squinted to see inside the dark space, stilling once my eyes adjusted enough. Lucy and Mrs. Pike were within. Both women stared back at me, Lucy with wide, frantic eyes, Mrs. Pike with tired, drooping ones.

"Diana!" Lucy cried out in consternation. Somehow, her eyes widened even more as she looked behind me. "Uncle Duke!"

Chapter Thirty

It took me a moment to understand what I was seeing. I had certainly not expected to find Mrs. Pike part of the elopement party.

"Could I have a word with you, Lucy?" I asked in the most composed voice I could manage.

Her surprise gave way to wariness. "Whatever you have to say to me, you can say here."

"You may come out of your own accord," said Duke calmly, "or I will carry you out myself. It is your choice, Lucy."

"You are a tyrant!" she said, her hands balled into fists in her lap. "A despot determined to make everyone as miserable as you, and I hate you!"

I glanced at Duke and saw in his expression a flash of pain.

"He is a guardian trying to save his niece from a fortune hunter," I replied, trying to keep my rising temper under restraint at Lucy's complete lack of gratitude.

"Edwin is not a fortune hunter," she retorted. "Just because he needs the money does not mean he is marrying me for it."

I was momentarily bereft of speech, left with nothing to do but look to Duke.

His brow was knit, and after a quick glance at me, he directed his gaze at Lucy. "You know of the fortune?"

"I told her of it."

The voice came from behind us, and Duke and I turned to see Mr. Pike standing a few feet away, a plate with bread and cheese in hand. "She deserved to know."

Lucy rose from her seat within the carriage and came to the door, her eyes lighting up at the sight of Mr. Pike. He brushed past us and put out his free hand to receive hers, pressing it and looking up at her with a warm, reassuring expression.

"That was for her father, not you, to decide," Duke said flatly.

Mr. Pike gave a curt nod. "And I tried to honor those wishes. But at some point, I realized that my love for Lucy required me to stop keeping something so important from her—particularly when it had the potential to make her doubt my love for her." He looked over at her. "And I loved her before I ever knew of the fortune."

"And apparently enough to put it forever beyond your grasp," Duke said drily.

Both Mr. Pike and Lucy looked over at him, frowning in confusion. "What do you mean?" Lucy asked.

"As Mr. Pike undoubtedly knows from his familiarity with your father's will," Duke continued pointedly, "you stand to inherit a mere fraction of the five thousand pounds if you marry without my approval—even if that marriage takes place in Gretna Green."

The slack-jawed expressions that met this comment were enough to make it clear that neither of them had known of this particular stipulation.

Lucy looked to Mr. Pike, and he shook his head, bemused. "I had no notion . . . ."

"I am surprised to hear you admit as much," Duke said. "If you *had* known of the provision, your flight to Gretna Green would appear noble—irrational, perhaps, but noble, all the same, for it would have been inarguably motivated by love. But now it is clear that you believed you were on the cusp of inheriting—"

"Gretna Green was *my* idea," Lucy said, stepping down next to Mr. Pike. "Edwin resisted and resisted, but in the end, we became desperate. His mother needs treatment now, not in two years"—she shot a chastising glance at her uncle—"and it was becoming clearer by the day that Diana no longer intended to help us because she had fallen in love with you."

My cheeks burned, but I kept my eyes away from Duke, knowing he would see the truth in my face if I allowed him the chance. I had been silent, unsure what to say, what to make of Lucy's fervent loyalty to Mr. Pike under circumstances when any woman would have been forgiven for doubting his intentions. How could she possibly trust him so easily when he was in such dire need of the money she could offer?

All eyes were on me, but I didn't have the opportunity to respond to the accusation.

"I wish you would inform *her* of that fact," Duke said, holding my gaze with wryness and a hint of amusement.

"Informing Diana of something is the very worst way to go about things." I didn't need to turn to recognize my brother's voice.

"For heaven's sake! Isn't there a pint or a dram inside to tempt you, Valentine?"

Duke's mouth quirked up in a smile, and I turned to find my brother with just such a pint in hand. He held it up as if to toast my suggestion.

"If you want Diana to marry you, Russell," he said, "all you must do is prohibit her from doing so under any circumstances."

"Back to the matter at hand," I said through gritted teeth, flashing Valentine an expression that I hoped would send him back into the inn. He shot me a smile but turned back toward the entrance to The White Hart.

I faced Lucy and Mr. Pike. "Now that we have established the unwisdom of an elopement, I think it behooves us to find your mother a place to rest for the night, Mr. Pike. She is not looking well."

"What possessed you to bring her along?" Duke said.

"She insisted she was well enough," Mr. Pike answered, though his face looked to be reddening in the dark. "The journey *has* been more taxing on her than I had anticipated, though. We have been obliged to stop a great deal." He stepped up into the carriage and sat across from her, offering her the food. They exchanged a few unintelligible sentences in the darkness while Lucy stood on the step nearby.

Duke came up beside me, and I braced myself for a reference to Lucy's comment about my having fallen in love with him.

"What would you do?" His voice was soft, his eyes trained on Lucy.

I looked up at him, and he met my gaze, his eyes filled with questions and uncertainty.

I tried to leave my own problems aside, sucking in a breath and watching Lucy reach into the carriage for Mrs. Pike's hand.

"At some point, Lucy must be allowed to make her own decisions, even if they *are* mistakes." I returned my focus to Duke. "You have done your best to guide her, to encourage her to be wise, to honor your brother's wishes. And if she chooses to marry him now, she does so with a full knowledge of what she is choosing."

His lips turned down at the sides. "Do you still believe Pike's affections to be sincere?"

I bit the inside of my lip and looked away. "I do not think myself the best judge of such things."

"I trust your opinion, Diana. I need it. The weight of this

decision is too much to make myself. Please give me your true thoughts."

I swallowed, moved by his vulnerability and confidence in me.

Mr. Pike stepped down from the carriage, and he and Lucy faced one another. As they conferred, he reached for her hand, and my own heart ached at the subtle but tender display of affection. I could so easily remember when Duke had reached for my fingers in just such a way.

I took in a breath and looked at him. "I have learned nothing of his character that has given me reason to think he will make anything but a good husband to Lucy."

He nodded slowly. "And his debts?"

I lifted a shoulder. "If you are concerned about them, might you not write something into the marriage contract that determines the amount of Lucy's fortune he has control over until he has proven himself?"

"I had that same thought once," he said, "but I worried about sending Lucy into a marriage with such doubts hanging over my head. But I think you are right. It seems the best way forward." He looked at me, those light green eyes piercing me. "Thank you. For everything."

I hated those words, as much for the fact that I had done nothing that merited his thanks as for the farewell they sounded like.

He turned away and stepped toward Lucy and Mr. Pike. "Will it suit your mother better to remain here for the night, Pike? Or would she prefer to return home? Either way, there is no need to continue the elopement." His chest rose with a slow breath. "I will give my approval for you to marry. *But*"—he looked at Mr. Pike—"until you can prove more financial wisdom than you have displayed in the past, Pike, the amount of money you shall have access to will be limited."

Both Lucy's and Mr. Pike's eyes widened, and they stared at

Duke for a moment before turning their faces toward one another. There was a moment of hesitation, then an embrace, fervent and overjoyed. That they should rejoice so fully despite knowing the stipulations their union would occur under was a testament to the genuineness of their affection for and devotion to one another. I looked to Duke to see what he thought of it.

He was smiling softly. But as his eyes darted to me, there was a hint of sadness there.

M y heart and mind were too muddled a mess to even consider the prospect of another carriage ride like the one I had endured on the journey to West Kingsdown. Grasping for any excuse to prevent such a thing, I suggested that Lucy should ride with Valentine and me on the journey back to Blackwick—for propriety's sake.

It certainly occurred to me that no one would think it more appropriate to send a young, unmarried woman in a closed carriage with my rake of a brother rather than with Mr. Pike, and I was fairly sure it also occurred to Duke and Valentine, but neither of them said anything. Duke's eyes lingered on me after I made the suggestion, though, as though he knew the reason behind it.

The chaise had seemed entirely too small to carry three people on the way to West Kingsdown. But now, with three of us on the way home, the same space somehow felt empty.

"You're a fool, Di," Valentine said as the carriage rumbled out of the inn yard and onto the dark roads. Leaning his back against the carriage wall, he closed his eyes and was soon asleep.

Just as his head lolled back and forth with the motions of the chaise, so his words bounced around in my mind, jostling my emotions and preventing them from settling any place I could be satisfied with.

"You have a wedding to plan," I said to Lucy, hoping to direct my thoughts elsewhere.

"Yes," she replied, the smile in her voice apparent even in the dark of the chaise. "Though, I shall be content even if it is only Edwin, Mrs. Pike, and me." There was a brief pause. "And I would be honored, of course, if you were to come, though I quite understand if you feel unable to do so after . . ."

I took her hand in mine. "I wouldn't miss it."

She smiled back at me and returned the pressure of my hand. "I am so sorry for everything, Diana. For doubting you and being unkind. I do not deserve you as a friend."

"Nonsense," I said. "You deserve much better."

She shook her head. "What I said was untrue and terribly hurtful. You have done nothing but help me, and, out of my fear of losing Edwin, I let myself say and do terrible things. I have always wished I was more like you. You are the most amazing woman I know."

I swallowed, more moved by her words than I cared to show, so I settled for squeezing her hand again. Silence reigned for a time against the backdrop of the rattling and rumbling of the chaise, and my mind immediately returned to its agonizing thoughts.

"Lucy?" I said quietly.

"Hmm?" she replied with a sleepy edge to her voice.

I hesitated a moment, feeling a lump rise in my throat. "How did you agree to marry Mr. Pike when it was possible he was marrying you for your fortune? When it was possible it could crumble the moment the money became his? Such trust . . ." I shook my head.

She took time before responding. "I *do* trust Edwin. And that is what trust is, isn't it? A choice to put your faith in someone, knowing there is a possibility, however small it might seem, that you could be wrong, that they might hurt you. But I know Edwin enough to believe that he would never hurt me on purpose."

I nodded, and she looked at me thoughtfully. "Do you love Uncle Duke, Diana?"

I pulled my lips in, taking my time before responding to such a weighty question. "I do. But I am finding it hard to trust him —or perhaps to trust myself."

She smiled sympathetically. "I have not trusted him as I should have, either. And I can see how wrong it has been of me to assume the worst of him."

"He does love you, Lucy," I said. "More than you know."

She sighed. "I believe you, and I hope I can mend things with him with time. Any man who loves *you* cannot possibly be anything but the best of men. And it is clear that he does love you, Diana. But trust is like a key, and without it, all the best parts of love remain locked away." She gave a large yawn. "And you deserve the best parts of everything."

Her head soon tipped onto my shoulder. While she slept, my eyes stayed alert, my mind wide awake.

Chapter Thirty-One

B y the time we reached Blackwick, I estimated the time to
be somewhere nigh on one o'clock in the morning.
Valentine and Lucy had slept the entire way home,
including through the changes of the horses, whereas I had been
unable to sleep a wink, despite how tired I was.

I stayed seated for a moment, looking between Lucy and
Valentine. I had been cross with Valentine for his meddling, but
I felt a surge of appreciation for him. I gently roused them from
their slumber, and both of them stretched their limbs before
descending.

Once I had stepped onto the gravel drive, I looked down the
lane behind us for the carriage Mr. Pike, his mother, and Duke
were in. There was no sign of it, though, just a dark abyss. Duke
was evidently not returning to Blackwick. My heart gave a little
twist as I turned back toward the house to find my brother
watching me.

"It looks as though you've won your war," he said. "Sweet
victory." The last words were delivered in an unmistakably
ironic tone. His eyes bored into me until he turned away toward
the house. He glanced over his shoulder when he reached the

door. "Or perhaps this whole time you were fighting against the person you should have been fighting *for*."

He didn't wait for a response before opening the door and stepping inside. I stared at the closed door for a moment, then turned to Lucy.

"Let us get you in bed, shall we?" My words sounded overly energetic and bright, but Lucy didn't seem to notice. I helped her to her bedchamber, ensuring she had someone to help her undress for the night, then I went to my own room, with nothing but Valentine's words to lull me into a restless sleep.

T nearly ordered my breakfast to be brought to my room, for I was under no illusion that last night's escapade would have slipped past my father's notice. And while I was hardly eager for the inevitable exchange, I owed it to Valentine to ensure the finger of blame was not pointed at him.

My father looked up at my entrance into the breakfast room, astonishment in his expression. "Diana."

Perhaps he was dismayed by my tired appearance. I couldn't blame him for that. I did not look particularly well.

"What are you doing here?" he asked.

I stood still, facing him, my brows drawn together. Perhaps his age was beginning to affect his mind. "I live here, Father."

A flash of irritation crossed his face. "I am well aware of that fact. But you left last night."

I didn't respond immediately, for I was uncertain what to make of the conversation so far.

His mouth turned down in a frown. "I had thought you might be eloping with Mr. Russell."

I was well and truly speechless for a moment, too many questions forming in my mind for me to verbalize any single one of them. My father, however, didn't even bother waiting for a response, merely frowning deeply as he turned back to cutting his mutton.

"But I left with Valentine," I said, finally managing to point out only one of a hundred problems with his madcap assumption. His jaw hardened at the mention of my brother, and I hurried to explain. "Lucy and Mr. Pike took it into their minds to elope, and I felt it behooved me to go after them. Valentine worried for my safety, so he insisted on accompanying me."

My father gave a little *hmph*.

I had not expected such a mild reaction to an expedition hardly meant for a lady, but I was not ready to let him go back to his breakfast, either. "Why in the world would you assume I, of all people, had eloped, of all things, with Mr. Russell, of all people?"

He stabbed a piece of mutton with his fork. "Perhaps elope is the wrong word. When you were found to be gone, I rather thought he might have abducted you. I assumed Valentine had spent the night carousing in the village, as is his custom."

I let out a loud, incredulous laugh. Surely, this was the most bizarre conversation in all of history. "And, believing that your only daughter had been abducted by a man intent on taking her to Gretna Green, you chose to enjoy a full night's rest, then sit down to a leisurely breakfast this morning?"

He set down his utensils and turned his focus on me, visibly exacerbated. "When Russell asked my permission to pay his addresses to you, I told him he was wasting his time, that the only way you were likely to be found at the altar was if you were forced there—and heaven help the man brave and foolish enough to try such a thing. He told me he would keep my suggestion—and warning—in mind."

"He asked your permission to pay his addresses to me," I repeated dazedly. "When?"

He waved a dismissive hand, as though my question was a mere annoyance. "A few days ago."

There was silence as we stared at one another. "Why did you not tell me?"

He frowned. "You made it clear to me you had no liking for him, and I thought better of creating more awkwardness amongst the guests by informing you of something you would find distasteful. Now, if you will excuse me, I mean to eat my increasingly cold breakfast in peace."

I nodded vaguely, all thought of eating my own breakfast long gone, and walked dazedly out of the room. Mr. Russell had asked permission to pay his addresses to me.

I had been doing everything in my power to drive him away, to give him a distaste for me, and somehow, he had still wanted me.

And I . . .

I swallowed. I wanted him too.

I wanted to unlock every door that stood between us, keeping us from one another. And just as Lucy had said, I alone had the key to do so. I had been using it to bolt every door I came in contact with, but I was done being so confined, so alone, so obsessed with protection. Protecting myself had come to feel more like a cage than anything.

Duke was gone, but there must be something I could do to convince him that I was ready to surrender my key to him. Forever.

Chapter Thirty-Two

The next evening, Valentine heaved a large sigh and stepped down from the carriage. As though our chase toward Scotland had not been enough, we had just spent the greater part of another day in the chaise together. "You may end the night with Russell, Di, but that will hardly do you any good if Father murders you afterward."

"Hush," I said, handing off my burden to him as I stepped out of the carriage in front of the public assembly in north Kent. "He shall never know." It was a strange thing to carry a book to a night of dancing, and if things went awry, it would be terribly awkward to heft around all night, but it had felt important to bring along with me.

Besides, I had no patience for Valentine's cynicism at the moment. I seemed to be made up entirely of nerves, crushing doubts, and impossible hopes, and Valentine couldn't help but tip the balance the opposite way I was hoping for.

I wasn't even entirely certain Duke would be here. It was possible I had misremembered what he had said about the assembly, in which case, today's long journey would be for naught. But here I was.

I smoothed the white crepe of my overdress. How could I be concerned over something as inconsequential as my appearance when my heart and future were in the balance?

"Look on the bright side," Valentine said, watching my nervous gesture. "If things go badly, you have this to throw in his face." He held up the heavy book.

I gave an impatient groan, turning away from him. That's when he surprised me by taking my hand, moving in front of me until my only choice was to look him in the eye.

"Only a fool would refuse you, Di," he said, handing me the book. "And Russell is no fool."

I rubbed my lips together, nodding nervously. Of all my brothers, Valentine was perhaps the least obvious choice as a companion tonight, but he was the one I trusted to keep me sensible if the worst scenario became a reality.

He squeezed my hand and jerked his head toward the door.

I sucked in a deep breath and led the way up the steps. Warmth and music rushed around us as we stepped inside, and my eyes searched the throngs of people for any sign of Duke. I was only here for him.

I caught sight of him, standing in conversation with a gentleman, and my heart immediately set to pounding. He was the most strikingly handsome man in the room—not that I had bothered to verify such a thing—and I was suddenly seized with the madness of what I was doing. Any woman here would be fortunate to call Marmaduke Russell her husband. I made a quick surveyal of the room: the young women dancing, those in laughing conversation with their friends, those glued to the sides of their chaperones. Surely, I was the least fit for the role.

I straightened myself, pulling breath into my unwilling lungs. I was the daughter of Admiral George Donovan. I had been taught to fight for what I wanted, and I wanted Duke Russell more than any woman in this room wanted him. It was whether he still wanted me that I was set to find out, and the prospect couldn't but make me quake in my slippers.

But I would not turn back now, I wouldn't shrink at the prospect of possible—even likely—defeat. Love might be a battle, but vulnerability rather than brute strength was the only way to victory.

The last notes of the country dance faded, and the couples in the set bowed and curtsied to one another. My eyes, however, shifted between the Master of Ceremonies, who stood at the head of the dance floor, and Duke, who was still engaged in conversation. The former waited for the buzz of chatter to lessen slightly before announcing the next set.

I turned to my brother. "I know it is against your nature to stand stationary at a place like this rather than attempting to lose a fortune at cards, but please try to resist for the next twenty minutes."

"Hard to lose a fortune when you haven't one to lose," he replied in annoyance. "But lest you be concerned, I will stay over there by the window. After I find something to drink, that is."

I gave a nod and turned my focus back to the Master of Ceremonies, my first obstacle.

But Mr. Arnold was a jolly fellow, and when I managed to speak with him, he was more than happy to comply with my request, be it ever so strange. For I had no chaperone with me—other than Valentine, of course, who might be considered the *opposite* of a guarding influence.

"Mr. Russell has not yet danced this evening," said Mr. Arnold, "and it would give me great pleasure to change that, Miss Donovan."

I thanked him, trying not to think of the very real chance that Duke might refuse.

His gaze dropped to the book in my hands. "Is there someone you could leave that with?"

"Thank you, but no."

He gave me a strange look but seemed to decide against saying more. He turned and led the way, blissfully unaware of how my heart struck against my chest like a whip to a horse's flanks with each step we took.

He stopped suddenly, and I nearly ran into him.

"He was just here." He searched around the room until his eyes alighted on something. "Ah, there he is. He looks to be making his way toward the door. Escaping early, it would appear." He turned to me with a grimace. "I am so sorry, Miss Donovan."

"I think we might still catch him," I said, though the possibility that Duke might have seen me and decided to leave as a result certainly crossed my mind, sapping some of my courage.

Mr. Arnold's eyebrows went up. "I . . . he is not . . ." He met my pleading look, then pinched his lips together. "Oh, very well. Let us hurry, then."

The crowds parted willingly once people took note of who was begging their pardon, and while I was aware that many eyes lingered on me, my own were trained on Duke, who was almost to the door.

By the time we reached him, he had already passed through it.

"Mr. Russell," Mr. Arnold said. "Leaving so soon?" His voice was a mixture of forced levity and obvious nerves. He was afraid of Duke, of being given a set-down by him. The realization made me smile, even amidst my own nerves.

Duke didn't turn immediately, as though he was gathering his patience before responding. With a breath that made his shoulders rise, Duke slowly turned toward Mr. Arnold, who swallowed and pressed on.

"I hoped you might find the time to join the next set—and permit me to introduce you to a very eligible partner."

Duke's eyes flicked over to me, and he stilled.

"Allow me to present you, Miss Donovan, to Mr. Russell."

I held Duke's gaze, desperate for a sign of how he regarded my sudden appearance, then dipped into a curtsy—an awkward affair, given the book I was holding.

"Splendid," said Mr. Arnold, unaware of the fraught situation he was in. "Now, if you will excuse me, I have duties to attend to."

The door creaked closed, shutting out the din of conversation and music, and silence overcame us. We were surrounded by nothing but darkness and a few horses pawing at the ground while carriages waited for those dancing inside the hall.

"Shall we dance, then?" Duke asked, gesturing to the door.

"I don't want to dance," I said. Not that I could have done so with the book I was holding even if I had wanted to.

"I am relieved," he said with a little half-smile. "The last time we danced, the damage to my feet was significant enough, I thought I might need Dr. Chisholm to amputate."

I couldn't help releasing a laugh, and with it went some of my anxieties. "I could see no evidence that my efforts to crush your feet were having any effect upon you at all."

"My entire existence since our first meeting has been trying to persuade you I am unaffected by you."

My breath caught in my chest, and I swallowed. "Why?"

"Because no sooner do you feel pressure to do something, Diana, than you fight against it with everything inside you."

My grip tightened on the book in my hands, the words I had used as a guide almost my entire life.

"Perhaps you were too persuasive," I said.

"Perhaps," he said. "Or perhaps my hopes were ill-conceived from the start. Perhaps it was folly to think I could ever force my way into your heart."

I shook my head, my heart beating fit to burst, for I recognized the moment I had been both fearing and anticipating. "I have not been fighting to keep you out of my heart, Duke. I have been fighting the fact that you were already there. I was fighting myself." I inhaled another shaky breath. "But I don't want to fight anymore." I held out the book toward him.

His eyes were fixed on mine, but he reluctantly pulled them away to look at what I was holding. He took it from me, squinting to read the title in the darkness. He looked up at me, and I could see in his eyes that he understood the significance of the gesture.

"I cannot take this," he said, extending the book toward me. I did not take it back. "Who is Diana Donovan without her beloved war strategy?" His gaze grew more intent. "I love the fight in you, Diana. It was what drew me to you in the first place. But one cannot fight forever. The purpose of war is to preserve the things we cherish, to protect the people we love. I will fight alongside you as much as you please; I will even fight *with* you. But I want to be the person who is there when the fight is over. I want to be the one you are fighting *for*."

My throat thickened. "Why would you wish for such a thing?" I glanced at the door to the assembly. "Inside that door, there are fifty eligible young women more suitable for becoming your wife—docile, entreatable, kind."

He let the hand holding the book drop down to his side and stepped toward me, looking down into my face. "I do not wish for a wife who needs to be taken care of, Diana. I want a wife who can take care of herself but who *chooses* to be with me because she loves me." He put a gentle thumb to my cheek. "Do you love me, Diana?"

I held him by the wrist and met his gaze, pressing his hand to my cheek more surely. "Heaven help me, I do."

For all the darkness around us, his eyes lit up at the words, an energy coursing through him and into me. "Heaven *must* be the one to help you, then, for I promise you I shan't." Searching my eyes with his, he dropped his lips to mine, and with a little shudder of bliss, I leaned my body into his.

He wrapped his other arm about my back, and the book he held knocked into me. He let out a sound of annoyance, breaking us apart and holding it up. "This blasted book has given me nothing but trouble from the beginning."

I laughed, my body feeling free and light as never before. "Valentine tried to persuade me to leave it home."

"Your brother is a wise man."

I raised my brows. "He also suggested I could throw it at you if you rejected me."

"Your brother is a fool." He let go of me and moved to set the book on the nearby stone baluster.

"Gently," I said, clenching my teeth. "My father will have my head on a platter if it is ruined."

Duke turned toward me, amused exasperation on his face. "And here I thought you were giving it to me—surrendering it."

I pulled my lips between my teeth guiltily. "It was meant as a gesture."

He chuckled and came over to me, wrapping me in his arms and pulling me forcefully against him so that I had to lean my head back to look up at him.

"You, Diana Donovan, are the most delightful and maddening woman I have ever had the pleasure of knowing, and I mean to marry you as soon as can be managed."

I raised my brows, even as his words sent a thrill through me. "Even if you must abduct me and take me to Gretna Green?"

"Nothing shall deter me." He dropped one of his hands from my back and threaded his fingers through mine, sending shivers throughout my body.

"It is not the general practice for a man to ask a woman's father for permission before abducting and marrying her."

He frowned exaggeratedly. "No? I am certain there is something in here about that." He stretched an arm out, reaching for the book, and I swatted his hand down.

"For heaven's sake, Marmaduke. Enough about the book." Wrapping my arms about his neck, I pulled his lips down to mine, savoring every second of a shared victory.

Epilogue

OAKWORTH PARISH CHURCH, KENT, ENGLAND

Of all the things I had never thought to experience in my life, my own wedding in the fullness of a Kentish summer was chief among them.

The weather was such that both my family and Duke's had congregated outside, reluctant to leave the warm sunshine and the gentle morning breeze for the confines of the dim church. The vicar had been obliged to step into the village, providing the perfect excuse for us to linger outside a little longer.

My eyes strayed to Duke. My heart thumped more strongly at the sight of the man I would be married to within the next hour. He was truly everything I had never known I needed, and the sight of him smiling so fully on the morning of our wedding did strange things to my heart. He stood beside his brother, Roger, come from London just last night.

Nicholas was present in the form of the broken watch that dangled from Duke's pocket. Just within the pocket sat a letter from Lucy, congratulating us and expressing anticipation at our impending visit to Harrogate on the way to Northumberland.

"Well, my dear," Mrs. Westwood said, her chin lifting high in pride, "the day has come. The pinnacle of your existence."

Normally, I would have rolled my eyes at such words, but today, they felt surprisingly apt. Joining my life with Duke's *did* feel like the pinnacle of my existence thus far. My only disagreement with Mrs. Westwood lay in the fact that I believed there was even better to come.

"Have you heard from Lucy?" I asked, preferring not to express my opinion on the subject at the moment.

"Just yesterday, in fact," she said. "She reports that her mother-in-law is responding well to Dr. Chandler's treatments. She cannot be cured, of course, but she is much more comfortable, and that is what the hope was. Lucy seems to be quite content. Marriage suits her, I think."

"Yes, I think so too." I would see for myself soon enough, though. Tomorrow, Duke and I would set off on a small wedding tour, stopping in Harrogate, where Duke had promised to help Mr. Pike gain a better understanding of proper financial management. After that, we would take a few days in Cumbria before fetching Rebecca from Northumberland. Rebecca, Duke's sister, would come to live with us.

Mrs. Westwood gave me a smile and pressed my hand. "I think I shall go in and prepare for the service now."

"Of course," I said. Once she had left me, it didn't take long for my gaze to stray back to Duke. How was it possible to be on the verge of marrying a man and to still be impatient to be near him?

Valentine came up beside me, looking dapper in a dark tailcoat and blue waistcoat. "Well, no one could mistake *this* as a marriage of convenience."

"What do you mean?"

He cocked a brow. "The way you look at Russell has 'lovesick match' written all over it. Besides, there is nothing convenient about it for me. It means you are leaving Blackwick."

I slipped my arm through Valentine's, pulling him closer to me. "It does seem cruel to leave you with Father. Of course, Phineas is still there, but I am afraid he is little help to you."

"None at all," Valentine agreed.

"Perhaps it will be a good thing, though. You and Father shan't be able to avoid one another, and you can settle your differences."

He turned his head to look at me. "Only a woman about to be married could express such a nonsensical hope."

I shrugged. "You could always marry."

He let out a laugh and patted my arm. "I cannot decide whether your absurdity is inspiring or pitiful."

Phineas approached, his silver waistcoat matching the metal frame of his glasses. "A happy day, isn't it?"

"It is," I agreed. "And Duke and I owe a great deal to you, you know, for you acted as an informal chaperone to our meetings in the library."

He smiled in his subdued way. "I am very aware of that. I do not generally prefer to do my reading to a backdrop of flirting, but for the potential I saw between you and Russell, I was willing to make a sacrifice."

Eyebrows raised high, I glanced at Valentine, who looked just as surprised as I.

"You mean you heard . . . everything?" I asked, half-dismayed, half-amused.

He chuckled. "I heard . . . enough. Thankfully, my ability to focus is strong, and I was able to willingly ignore a great deal at will."

"Oh, for heaven's sake," I said, "we were not so bad as *that!*"

Phineas and Valentine shared a glance, and I hit them, one after the other, as they both laughed.

The gate to the churchyard creaked, and we all looked over to the vicar, hurrying through it, dressed for the ceremony and pleading for our forbearance with his tardiness.

"Diana," my father said. "It is time."

I nodded, my heart doing a sequence of trips and flips as I sought Duke with my gaze.

He was walking over toward me. "Could I have a moment with the bride?"

"Too late to back down now, Russell," my father said. "She is as good as yours."

Duke laughed, taking my gloved hand in his. "Believe me, Admiral, I would be glad if that were true, but in the eyes of God, a few items of business are still lacking for her to be well and truly mine and I hers. We will only be a moment."

My father nodded, and Duke pulled me by the hand, taking me around the side of the ivy-covered church to a place of relative seclusion.

"What is it?" I asked, unable to quell just a hint of anxiety at the unexpected detour.

He pulled in a breath and looked down at me, brushing at a wisp of my hair with a finger. "I just . . . well, I am selfish enough to want a moment with my bride alone before she becomes my wife."

The last two words were dizzying in their power. I had never thought to become a wife, and yet, here I was.

"Diana," he said, looking down at my hand and thumbing the silk of my glove. "We shall be making vows to one another soon."

"Yes," I said, unsure what was in his mind.

"We shall repeat them after the vicar." He began pulling at the fingertips of my left glove, removing them one by one. "But I know them by heart, for I have been thinking of them for weeks. And I want you to know that I am not simply saying them because it is what is expected." He pulled at my glove, and it slipped off my hand, leaving my skin to tingle in the breeze. He looked up at me, and I felt suddenly faint.

Reaching into his pocket, he brought out a ring, a simple gold band. Holding my gaze, he spoke, "Diana Donovan, with this ring, I thee wed, with my body I thee worship"—my heart quivered, and my knees went weak—"and with all my worldly goods I thee endow." He slipped the ring on my finger and looked up at me again. "I love you, Diana, and I promise to fight for that love—for our love—as long as you will let me."

I took in a trembling breath and grasped his hand with mine, meeting his gaze. "I love you, Duke, and I promise to fight alongside you." Reaching my other hand around his neck, I pulled his lips down to mine, sealing our vows with a kiss.

When we pulled back, our gazes met, and we both smiled as only two lovesick people on the cusp of a wedding could smile.

"Now," he said, "you had better give me back that ring or the vicar might refuse to marry two heretics."

"And here I thought you were giving it to me—surrendering it," I teased.

"It was meant as a gesture," he countered, knowing exactly what conversation I was echoing.

I laughed and pulled it from my finger, giving him the ring in exchange for my glove, my hand still trembling from the intimacy of the moments we had just shared.

I pulled the glove back on, and we looked at each other one last time, Sun Tzu's words repeating in my mind. *If you know Heaven and Earth, you may make your victory complete.* In Duke, I had come to know both heaven and earth, and when we emerged from the church in an hour, our victory would be complete, for we would have achieved together what had only recently seemed impossible.

THE END

R ead the next book in the series, Valentine's story:

Other Titles by Martha Keyes

Goodwill for the Gentleman (Belles of Christmas Book 2)

The Christmas Foundling (Belles of Christmas: Frost Fair Book 5)

The Highwayman's Letter (Sons of Somerset Book 5)

Of Lands High and Low

A Seaside Summer (Timeless Regency Collection)

The Road through Rushbury (Seasons of Change Book 1)

Eleanor: A Regency Romance

Author Note

The Art of War, the famous military treatise, has been around since the 5th century BC, but it was not until the 20th century that a full English translation was made available. During the Regency Era, a French translation by Jesuit Jean Joseph Marie Amiot existed, which is what I have given my characters access to in *The Art of Victory.*

While there are scholarly debates around the true authorship of *The Art of War,* I have attributed the work to Sun Tzu for the sake of simplicity.

The quotes you see in the book come from one of two places: my own translation of the French version, or the English translation by Lionel Giles, which is in the public domain.

Acknowledgments

The idea for this book has been in my mind for quite some time, but it is only thanks to the help of many people that the final product is in readers' hands.

My husband deserves all the praise in the world for his support in this all-enveloping business. None of this—none of it —happens without him. The meals, the cleaning, the child-care, the plotting, the confidant. He does it all.

My kids are patient with my constant preoccupation, even though they don't understand how somehow my books are never finished.

My critique group—Kasey, Jess, Deborah—you are my people, and your friendships are the best part of this gig by far.

To my beta readers—Mom, Madi, Kelsy, Brooke, Miranda— thank you for reading the first version of this and for making it better than it ever would have been without your careful eyes and feedback.

Thank you to my editor, Molly Rice, for her wonderful work and for cleaning up the messes I make.

Thank you to my Review Team for your help and support in an often nervewracking business.

And thank you, finally and most importantly, to God, for blessing me with everything I have.

Whitney Award-winning Martha Keyes was born, raised, and educated in Utah—a home she loves dearly but also dearly loves to escape to travel the world. She received a BA in French Studies and a Master of Public Health, both from Brigham Young University.

Her route to becoming an author has been full of twists and turns, but she's finally settled into something she loves. Research, daydreaming, and snacking have become full-time jobs, and she couldn't be happier about it. When she isn't writing, she is honing her photography skills, looking for travel deals, and spending time with her family. She is currently traveling the world full time with her husband and twin boys.

Printed in Great Britain
by Amazon

39567917R00169